Confessions of a Carnivore

Also by Diane Lefer

Short Story Collections

California Transit (Mary McCarthy Prize)
Very Much Like Desire
The Circles I Move In

Novels

The Fiery Alphabet
Nobody Wakes Up Pretty
Radiant Hunger

Nonfiction

The Blessing Next to the Wound: A story of art, activism, and transformation
(with Hector Aristizábal)

Confessions of a Carnivore

Diane Lefer

Fomite
Burlington, VT

ISBN-13: 978-1-937677-96-1
Library of Congress Control Number: 2014953996

Fomite
58 Peru Street
Burlington, VT 05401
www.fomitepress.com

For Ted Gottfried,

who inspired me as he stood up for justice in unconventional ways,

and sadly didn't live to see this in print.

Chapter One

IT WAS HEAVEN TO BE DRINKING AGAIN and for that I could thank Jennie.

It's not that I ever actually quit, except for the years when I was agonizing over my alcoholic ex, but I had stopped drinking for pleasure. I had forgotten what it was like to be reckless. My conscious mind had repressed the exhilaration of risk but now the memories were back: the blissful irresponsibility, all those moments when I'd given up fighting him for the car keys and had left us in the hands of fate; the intoxication as again and again I surrendered, even though I knew it was wrong, even knowing it might cost my life and the lives of innocent others. And each time, after the struggle? No conscience, no fear. The oceanic thrill of not caring.

I thought that was over for me. I'd seen the cost, even if he hadn't. Living in LA and not being the world's best driver even when sober, I didn't allow myself so much as a taste if there was any chance I might end up behind the wheel which, until I became friends with Jennie, was more or less all the time.

Every time you get in the car, you're demonstrating your faith in other people. Every time you reach your destination alive, your trust has been repaid. For this reason, I love the freeways. I don't, however, love to drive them.

Where's the lane markings? Is that a stripe, or a popped seam filled with tar? Is this one of the ramps where you have to merge at speed or one of those where if you don't stop though it isn't marked you're gonna get killed? Why don't the stripes and the reflectors coincide? Where are we anyway? The exit signs are draped in black. All I see are billboards for titty clubs. Right lane must exit. Let me over! I don't want to get off. Or do I? Three left lanes exit west. Which three? Does that include the car pool lane? Use your turn signal, asshole. There's debris flying off the back of that truck. There's an axle in the middle of the road. There's a piece of black plastic that just blew onto my windshield and now it's caught in the wipers and oh my God I can't see a fucking thing!

Jennie freed me from all this. Once we started going everywhere together, she preferred to do the driving. I preferred to sit back and revel in trust. Plus it seemed all right to have a thermos of margaritas in the car and for me to be drinking them.

I warned her: "Once we get to the reservation, alcohol is strictly forbidden. If it's like other reservations I've been to, though I've never been to Basoba, I don't really know, but in general, it's a matter of sovereignty and the tribal police will at the very least confiscate it and maybe even fine or arrest us."

"Public Law 280. California Indians aren't allowed to have tribal police or enforce their own laws, if they have any," Jennie said. "Anyway, how can you have a casino without liquor?"

"I don't know. Maybe the casino isn't on reservation land."

"If it isn't, the State wouldn't allow them to have a casino," Jennie said.

She held out her thermos cup for me to pour her another. Illegal, of course, but according to Jennie, Koreans had been oppressed for so long, they were no longer interested in following rules. According to me, if she was comfortable drinking and driving, well, that wasn't my business. It was her choice. This kind of deluded thinking reminded me ever so pleasantly of my youth.

It's sad to have become this stereotype, an older woman with a romantic past. As a useful aside, I should point out that in animal behavior studies, stereotyped behavior, or "stereotypy," refers to the mechanical repetition of an action or gesture, seemingly beyond conscious control and indicative of psychological stress.

Jennie and I had been carousing ever since she took the bar exam and then decided not to look for work until she got the results in November. The truth is, she hadn't done much studying for the exam. "If an idiot like Pete Wilson could pass," she'd said, referring to a particularly unpleasant former governor, "why should I worry?" Being a true friend, I didn't try to dissuade her from a course that led to all but certain failure. Success would mean being a lawyer which I was sure would lead to all but certain boredom and grief.

"When we get to Basoba," I said, "don't ask any direct questions. I mean don't ask any questions at all. With Indians, it's impolite. Even if the question is polite. Like right now, if I wanted to say, Do you mind if I roll down the window? what I'd do is say,

Well...I'm thinkin' 'bout rollin' down that window, and then I'd wait and see your reaction."

"Roll down the friggin' window," Jennie said. "I don't care."

It was amazing to have a friend again and to be drunk.

The sign at the side of the freeway said, *Lane closed ahead. Merge left.* But as we came around the curve it was the left lane that was closed and there was much honking and screeching of brakes and Jennie's car was a sure bet to rear end the red sports car in front, but she turned hard to the right, we went up on two wheels, wobbled, then slid onto the shoulder and jerked to a stop as Jennie pulled on the parking brake.

"My God," she said. "That was close."

"Someone should sue Caltrans. Putting the sign—"

"It wasn't them," Jennie said. "It was me."

"The sign said *Merge left.*"

"Didn't you see what just happened?"

"I saw a sign that said *Merge left* but—"

"I could've really fucked us up," Jennie said.

"It's not that big a deal," I said. "It would just be the continuation of your life with certain changes," I said, "that's all. Facing and fighting societal and architectural barriers every day of your life, for sure, but—"

"Jesus," Jennie said. "Give me the thermos."

I said, "The prospect doesn't frighten me."

I poured margaritas, one for Jennie, one for me, and marveled at our closeness. Like many women—stereotyped again—I'd gone from trying to love the whole world to settling all my affections on a few, then on one, and then, the ultimate older woman cliché—i.e., those who cannot rely on humans turn their affections to animals—I fell in love with Molly, my cat. I'd come to a point in my life when instead of trying to make new friends, I was doing my best to lose the old ones. Jennie had come along and changed that.

In her company, I regretted what I'd lost. With her, I was able to expose myself and be honest: "Jennie, when you talk to your cat, do you just automatically say I love you? I mean does it just flow out of your mouth without the slightest inhibition? Do you call her angel and sweet girl—OK, I know yours is a boy—and darling? I do. But you know I used to actually feel a thrill watching her cat food come down the conveyor belt in the supermarket. The sight of those cans rolling over to the cashier and the scanner would set me aglow because it was food for *her*, and I could almost hear her purr and feel her head brushing against my hand, I swear I'd get orgasmic right there in the checkout line. I loved leaving the apartment because even on my way out the door I was imagining what it would be like when I got home and she'd come running to greet me. And Jennie, it's gone," I said. "I still say I love you I love you I love you but it's just habit. Do you think that's what happens after a long marriage when people suddenly realize there's a total absence of feeling and after years of saying The Words they suddenly turn to each other and say, I never loved you. If that's—"

"Your cat?" she said. "We're talking about your cat when we almost got killed!"

"Yes, my cat."

"I tried to brake and my foot went down and down and down and I felt nothing! No contact. No connection."

Connection was the point, exactly. Sociologists say we need autonomy, security, and relatedness to be fully human. Sometimes I swear Molly is more human than I am.

"You need to trade this in for a reasonable vehicle," I said. "God, it's embarrassing riding around in an SUV!"

"This is not an SUV. It's a big car."

"Connection. That's the whole point, Jennie."

Jennie said, "I am not ecologically unsound."

"No? You are such a brat." What else can you call a vegetarian who loves red Naugahyde, who goes to steak houses to munch on iceberg lettuce and drink whiskey neat?

"And you're a pest," she said. "A real pest." She turned the key in the ignition.

"Jennie," I said, "are we friends?"

"What? You want permission to say something shitty to me?"

"No. I mean friends who care about each other? Do you think I care about you? I want to. You know I really want to."

"What is this?"

Oh, God, I was crying. "Do you love your cat? You picked a good one. Castrated males are the most affectionate, don't you think? My little girl isn't a lap cat, Jennie. She just isn't. And drinking and driving is bad. Really really bad. I think you have no idea how bad it is. It's wrong, Jennie, I know it's wrong, but I don't cry anymore, did you know that? Thank God for tequila. Something to make my hard heart melt. Hey, we've got to get out of here before the highway patrol stops to help."

"How can I drive without brakes?"

"The parking brake. Use the parking brake."

She also needed a break in the traffic. She got it when two cars coming around the curve veered to the right lane and collided.

"I hope no one's hurt," Jennie said, not waiting to find out.

Out onto the road we ventured again, exited the freeway and, using the parking brake at intersections, made it to a service station. Jennie's big car up on the lift, we crossed the street, drawn by a poster that said Gorilla Theater, my heart heavy with my own admission.

I'd lost sympathy with myself because I no longer loved my cat. My beautiful and personal representative of the species to which we owe our civilization.

Until they killed and chased away the birds, we couldn't plant. Until they killed the mice, we couldn't store our grain. Living in one place, instead of being nomadic, building cities, none of this could have happened without them. And then... even when we didn't need them anymore, even when they are of absolutely no practical use, we keep them and feed them. It's no longer symbiotic. They don't protect our property the way a dog does. They don't behave like slaves to enhance our shaky self-esteem. We continue to live with cats because they awaken our most noble sentiments. It is only through our relationship with them that we learned altruism, caring about the well being of a creature that does nothing for us and does not perpetuate our gene pool. Cats awakened our inherent but unevolved aesthetic sense. They left us startled and breathless, contemplative with their beauty. They insist we be our best selves. You can beat a dog and you're still the master and it will still love and obey but mistreat a cat, and she'll leave. She'll cooperate with you only if she values you. You cannot control her.

Yet at any moment for any reason I can have Molly put to death. What kind of legitimate relationship can there be between us? Though I didn't "buy" her, though I "adopted" her, and though she is my "companion," not my "pet," in reality—though she is not a thing—by law she is thing-like, my possession. She doesn't know it. But I do. Is it any wonder I hate the law? What does it do to a human being to have such power over another living thing, all the while using the word "love"?

Still, in spite of my hard heart and ultimate power, I let her guide me, as I expect she is leading me to a more evolved state I cannot, with the limitations of human vision, even imagine.

Weezie Wickham agrees with me.

There, I've mentioned Weezie—Louise. You'll meet her later. Now, back in the auto repair shop, any minute now, you'll meet Marcia. But for the moment, you're still with me and my guilt.

I was guilty, during these dark days of world crisis, to ignore the state of the Union and instead spend hours at the LA Zoo watching the traumatized little markhor. If they'd given her a name, I didn't know it.

I watched her nibble on browse. She took a few steps to the right, stamped her left hind leg three times in nervous succession, and reached for another leaf. She bent her head back and twisted her neck and I did the same to see if there was anything up in the sky. The big male moved closer to get at some leaves and she tripped daintily to the door and off-exhibit.

"Bambi!" cried a child. "Bambi! Don't go!"

“That’s not a bambi,” said the mother. “That’s a sheep. Baa baa.”

The markhor is not a fawn or a sheep. She’s a refugee. A mountain goat, a species highly endangered, in greater danger of extinction each day, and this particular markhor was evacuated from a war zone in Afghanistan. Traumatized for sure, but by war, captivity, or by the big ram?

As I watched, she returned and thrust her front legs up against the wall and she stretched her head and twisted her neck. Stereotypy. When she stepped down, the stripe on her back trembled and quivered like a spinal cord made visible. She bent her front knees and lowered herself to the ground. Her tail beat against the planet with flashes of white. I watched her nod her head again and again, then bend her neck backwards till her head touched that spinal stripe.

We research department volunteers watch them to try to know how to make their lives better. What if we watched other people that way, not judging them, only judging how to bring them greater comfort?

And that’s how David hooked me. He was precisely not my type. Just the kind of white guy who thinks the earth and its inhabitants were created for his use, and I knew I’d be a better person than I’d ever been before if I could bring myself to know him and not judge him.

I’m throwing a lot at you all at once. Just relax. There’s no other way when you’re talking about the whole web of creation and all that cosmic blah blah. David never liked the way I tell a story. “The human mind is suited to linear thinking,” he told me. “You have to build a logical chain.” And be shackled in it?

And you, do you really want to be like David? Anyway, he's wrong. There's nothing linear about us on a molecular level.

So hang on a bit and I'll back up and introduce you to David and to Lyle. In the meantime, the markhor raised her legs up on the wall again and again in a mechanical stereotyped way without frenzy or passion or terror, as if resigned both to captivity and to a lifetime of ineffectual attempts to escape it.

But I was about to tell you about Marcia. A distraught partial blonde in tight shorts and ruffled midriff-baring top—her clothing as unsuited to her ungraceful middle age as my demeanor some would argue is to mine—who rushed into the garage soon after Jennie and I returned to find the big car still up on the lift.

"Hello, Marcia," said the owner from behind the counter.

"Hi, Marcia," said a mechanic passing by.

"Marcia! Hey!" called the guy who was working on Jennie's car.

"Do you think she's fucking all of them?" Jennie asked me.

"Is anyone that hard up?" I said, though her large breasts were very much in evidence and that often counts for a lot.

"You've got to help me!" Marcia said. "I'm in trouble!"

The owner said, "Sure, Marcia, what's wrong?"

"I forgot to go to jury duty and they're fining me $1500. So can you write up an invoice that claims my car broke down so I'll have an excuse?"

"Sure, Marcia," he said. "What date was it?"

"How the hell do I know?"

Then she sat down beside me, put a hand on my knee and said, "I'm an alcoholic. But the good part of it is, I've been certified mentally ill."

I said, "That sounds like a good enough excuse to get off jury duty."

"Not in California," Jennie said.

The mechanic broke us the bad news. "Your brake cylinder went, but that's not all. It's the..." many more things there's no way I'm going to remember. He said, "You're going to have to leave it overnight."

"No powwow," said Jennie.

"Powwow?" Marcia's eyes were wide.

"We were going to Basoba."

"Hey-a-hey," she said, "hey-a-hey. I'm a shamaness though I don't practice anymore. At my job, they accused me of witchcraft. Me? Witchcraft, me? Of all people, when I'm a survivor of satanic abuse. My grandfather and the Governor of Ohio kidnap Amish children and eat them. You know in traditional societies, among the primary peoples, when someone exhibited signs of what we so ignorantly call schizophrenia or was in some other way different, that person was believed to have the depth of complexity of soul, the open communication to the spirit world, the vision and capacity to be a shaman. So when I was diagnosed as mentally ill, I started shamanic training. But you don't get the same respect here. If you want to go to Basoba, I'm overdue for a visit. I'll drive you."

"Wow! Great! Thanks!" said Jennie.

And I remembered why I'd stopped hanging out with drinkers. The bad judgment thing.

Jennie passed the thermos to Marcia.

Chapter Two

OK, I PROMISED YOU LYLE. Here's how we first met: He approached, twisted his head in a friendly way and began to masturbate. He was in the breeding program, an adolescent drill baboon, so we were curious about his sperm count. A semen sample would have been nice, but as soon as he came, he ate it.

David's introduction to Rosie didn't go like that at all. It didn't occur to him she had a name. The techs had already put her in restraint: thoracic and shoulder straps tightened, fiberglass backpack in place, all suspended from the ceiling by a tether of stainless steel. The catheters inserted in her arteries and veins were more or less permanent now that her arms were encased in plaster and she could no longer pull anything out with her hands. Through tubes, at David's (or the protocol's) mandate, flowed a variety of drugs, while through others her heart's blood was withdrawn for further testing.

Rosie had a history as a shrieker and a shitter, constantly befouling herself and the cage, but now she swung over a floorless cell and her body wastes fell into the channel below to be flushed away with a hose and she was mostly silent, or, if she made any sound—whimper or cry—it was inaudible over the shrieking of other lab baboons who hadn't been around quite so long. Her eyes, when David let himself meet them, held no light.

THESE PAGES WERE MEANT to be the simple yet scientifically accurate chronicle of a year's observations, Autumn 2002-2003. When I began charting behavior and human crimes against other species, I had no idea the crimes of the Bush administration would go into the record as well. How could I anticipate that politics—something I preferred to ignore—would shake my life hard? Or that, a decade later, the abuse of power would go on—no aberration but simply American. Can we learn from the past? I don't know. I just observe. So here it is, the record I kept of that single year of efforts I made on behalf of Lyle and Rosie and their kind, while Lyle lusted for me and I lusted for David.

My first glimpse of him, engraved in memory, retains its erotic jolt. In the audience at a weekend conference of the Southern California Primate Research Forum, he sat in the row behind me. When I turned around, he caught my attention through the bad posture that comes with bad faith: the shoulder-slumped self-hatred of the body that certain men can flip into a mild-mannered yet vicious display of superiority. He sat still as a shoe box. I saw him and shivered.

I could never return Lyle's feelings as I've always been attracted not to the *me* but to the *not-me*. I saw myself in each and every baboon. I looked at David and saw unbridgeable difference.

We weren't actually introduced until some time after the conference, and then it was through his 15-year-old daughter, Devon. She, in reaction to his work, had joined a street theater troupe going by the provisional name Gorilla Theater, and, as you already know, my best friend Jennie and I had walked in on what turned out to be their organizational meeting after that breakdown en route to the Basoba reservation, a place that would later figure in such different ways in David's life and my own.

There were no great apes at the meeting, only humans, and luckily enough for those of you who may find it hard to keep track of lots of characters all at once, they represented a range of distinct types.

When I still taught high school, 35-45 kids in a class, diversity was a teacher's best friend. If all your students are the same color and race, it can take weeks to tell them apart. These days, watching chimps, I've learned you look for who's biggest, who's got breasts, who's got bald elbows and so forth, and you don't stop watching just because you find some behavior unattractive, and even if there's too many individuals running around doing too many different things and there's no way you're going to keep them straight, working with primates still beats trying to distinguish one gray kangaroo from another by their ear notches while their ears never stop flicking.

The people at Gorilla Theater were even easier to ID than chimps: a woman seated in a wheelchair with a little black dog sprawled across her lap; a middleaged Latino wearing his hair in a long white ponytail; two teenagers—one female (David's daughter), one male; a 40-something woman who looked familiar, or maybe it was just her glasses I'd seen before—diamond-shaped lenses inside thin green metal frames. Obvious differences, but still, as I've learned to do, I started with the most striking characteristic, so it's natural I learned Sara's name—she was using the wheelchair—first.

And how fortuitous that less than an hour earlier I'd instructed Jennie as to sensitive contemporary terminology. This was following our close call on the freeway when she was all freaked out about how bad an accident it could have been.

"It's not really that big a deal," I'd reassured her, "as long as you don't hit a child."

Even strangers mourn when someone dies young while we—I, at least; Jennie's much younger—had reached the age when your death can only be tragic to those who still love you. Once upon a time, I'd worried who would take Molly if anything happened to me, but Jennie had promised. Once upon a time, I'd been afraid of losing a limb or having to use a wheelchair.

"Once upon a time?" Jennie said. "And now you want to be confined to a wheelchair?"

I took the opportunity to explain a person *uses* a wheelchair. It's the *person* who counts. The wheelchair is just a tool. You don't say the carpenter is confined to her hammer...etc.

"I'm Bernice," said the woman with the distinctive glasses. "Join us," and we did.

We chanted, we cleansed the space with sage, we honored one another, we went to grab folding chairs from where they leaned against the wall.

"The mission of Gorilla Theater is to change the way people view other species," said Bernice. "Once we start to regard non-human animals as persons, we'll have to change the way we treat them."

"That might not be a change for the better," said the male teen. His name was Amory—where do they get these names?—and his T-shirt read *Regime Change Begins at Home.* By winter his shirt would read *No Blood for Oil.* "Besides, this gorilla stuff is just wrong. We should represent all species."

"But primates are our brothers," Devon said.

"Sisters," said Sara.

"You're privileging gender over species," said Bernice.

Amory said "Siblings."

"I work with baboons," I said.

"So does my father," Devon said.

I started to explain that the drill baboon was even more endangered than the mountain gorilla.

Devon said, "He tortures them. In the name of Science, of course, but it's pseudoscience. He tortures them in the name of funding."

Bernice got up and hugged her. "See how interrelated we all are? Devon doesn't want baboons to suffer, but she also doesn't want her father to be a human who makes them suffer. What happens in one species affects us all."

I looked at Devon with her nose ring, silver charm jiggling in her navel, and her A-inside-a-circle anarchist's tattoo barely visible on an arm covered with bruises from, she said, a wrestling lesson with Oleg the Russian Bear Taktarov, and I reached the conventional conclusion that she was trying to torture her father.

"Can we hold a protest in front of the lab?" she said.

"Actually," said Bernice, "I was thinking the LA Zoo."

I decided not to mention the LA Zoo was where I worked, if you can call it work when you don't get paid.

"At least they don't eat the animals at the zoo," said Amory. "In Third World countries—"

At this point in time, I wasn't political. I was merely a know-it-all and couldn't stop myself from interrupting: "We don't say Third World anymore."

"What do we say?" Amory asked.

Oh, God, I couldn't remember. Developing nations? Emerging nations?

Everyone looked toward the Latino guy, Bobby. "Hey, I'm just here to paint your sets,"—and then their eyes slid to Jennie. Everyone else in the room was white.

"I never understood it anyway," Amory said. "We were the First World, right? They were the Third World. Who was the Second World?"

"Must've been the Russians," Bobby said. "Everything used to be about the Russians."

"Soviets, actually," I said. "They were Soviets then."

"But were they Second World?"

That's the way it always is. People remember the winner and the loser. No one ever remembers the runner-up.

"Should we call them cousins?" said Devon.

"The Russians?"

"No, the gorillas, chimps."

"Our closest kin." Bernice reached into the pocket of her work shirt. What I'd taken to be cigarettes turned out to be a pack of Kleenex. She pushed up her glasses and dabbed at her eyes and that's when I remembered who she was. Just the other day I'd been with the gorillas when she came up to the gate and stared at the silverback in the way a primate living free would interpret as threat.

"I'm sorry, Kelly," she whispered.

He knucklewalked toward Evie who fled.

"I'm sorry, Evie." Bernice took out a Kleenex. "Allergies," she said to me and dabbed. "Every Yom Kippur I visit the apes. I spend the Day of Atonement asking their forgiveness for what we've done."

Then she hurried off, in the direction of the chimps.

"We have the same chromosomes," she told her actors. "We share a history, we—"

"That's exactly why we shouldn't privilege them."

"What are you? A human-hater?"

"I just don't think we're the be-all and end-all." (My memory is faulty. If I were to attribute all this dialogue, I'd just be guessing.)

"If you read the Bible—"

"What do you expect?" Jennie said. "The Bible wasn't written by a mountain goat." (I'm sure it was Jennie who said that. You can't get away with Bible stuff in front of Jennie.)

"Of course not. Mountain goats can't write."

"Only humans—"

"But if a mountain goat had written the Bible..." Bernice said. "Try for a moment, think like a mountain goat."

"Is this an acting exercise?"

"No. It's re-earthing," Bernice said. "It's expanding your consciousness beyond the ego to embrace other life forms. The great Aldo Leopold taught us we must learn to think like a mountain. It's—"

A tinny carillon played the theme from *Star Wars*. "Hello?" Devon answered her cell phone. "Hello?"

"Gorilla Theater is just a pun. It's not just about gorillas."

"Then it's exploitation. Appropriation. It's the same old same old. If it's not about them—"

"Enough arguing," said Bernice. "Let's try something. Lie down on the earth. Feel it breathe beneath you."

"This isn't earth. It's industrial carpet."

"A dirty carpet."

"It's called acting. Lie down."

I did and Jennie followed suit. It's not the sort of thing she's into, but though I'd never wanted to be a leader and Jennie was definitely not a follower, for some reason, it pleased her to humor me. If you think you know Jennie, you probably don't. All Korean women in the US have one of three names, Jennifer Kim being one of them, and so people are always confusing her with someone else.

So we're re-earthing ourselves at rehearsal, all of us but Bernice stretched out face down on the floor, when Devon's phone played its tinny bells again. She tried to stand and let out a bloodcurdling shriek when her bellybutton jewelry got caught in the rug.

I didn't feel her pain, though I wanted to, which is probably why I put this moment right up front, to state right at the outset that I was trying to overcome what I'd become: a person who managed to be both scrupulously ethical and thoroughly insensitive to others' suffering.

For example: Jennie won't eat anything with a face. I do. I eat animals who have eyes, ears, legs, hearts, lungs. My cat is a carnivore, and I refuse to be morally superior to Molly.

I buy meat in the supermarket, but that doesn't mean it's sanitized. The fact of the slaughter is part of my pleasure. I love chicken—not nuggets, not boneless skinless breast. I like to see the bones pile up. I like the neck, the evidence on my plate of carnage. And ribs! There's no word-disguise, no camouflage, no steak or roast or filet. You know damn well you are eating a living thing's RIBS. I can hardly look at an animal without wondering what it tastes like. Which may explain why Molly bolts and runs when I try to kiss her.

This is not a perpetuating-the-cycle-of-violence-type of thing. I felt this way even before I got shot.

Southern California doesn't have too many cars. It's got too many vegetarians and too many guns. I was in the health food store because vegetarian colleagues from school were coming over for dinner. I was buying seitan and tofu and organic this, organic that when my ear got blown off by a jittery security guard. It could have been my head. This experience did not make me hypervigilant, but rather indifferent to my own fears. I figure how many times is it likely for an ordinary person to be shot?

The settlement paid for my auricular prosthesis, nicely sculpted silicone held in place by titanium clips implanted in the bone. I asked the surgeon if he ever implanted Goth horns in foreheads. He said no, but a friend of his in Santa Cruz did.

In the lawyer's office, that's where I met Jennie. She'd finished two years of law school in a class probably 75% women—all diligent, patient, detail-oriented and, as I would soon try to convince her, tricked into considering the stultifying work and long hours empowering. This was her summer job and probably where she developed her insensitive vocabulary. (A client who's "wheelchair-bound" gets more from a jury.)

So, yes, there was a settlement. Not enough, given my debts, to buy a house, though I could have finally visited Africa and lived out my fantasies involving mountain gorillas and chimpanzees. My God, but I wanted to be Jane Goodall. To be thin and blonde and have an English accent and maintain my dignity even when pant-hooting to a crowd. I had never been adventurous enough, that was my problem, and now I had my chance. But when it came down to it, I couldn't leave Molly. So I stayed home and got the prosthesis which nicely keeps my glasses from sliding off my face. I paid off debts which still left me, if I stuck to a budget, with enough to take the year off from teaching English and become a volunteer at the Los Angeles Zoo.

Let me take you there now, on a little tour amid palm trees scaly and shaggy, past rock caves where peacocks strut. If you don't like meandering, go home now. But stick with me and we'll stare at turacos, pudus, and fossas that never made it into a box of animal crackers, ghostly sifakas sitting straight-backed, cross-legged, and alert, locust pods rustling overhead and the sizzle of the sprinklers, up to where the paved path curves around higher still. Don't worry where we're going, just look. There's a water fountain painted green, a trash can, the gate still locked to keep the noisy public from disturbing the drill baboons that are no longer there. Inside: broken logs, hanging gourds, trees now safe from Lyle's fury.

He was my primary involvement, though I did get quite attached to Michael and Melissa who were so passionately attached to one another.

I've got plenty to tell you—about deep ecology, Basoba Indians, David (bless his heart!) and the Church of Neoproctology, Gorilla Theater, war, peace, mountain goats, cats, frontal lobotomies, and Weezie Wickham's secret files—but their story, Michael's and Melissa's, is where we'll have to return. In the end, their plight is what it all comes down to: What are the rights of two individuals in a society that won't respect their love?

And though it's time to get back on the road and though I plan to take you sooner or later from the high desert to the beaches of Malibu, we'll return again and again to the zoo. For all the ethical quandary it presents, it's the place where I used to feel most at home: this simulacrum of wildness, where people have carved their names into the flat paddle faces of the cactus, into the broad leaves of maguey, even into the desert tortoise's shell, where we're all prisoners of late capitalism, where the infrahuman organisms are as real and artificial as we are.

Chapter Three

"JENNIE KIM!" Marcia said. "So you're the woman who broke my brother's heart."

"Some other Jennie Kim," said Jennie Kim.

We were in Marcia's boat of an old Buick and she and Jennie were bonding over their respective why-I-became-a-vegetarian stories. Jennie had always refused to tell me. Too disgusting, she said. Now, eavesdropping from the backseat I heard:

"First it was just red meat. We went out to dinner and Loy ordered yuk-hae. That's strips of raw beef. I grew up eating it, but there I was, staring at these bloody red strings and suddenly I thought I saw them move."

Outside at every strip mall, flags snapped meanly through the air, like wet towels in high school locker rooms.

"I don't eat meat for moral reasons," Marcia said, "but I can't be an ethical vegetarian because I'm not an ethical person."

"Then we had a case at the firm," Jennie said. "Product liability. This guy drops his hairdryer in the tub and electrocutes himself. And the hairdryer stays on and brings the water to a simmer. By the time they found him two weeks later, he'd been poached in his own juice."

She was right. It was too disgusting to tell.

"You're a lawyer?" Marcia asked.

"Uh, no, it was a summer job," Jennie said, very quickly.

"I'm not asking for me," Marcia said. "My friend, Weezie. The city's condemning her house because she has cats."

"She'll be a lawyer any day now," I said. "Just waiting for the bar exam."

Marcia swerved to make the exit ramp and headed out into the foothills.

OCTOBER WILDFIRES had the air heavy with ash and smoke. The sky was yellow and the sky was black and I thought of the skies over New York on 9/11 and I thought of the little markhor, frantic in her native habitat with the bombs falling. I thought of Jennie wanting to be a human rights lawyer, as though only humans had rights.

"It's not her fault," Marcia said, parking on the street. A border of star jasmine along the sidewalk spiked fragrance through the smoke and car exhaust and we looked up at a hillside covered with mattresses and rusty stoves and, if I had any real idea what tractor parts look like I could with more confidence add, tractor parts. "She goes into the clinic for a couple of weeks and people use her yard as a dump."

Jennie said, "If she's been served by the Nuisance Abatement Board, I guess if she can get this all cleared off..."

"No one cared what Weezie's place looked like till this developer decided to put in a subdivision," Marcia said.

I was short of breath as soon as we started up the steep stairs. At last the lopsided green house came into view. Along with its owner.

Weezie Wickham. That was a name you could picture in hat and gloves. I could see her wearing pearls, and going to Wellesley, and learning to pour tea. She met us at the front door in a blue plaid house dress, her gray hair up in a French twist half undone. Cats ran out. Cats ran in. She smiled.

The smile was what you had to see. It was not a dazzling smile. It was not a placating smile. It was not a forced, rehearsed, smile-on-command calculated to guarantee the efficacy of some brand of toothpaste or religion. It was effortless. It matched the mildness in her eyes. She could no more keep her mouth from turning up at the corners than a turtle can. It was a pleasant smile. And this in spite of bad bridgework and a couple of gaps.

"Did the Senator send you?" she asked.

"The Senator is dead," said Marcia.

"Oh, that's right." She gave us all her vague pleasant smile. "Did you phone me? I don't have a phone, but come on in. If I'd known to expect visitors, I would have done my hair. I've let myself go gray. There's so much ammonia in that hair color, Smoky climbed up on my head and peed."

Cats—more than I could count—ran over to be petted and stroked.

She said, "You can hardly blame him."

We wended our way through newspapers piled like snowbanks. I had just caught my breath from the stairs and now with the stench I no longer wanted to breathe.

"This place could go up like a torch," I said.

"It's not her fault," Marcia said. "She's a senior citizen. How's she supposed to carry stuff all the way down the hill to the bins?"

"Call me Weezie," she said. "All my friends do."

Unidentifiable substances squished underfoot. From dark corners, growling, yelps of outrage, mouths opening instinctively to hiss, red mouths, white teeth. Flies settled on bowls of cat food, darted and buzzed and cats leapt in the air to bat at them, spun themselves in cartoon-cat pirouettes.

"I've brought you a lawyer," said Marcia. "Jennie's going to help you."

"Maybe," said Jennie. "Have you been served with papers?"

"Oh yes."

"Do you have them?"

"I save everything," Weezie said.

We followed her to a room with a desk and a manual typewriter and ten-twelve litter boxes lined up against the wall and cats burrowing around and under and through the piles of paper bags filled with trash, ambushing bugs and each other, scuttling, pouncing at every rustle.

"It's hopeless," said Jennie.

"Every wrong has a remedy," I reminded her.

"Yeah, and the remedy for this place is demolition."

"Please do have a seat," said Weezie.

Jennie preferred to stay on her feet but I felt faint and found a relatively dry chair.

"I see it's not just the situation outside," Jennie said.

Cats landed with soft thuds, scrambled up my legs, tumbled

over me. One cat stretched out in my lap and purred. Another rubbed his head in my hand while straddling the purring cat. There were more: one with its paws on my shoulders, and one on my leg, touching and brushing against each other but interested only in me, the way ostensibly straight men touch each other fearlessly in a threesome with a woman.

"Are you taking medications?" Jennie asked.

"No, dear. It was surgery. And now they've cut off my phone." Weezie stroked a beautiful Abyssinian with a russet coat. "Nefertiti here likes to fetch." There was a cat wheezing from allergies. A big Himalayan in my lap. "How anyone could live with fewer than three, I just don't know."

Cats throwing up. Hair balls. Vomit. All those big green eyes watching you. Eyes everywhere. From the floor, from the ledges, from overhead, from the baskets, peeking out from piles of trash.

"I don't care for Siamese, but they need homes, too," Weezie said.

Calicos like Molly. Black cats with long matted hair. Tuxedo cats. Buff cats. Gray cats.

"That's Daisy. She'll always roll over to have her belly rubbed. Some of them like the brush. Some only like your hand. If you are brushing one of them, Abner will come over and groom the cat you're brushing and then look at you, like, see what a nice guy I am, give me some love."

Three-legged cats, a big one with a bobbed tail. Cat hair in your eyes and mouth and coating your throat.

"Of course the last time the Senator saw me, I didn't have hair. They shaved it off. For the surgery. How is he?" she asked Jennie.

"What Senator?" Jennie asked.

"My Senator," she said.

A soft wet nose pressed against my hand.

"That's Nutley," said Marcia. "He only eats Whiskas."

A tail draped over my arm. "Chessie. She likes French fries."

"Senator McManus," Weezie said.

"Never heard of him," said Jennie.

I said, "I don't vote."

"He's dead," Marcia said.

Weezie sighed. "Mistakes were made."

A paw tapped my shoulder, the vibration of the purr, the slither into my lap and the tumble of one over another, competing peacefully for love.

"Was he a California senator?" Jennie asked.

"Oh, no, dear. We're from back east. After my surgery, I found I couldn't care for myself so well. I had a marvelous nurse who used to wrestle with me and spank me, and Flori, dear Flori, stayed with me a while but then... I saw his name in the paper. Walter Wickham, an attorney in Sierra Madre, so I took the train to Pasadena and went to see him. He denied we were related, but I stayed. Ask Marcia about it," she said. "I get tired when I talk too much."

Heads fit themselves into my hands.

"I think I'm probably as smart as I used to be," she said, "but it doesn't seem worth the bother."

A cat with a large red cancerous tumor. One who wrapped his smoky paws around my neck and put his face out for a kiss. Scrawny cats, fat ones. A hiss.

Something dropped and a dozen cats startled.

"She used to be a very important person in Washington, DC," said Marcia.

"Oh! I still keep up," Weezie said. "With the Imperial Presidency. His Fraudulency. Our elected representatives abdicating their responsibility. I know what's happening. I have very strong opinions."

"That's good," Jennie said.

"But, somehow, I don't care."

"Can I see the papers?" Jennie asked.

Weezie looked under her desk and pulled out newspapers with stained pages.

"I mean the legal papers."

"I care passionately," Weezie said, "but in a rather vague sort of way."

"I don't understand," said Jennie.

"Neither do I." Weezie kept smiling. "I'm just repeating what I've been told, mixed up a bit with what I think I feel. There's a disconnect, you see, between what I know and what I feel. And I know a responsible person acts on knowledge, not on emotion, but my dear, without feeling, I forget to act."

Cats with fleas scratched at their ears, hindlegs sawing the air.

Weezie said, "Something, something, something, is missing."

"I'm not sure we can help you," Jennie said.

"That's all right," said Weezie.

Wires sizzled between her and me. "Yes, we can," I said.

"I cared too much," she said.

Everywhere, the reek of cat shit and cat piss and an unfamiliar stench that must have been unaltered tomcat spray, and the creatures moved over me, more cats than I ever could have imagined, like hell and heaven all at once, like being in love.

"In some cases, there were terrible side effects," Weezie said. "In my case, it worked just as it was supposed to."

"It did?" I said.

"No more anxiety. And there was so much pain before." She touched her chest and maybe meant her heart. "It's gone," she said. "I think it's gone. I may not have a good grasp anymore of what pain feels like."

Frantic scratching at the wooden floor, cats unable to bury their shit.

"I was a very important person. I had a lot of influence. For a girl." She kept smiling. "Marcia tells me they're going to bulldoze my house just like Palestine. The cats will be homeless and the papers will be buried."

I said, "You still have them?"

"All the reports." She waved a hand. "I've got them here somewhere. People need to know."

"Can I see the reports?" Jennie asked.

Weezie smiled. "If the cats haven't used them for a litter box."

"What are you going to do for her?" asked Marcia.

"I don't think I..." Jennie began. "Health hazard, fire hazard, it's too far gone."

"OK," said Weezie. "How many teeth does a horse have?"

"I don't know anything about horses," I said.

Weezie said, "What I'm talking about is knowledge. There were monks who tried to find the answer in Scripture. Till one went and looked in the horse's mouth. They beat him. To seek knowledge in the world is to be tempted by the Devil. Tell me: who dares touch what's real?"

"I want to help," I said.

"You're a very nice girl," said Weezie Wickham. "The kitties certainly think so. But you'll have to remind me. Who are you?"

Chapter Four

If you're to understand who I am, meaning who I am now, though it's not necessarily who I was then, unless you believe that our inner self is godhead and the various phases and stages we go through and attitudes we strike are nothing but that indivisible godhead's multitudinous avatars, you need to understand my spiritual practice.

From Bernice, I eventually learned more about re-earthing and deep ecology.

Without going into the whole explanation, let me say that one can identify oneself as a deep ecologist upon endorsing eight general principles in spite of vast differences in fundamental belief-systems. I won't go into the notion of Levels except to say that we are each free to choose our own Level 1 of ultimate premises. Jennie, for example, became a militant atheist after breaking up with a very rich and unpleasant boyfriend—"If there were a God, he wouldn't have put such a big cock on a Republican." David, searching for meaning after his divorce, became an adherent of the Church of Neoproctology, the doctrines of which inspire much bathroom humor which tends to obscure the Church's iron grip on its followers.

I have my Level 1 which, as I've already explained, is the belief that we owe our civilization to the Cat.

Though the cat happily forms associations, by nature she is solitary and so her brain has no concept of hierarchy. The only relationship she understands is one of equality. Humans *should* be like cats. We *are* like baboons.

These are my beliefs, but thanks to Bernice, I learned to fit them into a fully elaborated belief-system.

My practice became to start every morning with a ten-minute meditation in direct contact with Nature. I could have walked to the park, or stood barefoot on the neighbors' lawn, but I chose to make things more difficult for myself, my way of asserting that we each can re-earth no matter where or in what circumstances we may find ourselves.

The apartment I rented then had no garden or yard. The patio was covered with cement. The cement was cracked but not a single blade of grass edged its way up. This complex was separated from the neighbors' by a cinderblock wall topped with a spiked sea-green fence, and a tree or shrub with clusters of hard dark green leaves just managed to hang over so that if I removed one shoe, stood on the other leg, lifted the bare foot in the air, I could touch those glossy almost-plastic leaves with my toes. Every morning, I clutched the bars of the fence to keep my balance. I never knew what kind of shrub or tree it was that I communed with daily. The plant doesn't name itself. With my leg up in the air, hoping the sanitation men wouldn't come into the alley and see my exposed crotch through the fence, I surrendered the human curse: self-consciousness. I would think like the plant, I would think with roots and bark, sometimes I swear to you I experienced photosynthesis.

With the return of human consciousness, I always felt a moment's deep regret. I wished my fingers were green glossy leaves. I wished I had a tail.

"Anti-Semites used to think Jews had tails," Bernice reminded me once.

"Yes," I said with longing, "but I've never been observant."

Leaves, branches, tails, horns, anogenital swellings. I stood firm on both legs and thought about threats to the planet. What we now call the planet is what we used to call the world, and as a child, I wanted to save it. Back then, we had to save it from the Russians. But I loved the Russians and their wonderful names. Ilya, Natasha, sheer poetry. My grandmother from Warsaw told of buying black bread from Russian soldiers, the best bread in the world, and a soldier saying to her, *nye boyitsa*, the only Russian words I know. *Don't be afraid*. I must have a Russian face. Old ladies walk up to me in Plummer Park, ask me questions in their native tongue, and all I can answer is *nye boyitsa*.

Don't laugh at the notion of re-earthing. It's instinctive. Why, after all, do people throw themselves face down on the ground when distraught? Why do we take comfort from the grass?

Re-earthing. It's through this practice that I have expanded my consciousness, without drugs, to the point where I can accurately and with full assurance tell you this story with more characters than you can count on your fingers. For the most part, I use a modified version of the methodology we employ when observing animal behavior. Modified because for example, in my line of (volunteer) work, you're not supposed to write, *The parrot ate*, but rather, *Grasping one piece of cooked macaroni in its left talons, the African gray parrot dipped its head to feed by breaking off approximately one-third of the food item and swallowing it*, which you have to agree makes for wretchedly bad prose. I will report acts, not inner meanings. It's not that we think animals lack consciousness; it's just not something we pay attention to. Therefore, while I can tell you that Amory bit his cuticles, that Bernice often wore sweaters with the sleeves rolled up to form cuffs in which she could keep Kleenex handy, that David, upon noticing a corner of the rug scrunched up beneath the leg of a chair wouldn't make a move to fix it but would point it out again and again till someone else did, I'll try to refrain from any speculation as to what these acts reveal.

Acts, of course, include speech acts, which have the capacity to exteriorize (or falsify) internal states. For example, you may have wondered why Armand Khanazarian of the auto shop was so willing to write Marcia a false report. Was he fucking her? Was he easily given to corruption? Did he realize he wouldn't have to make good on his offer? None of the above. He wanted Marcia kept off juries as he considered her too soft-hearted to convict anyone, not that he was a staunch law-and-order third-generation citizen, but rather he resented the new breed of criminals who were giving crime a bad name. Armenian organized crime? Pfui, he said, those punks couldn't find their way out of a file cabinet. As he explained to Jennie when she picked up her big car, his father had been a member of the criminal world's elite, a talented safecracker, who earned a good living for his family for decades in New York City without ever resorting to violence. Armand himself had inherited his father's ear, but instead of listening for the telltale aural signature of tumblers, he found himself preternaturally able to diagnose the malaise of engines whether piston or rotary with a simple listen. Jennie, when she paid the bill, pronounced him not just skilled, but an honest mechanic.

So: Speech acts are useful data vis-à-vis people (also parrots) and should by all rights include other species as well but I haven't yet got the knack of interpreting drill baboon vocalizations. I even hesitate with my most beloved species, the cat, because each one seems to speak a different dialect. And I lack even the most preliminary ethogram of cat behavior.

Why is it I can find experts to tell me exactly how elephants behave and why, and gorillas and ringtailed lemurs, but no clear, comprehensive, factual account of Molly? Are cats really so mysterious? Or is it just that when you live intimately with an animal, you can't help but be aware of her complexity. Wild animals are always Other, easy to schematize and explain. The cat I live with defies classification.

The other scruple that stops me from telling and interpreting just about everything is my respect for privacy. Do you have any idea how depressed a gorilla can become when deprived of visual barriers, when left with no way to remove himself from scrutiny? This is not a matter of hiding because of fear. It is the need of the individual to keep her thoughts to herself sometimes. Just as an animal needs both sunshine and shade, a healthy normal gorilla needs to take a rest now and then from social interaction. Sometimes a gorilla needs to be alone.

We all, human and infrahuman, have our boundaries, and mine was that much as I appreciated being introduced to Weezie, and much as I had determined to return to visit her, once we left her house, I'd had quite enough of Marcia. But it wasn't my fault that her tags were expired and we got pulled over and the highway patrol busted her for DUI. Was there a law on the books, Failure to Designate a Driver? Apparently not, as they took Marcia but let Jennie and me go which meant we were stuck somewhere outside Sierra Madre till she phoned her husband.

Are you surprised? I've neglected to mention so far that Jennie was married, maybe because for all my re-earthing wisdom, human pair-bonding still remains, to me, a mystery.

Chapter Five

THOUGH, NO KIDDING, I understood what she saw in Loy. Every time I saw Loy, he was running late, his blindingly white shirt still unbuttoned over his chocolate-brown chest as he dashed from car to home to wherever, looking like a TV commercial for laundry detergent or bleach.

He picked us up. We hadn't eaten? OK, let's eat. Maybe he was always auditioning, waiting to be discovered during that mad dash from car to restaurant. It's LA, after all. Someone might see him and make him a star and save him from his dental practice. Someone might see that chest and find it as irresistible as the Thai waitress who reached out her finger and touched it in wonder, startling them both.

We took a booth and Loy buttoned his shirt.

The waitress brought beer and Jennie put her through the whole rigamarole about could we get tom yum soup with vegetable stock, not chicken, and was she sure there was no shrimp or pork in the spring rolls while Loy, acting like this was just for my benefit, ordered more appetizers—the spicy salty fish and the larb.

Loy and I—fellow carnivores—got along well. The Army had put him through dental school and made his good posture second nature so that Loy, unlike David, looked at his most comfortable when standing straight. He'd enjoyed being stationed in Korea though, out of respect for local sensibilities, he kept his hands off Korean women till he returned to the US and found Jennie. They lived on the east side in a Latino neighborhood where no one was likely to question why they loved each other instead of hating.

I asked him once what he liked about Korean culture. "It wasn't Army culture," he said though he tried to be discreet in criticizing the military as he was still finishing up his service in the National Guard Army Reserve.

What Loy liked about dentistry was that, unlike in other professions, you had self-sovereignty. You took orders from no one and got to run your own show. What I liked about his being a dentist was he had Saturday hours, which left part of every weekend free for me to hang with Jennie—even those weekends when he wasn't drilling with his unit. What Loy didn't like about dentistry was the boredom. Jennie—and now I—did our best to keep him amused.

"We joined the Gorilla Theater," she told him. "You could come along next time."

I told him about Devon's bellybutton jewelry accident, but re-earthing just seemed to piss him off.

"Think like a mountain. Think like a mountain goat. Why

are those people so willing to make that effort, but they can't put themselves for even an instant in the shoes of a black man?"

"The mountain can't claim you're appropriating," I said.

Jennie said, "The mountain goat can't talk back and tell you you're wrong."

Loy doled out the soup which would have been a whole lot tastier with shrimp in it.

I said, "Molly's life matters more to me than some human being stranger."

"She's a pet," said Loy.

"I avoid that word," I said. "There's nothing surprising if your *pet* runs to you when you call. But when a *little animal* jumps up on the bed beside you and curls up to sleep, eyes closed in trust..." Didn't people see? The word *pet* was a diminishment of wonder.

"Hey, I love our Monk," said Loy. That was Jennie's cat.

"He does," said Jennie.

"I doubt it," I said. "Not real love. That's when someone or something looks like life itself."

Jennie reached for Loy's hand over the table. "Like when you feel you can't live without—"

"No, I mean it's synecdoche." Remember, I used to teach English, not that I ever used Greek words in front of my students. "The part representing the whole. You are captivated by his very breathing, by the thought of the blood moving in his veins, you are dumbstruck at the miracle of his existence and by terror at his fragility. He becomes everything, you are struck as if you'd never noticed before what a miracle it is that life was created on earth, and he is its manifestation. You are not just loving him, you are loving the whole of existence as he manifests it to you," I said. "Which means he, or she, doesn't have to be human."

"Molly's your baby," Loy said.

"No. She's a cat, and that's magnificent enough."

"The point," said Jennie, "is that love for any living creature can extend itself outwards, to other life forms."

"Even to humans," I said.

"Loy takes good care of Monk," Jennie said. She was always defending him to me because she assumed I didn't like him. Jennie was under the impression I only liked unattractive men.

"That video you show? The chimp flossing?" I said to him. "It's cute. It's real cute. Maybe little human children will take better care of their teeth. But do you have any idea how that chimp was trained?"

"Probably—" he began.

"Probably? Ask your wife. You can't build a chain of evidence with *probably*. You can be sure there were beatings, electric shock."

In those days, I still had a tendency of going into automatic lecture mode as the residual effect of my teaching career. The year before I went on leave, we were required to teach to the test using the No Child Left Behind script. No deviation allowed. The script told us when to sit, when to stand, when to make eye-contact and when to allow questions. It taught students who already tended to dehumanize anyone in authority to look at us as though we were videos, or holograms or adaptive learning engines, anything but real live people.

"That chimp was tortured," said Jennie, and then to me, "When do you want to go back to Weezie's?"

We told Loy about her, how she'd been someone important in Washington, and knew too much, and had a nervous breakdown, and they made her have a frontal lobotomy.

"She's got a stash of documents," I said.

"I thought you weren't political," Loy said.

"I'm not. It's more fun to be cynical."

"The lady doth protest too much," said Loy.

"No, that's the point. I don't protest at all anymore."

Jennie said, "Can you imagine the kind of stuff she's sitting on? It could be explosive."

"Really," I said. "It's just a crazy old lady, a trash pile and a hundred cats."

"A hundred—" Loy began. "What the hell were you thinking?" He started ranting about toxoplasmosis and my heart stopped the way it does when you sneeze, except I hadn't sneezed.

"My period came," said Jennie.

I looked at her. "You thought you were—?"

"We're trying," she and Loy said in unison.

I gulped beer to hide my dismay. It's not that I saw anything wrong with bringing children into this world. I just didn't want any in mine. If Jennie had her way, I was about to lose her to motherhood. Two utterly cool people were ready to submerge themselves in order to perpetuate the earth's most dangerous species.

AT THE ZOO, the females chimps kept getting pregnant though all the males had undergone vasectomy. We fussed over the babies and scrutinized the face of every male keeper and maintenance man.

At the drill exhibit, people who didn't know any better always thought Becky was pregnant—just her pot belly, the only exercise she gets being above the neck, her pissed-off aggressive head bobs.

I've never been pregnant. When it comes to breeding, I identify with Lyle. He'd been introduced to many an attractive female drill, but still preferred me. That was his right, though the drill is one of the world's most endangered primates and his sexual preference was an omen of extinction.

And as I would learn through my relationship with David, though there's currently what's termed an oversupply of Rosie's species, she too was expected to breed. At the lab, she was forcibly addicted to drugs and then artificially inseminated to test the effects of maternal addiction on fetal development, but she, and the other females with her, could not sustain a pregnancy. Maybe it was the cocaine. I prefer to believe it was her resistance, even on the hormonal level, to bringing a baby into a world of torture and captivity.

Chapter Six

JENNIE PHONED. "Devon wants us to join her and her father tomorrow night in Malibu for the grunion watch."

I was sure Devon had actually invited only Jennie who is beautiful and doesn't seem to know it. People were always trying to set her up with their troubled brothers, unmotivated cousins, and sad dads. When we first met, I too assumed Jennie was single. Maybe because Loy was so fine to live with, she came across as a happy person with the fresh unmutilated look of a woman who'd never been married, and what with a delicate ring on every one of her elegant fingers, who was to know one was a wedding band? So the *us* was a diplomatic modification—Jennie adding me and Loy to the invitation—but I said yes.

Grunion are fish. What's interesting about them (besides the name) is that on spawning nights, after high tide and at the right phase of the moon, they ride the waves and strand themselves on Southern California beaches. You can scoop them right up with your hands, but for this you need a license. You don't need permission to watch.

We were early and walked the boardwalk out to the dunes.

I said, "Someday there's gonna be vendors at the beach selling blinders." I could see whole phalanxes of people advancing for a glimpse of the ocean, eyes shielded from the piles of trash and hordes of humans. "Like the ones you put on horses in the city so they won't get spooked."

"You say that like it's OK," Devon said.

"Yankee ingenuity," I said. "You don't see a world destroyed but a marketing opportunity." I had more ideas, about selling tickets to people waiting in line to touch a tree, but Devon wasn't listening. She was staring at Loy, all the while holding tight to her much younger brother's hand to keep him from hanging on David's legs. David was clearly annoyed by the filial clinging but oblivious to the stranglehold of his tie and to his black shoes already filled up with sand.

"Daddy!" The little boy kept calling "Daddy!" His little mouth was smeared with pink as though he'd been eating raspberry ice. After switching his gaze back and forth between Jennie and me, I thought I heard him whisper to Devon, "Does one of them spawn with Daddy?"

Devon didn't answer, preoccupied with Loy—because he's gorgeous, I thought, but as it later turned out, she was merely stunned and excited to be seeing an African American person socially. In the most diverse city on the planet, there was brown skin everywhere but not, she explained later to Jennie, that you could talk to.

She said, "Is it weird being married to someone who isn't white?"

"I'm not white," said Jennie.

"You're just like white," said Devon.

"Is that meant as a compliment?" Jennie said.

"You're not different, the way black people are."

To me, Jennie said, "I don't know which is worse, to have your difference define you or to have it denied. Do me a favor: Keep that girl out of Loy's way."

"We've sort of met before," I said to David. "Gorilla Bachelor Societies."

"You were there?"

He'd been seated behind me at the presentation on the gender ratio of gorillas born in North American captivity. For no particular reason, males vastly outnumbered females, which meant most of the fellows would go through life without ever having a mate which meant zoos had to figure out how to handle and house them.

"Strategies for gorilla management," David said.

"That's from the human point of view," I said. "I'd rather we considered strategies for gorilla happiness."

He smirked and looked at me—really looked at me—for the first time.

I had judged him correctly, one of those men who will dismiss all radical points of view but consider the women who espouse them cute.

Two weeks later I took David to meet the white-cheeked gibbons, Luke and Lulu, the prettiest little apes in the zoo—Luke all soft black plush except for the white markings on his face and Lulu, creamy blonde. We watched their acrobatics, both of them swinging arm over arm from their branches, flying like trapeze artists with her right behind him, separating, then swinging back to meet one another in flight.

"The females are always blonde and the babies are born that way, to blend in. If it's a male, he'll turn black as he matures," I said, but David wasn't listening. "David?" He seemed anxious. "Something wrong?" and I realized at once he thought I'd brought him here to hint at commitment: As any primatologist knows, gibbons mate for life. Oh, please. That isn't what I was driving at. My point was that non-human animals—like those in his lab—have feelings. I wasn't holding the gibbons out as a model. Being monogamous, they are the least intelligent of the apes. Juggling multiple partners is what makes other primates so clever and I have always valued smarts over fidelity.

"You can recognize the subspecies by the differences in their testicle tufts," I said. Men like David love it when you talk dirty in a scientific way.

Luke had diabetes and being a guy, he tended to eat not only his own food but as much of Lulu's as he could grab, I explained. We couldn't seem to keep him on a healthy diet, and his blood sugar was way out of control. We had to separate them to save him. One of the keepers had the idea to try him on insulin. He learned to hold out his arm every day for the needle. He'd be cranky sometimes, no arm. But in a year's time, we had him trained, and he was healthy. We put them back together. No one knew what to expect. After all, they hadn't seen each other for at least a year. I slid back the gate. He walked in cautiously and then their eyes met. They stood, frozen, just staring. Then they ran toward each other and embraced, holding on for dear life and swaying in each other's arms.

"Happy ending," David said.

"Not quite," I said. "Once he started eating her food again, we couldn't seem to get his dosage right." He'd flop out. That is, he'd get the shakes and end up loose-limbed on his back, trembling on the ground. Never a coma, not quite an emergency, but obviously in trouble. "I was there once when it happened," I told David. "Lulu got all agitated. She'd look at him and look at me. Then she came over to the fence and put out her hand." At first I hesitated. Rules. Finally "I didn't actually take her hand. I just opened mine and let it hover there, and she grasped it, and then I squeezed back, and we stayed that way with the fence between us until Luke's episode passed and he got back on his feet and she left me to run to his side."

As I spoke, I put my hand out, and David took it.

On the beach at Malibu, David walked with his arms tight by his sides.

"May I tell you," he said to Jennie, "how wonderful you were in *Flower Drum Song*?"

"No," she said.

Several families had gathered, mostly Latino, plus a couple of little blondies wearing t-shirts from a progressive private school. Most of the families had brought buckets. The only little boy with raspberry lips was David's son.

"Tonight, you're all going to see a miracle of nature," said the ranger. "It's late in the season. So for probably the last time this year, hundreds, maybe thousands, of small silver bodies will be slithering and shining all over this beach. But first, let's learn about the grunion. Do I have a volunteer? A small body? You don't have to be silver, but you have to be a girl."

A little blondie raised her hand and stepped forward.

"You're a lady grunion," said the ranger, "and the wave has left you high and dry up on the beach. So lie down on the sand and wiggle to make yourself a nest."

"Do you think she's got a bellybutton ring?" Jennie asked.

"If you were a grunion, you'd be flopping your tail around to excavate a place in the sand. Twist your body, lady grunion! Now release your eggs!"

The ranger took David's son by the arm. "Now you're the Papa Grunion, and you have to do your part. Lie down on top of her—"

"Hey, wait a minute," said Loy.

"—and curve around all over her and release your milt all over her body."

The little girl's mother looked on, smiling. David looked nervous.

"Move," said the ranger. "Don't just lay there on her. Move!"

Loy grabbed David's son and pulled him off the little girl's body. Jennie got up in the ranger's face. "You're a very sick person," she said.

The girl's mother grabbed Jennie. "What do you think you're doing?"

"This is a science lesson," said the ranger.

"Someone should report you," I said.

"Science has no morality," said Devon.

The mother called Loy a pervert. "You're the one who's giving them ideas."

Sometimes you have this brief window in which to change your life. I had two semesters off from teaching. David had the disequilibrium of his divorce. He was at his most vulnerable. His wife had thrown him out after telling everyone including their children about his sexual inadequacy, his 6-year-old son had started wearing lipstick, his daughter treated him like a child, and he was having pangs of conscience over Rosie. I met him first. If only I had staked an unassailable claim before the Neoproctologists got him. (*Why are we here on earth? Are you baffled by the behavior of the people around you? Do you wish the hardness in your heart would melt?*) I do have to admit that after their regimen of high colonics he did relax and look a little less like a shoebox.

"Among the primary indigenous peoples," he eventually told me, "the stool is long and large in diameter. It floats and has no offensive odor."

I wasn't sure you could get any more primary than Caesar, the gorilla, and his feces, when he threw a handful at us, were not pleasantly aromatic.

"It's the artificial diet he's on," David said.

For a while, my sweet Lyle was throwing up at people and chucking stones. One afternoon, I saw him hunch and make a fist so I tried to head off a woman with her child. When I realized he was merely jerking off, I let them through. The mother snatched up her kid and fled.

We went up to visit the drills and I told David about Lyle's frenzies—tearing at and biting himself, and his aberrant behavior—rubbing a dead rat all over his body, scraping his penis hard against cement.

Drill baboons are stumpy-tailed, black-masked, mostly peaceful, big monkeys (related to the more colorful and popular mandrill). Their habitat is shrinking—just a small area in West Africa, including the island of Bioko. The forest gets logged, the logging roads bring in the hunters, and then there's a profitable trade in meat. The male baboons stand firm, holding the dogs off long enough for the females to escape, but the females stand by their men and—a species doesn't vanish. No poof!, no wave of the wand. What happens is, animals die. One by one, or two by two. They die.

And now we were supposed to save them.

But for what? Human consumption? I knew there was a difference between consumption for food and consumption for entertainment—you take a metaphor too far and your thinking's really fucked—but either way, we were generating a supply of product. I think the baboons understood that. We say we're only trying to help. They resist.

Take Michael. He was supposed to be the role model, give Lyle some pointers on having his way with female drills. So what happens? Michael falls for Melissa. There's Becky, with her anogenital swelling all rosy and ripe, offering herself to save the species, and all the big lug wants to do is cuddle up to an aging post-reproductive female with arthritis. And poor little Leona, ignored by all, walking around with a piece of burlap on her head.

"Just because something exists," said David, "it doesn't mean it must continue to exist."

Lyle had his big toe in his mouth. David and I watched as he grabbed at his own limbs and flailed and bit himself and pulled out his hair.

I stated the obvious. "He's upset."

"Is it me?" David asked.

I would have liked to imagine Lyle was jealous, but our thing was pretty much over. It was months since he'd jerked off in my direction in a friendly way. When he did masturbate at me, it was with hard aggressive thrusts, obviously not about sex, but power.

David said, "It's not scientific to give an animal a name like a pet."

"Trust me," I said, and hastened to add that was only a figure of speech. I've learned to run in the opposite direction whenever someone asks for trust. "Every animal in the zoo is listed in the stud book with a proper numerical ID," I said. "But it turns out they're happier and they stay healthier when spoken to by name, when they have a relationship with the keeper. It's a Stockholm Syndrome kind of thing. Everything runs better when we treat each individual with affection and respect."

As we watched, Becky presented to Lyle, that is, she positioned her rump right in his face. She turned her head and made eyes at him over her shoulder. I could see his erection but he just foraged around in the dirt for something to eat.

Leona had a hysterectomy, so her rump no longer swelled. Like Melissa, she was genetically useless. Becky carried around behind her what changed over the month from a deflated wrinkled pouch to something round and taut as a Crenshaw melon.

At full swelling, her shit came out the top and stood straight in the air and didn't fall till she'd break it off with her hand.

David and I held our breaths as Lyle suddenly noticed her again and approached. But all he did was stick a finger in the orifice, then sniff at his finger and lick it.

Poor Becky. She cycled for nothing. For a while, I explained to David, she tried being friends with Melissa, sitting beside her, grooming her—very junior high—just to get close to Michael. When she still couldn't get his attention, she began to attack Melissa. The next ploy was to sit down below, batting her eyes up at him. She got some response. Michael would approach every now and then and sniff at her swelling and then go right back to Melissa.

And there they were, the sweethearts, cuddled up together as usual, stroking each other's faces, gazing into each other's eyes, and kissing. He got so excited his teeth started to chatter and his lips smacked. Then the only thing powerful enough to separate them came along. A truck went by and Michael ran off to the fence to get a closer look.

It took forty minutes for him to get back in Melissa's good graces. David got bored with waiting.

"The science we do takes patience," I told David. That was true, but it was also spin. Those of us who worked closely with animals had to put up a good scientific front because our affections and loyalties were always suspect. "We don't just set up the infernal machine and let it run."

"Neither do we," David said. "There were...excesses in the past...but we have ethical standards now. It's thirty years since anyone bashed in the head of an unanaesthetized lab monkey."

"Progress," I said.

"Yes," he said. "I have a conscience. Or I'm developing one. But what you've got is an inordinate identification with animals. It's...unwholesome."

It could have been but wasn't. Years ago, I tried licking Molly's fur the way I thought her mother might. She looked at me like I was crazy and ran away. She chooses to be my companion only as long as I'm myself, no counterfeit. She recognizes what's real and what's unnatural. The attachment between us, in spite of our difference, is part of the natural world.

"Animals know when you're angry," I said. "They know when you're scared. If they can read your emotions, how can you imagine they don't have any of their own?" I told him how Molly used to climb into the litter box whether she needed it or not whenever I sat on the toilet. She could see the analogy between her and me. She could recognize our common ground.

"Who's Molly?" he said.

"See! You called her a who, not a what!"

At last, Melissa let Michael groom her again. She brought her muzzle to his. Another truck passed—and he was gone.

Chapter Seven

DES WAS DRUNK WHEN HE PROPOSED to me, he was drunk when we took out the license and got married. He was drunk throughout our intoxicating honeymoon. Okay, so was I. We lived on passion and tenderness and all-night conversations and laughter and booze.

The first time we made love, I had my period. Blood spattered all over the sheets, the floor, the walls. "This looks like a crime scene," I said.

"A Jackson Pollock," he said. Even his similes were classier than mine.

"You're not just sexy," he said one night. "You *are* sex." Then one day he woke up sober. "Rae?" he said. "What are you doing here?"

I'm talking massive blackouts, and I don't mean those caused in the great state of California by Enron, Arnold Schwarzenegger and George Bush. What does it mean when a life is made up of events that don't register when, to your mind, everything that happens never happened?

Maybe I'm exaggerating, but some of you, I'm sure, know exactly what I mean.

During his bouts of sobriety, my presence in his life seemed a puzzle. There were absences when he forgot me altogether and took up with others. I never called it infidelity or promiscuity but rather exuberance. It pleased me that he loved women, lots of them, as long as he kept on loving me. But what did it mean that every expression of my husband's love left no trace in memory? Everything—the passion, tenderness, the entwining of bodies, the promises, jokes, discussions, tears, the arguments and reconciliations, the kisses, plans, apologies, all my fears for him and my new growing fear of him, all that joyful fucking and sucking and touching and loving—it all disappeared into a black hole in his sweet sad substance-abused brain. I was the only witness to our life together. He might as well have been my fantasy.

When I told him we were divorcing, he looked more baffled than ever.

"I can't believe it," he said. "After all we've been through."

"What have we been through together?" I asked. He couldn't remember.

Which explains why Weezie Wickham's sweet vagueness didn't throw me for a loop. The holes in his brain were self-inflicted, hers were surgical, but her gracious confusion, like Jennie's boozing, brought back a nostalgic warmth along with that terrible ache, remembering all the days when I wished his life and my life could be different, and I wished and wished that there were something, anything, I could do.

WEEZIE'S NEEDS COMPELLED US to put other plans on hold—my pursuit of David, my trip to the Basoba reservation with Jennie.

It didn't matter that we'd missed the powwow which—though I'd expected to enjoy it immensely—was really just our pretext for crossing onto reservation land. Indian law intrigued Jennie, mostly because issues of sovereignty and the jurisdictional tangle of federal, state, and reservation law made it near impossible to determine accountability. Not to mention the federal doctrine of plenary power which allows Congress to unilaterally abrogate (that means abolish, nullify, do away with) any treaty ever made with any Indian tribe, making Indian treaty rights about as meaningful as my ex-husband's abrogated memory. At Basoba, the situation turned out to be even more sinister than we had imagined, but that came later.

The day before Weezie's toxic home was to be demolished, I rented a U-Haul and Jennie drove it.

Jennie wanted Sara to come with us. "She's a journalist. She can probably do more to help Weezie than I can."

Sara couldn't even use the media to help herself. When the neighbors in her gated community objected to her unsightly wheelchair ramp—"Does she need to have it at the front door?"—and to Ruby—"a pet!" they argued, "not a service dog as claimed!"—Sara figured she'd expose the situation in print but her newspaper advised her she was a journalist, not a columnist, the distinction being she was not allowed to write about herself.

And I didn't see how we could take her to Weezie's. How was she supposed to get up the stairs?

"I don't know," Jennie said. "But she must know. There are stairs everywhere. She must have a method."

"The method," I said, "is called exclusion."

"Oh."

I would say the realization sobered Jennie except she was already sober and I'd noticed she hadn't brought her thermos.

"Anyway," I said, "it's just wrong to inflict Marcia on someone."

We had arranged to meet Marcia at the house because she had offered Weezie a place to stay. Luckily only two could fit in the cab of the U-Haul, or Jennie would have insisted on picking her up.

"Be more tolerant," she said.

"I am more tolerant," I said. For that I could thank Sara. Despite my love for the non-human, I'd never liked dogs—nothing but thrill killers, snitches, and slaves. That was till I met her endearingly catlike little Ruby.

I said, "You're going moral on me because you feel guilty for not working."

"I feel guilty," Jennie said, "for being a self-indulgent useless waster of time and the gift of my whole wasted life. I've just devoted three intellectually and emotionally stultifying years in order to become a lawyer, and now I'm hoping I flunked the damn exam because it's not what I want. I really really really can't imagine doing law for the rest of my life. My parents will be so upset, and Loy's going to be disappointed in me."

"He just wants you to be happy," I said.

"It's pretty awful to be happy at a time like this."

I thought she meant Weezie and her cats about to become homeless, but she was referring to terrorism, anthrax, the loss of civil liberties at home, the Bush coup d'état, the restructuring of the US economy.

I added to her list: "People who drive SUV's."

"It's a big car," she said and continued with the craven irresponsibility of the Democratic Party, war, the threat of more war.

"I've got to quit drinking," she said.

"No," I said. I guessed, "You're not drinking because you're pregnant." How could Jennie fall for such a cliché?—a woman feels useless so she breeds.

"I've been drinking too much. Ever since the Twin Towers," she said, "I've been afraid all the time."

"The Administration is manipulating your fear," I said. "But maybe fear is good. Maybe we're supposed to feel it."

A week before, some dumb guy jumped in with the lions on a dare. Security got to him before the big cats did. Asshole, we'd all said, and angrily, because if he'd been hurt, it would have been his own damn fault but it's the lion who would have been put to death. But now it occurred to me what he'd done was honest, restoring the true relationship between man and beast. When lions are artificially in captivity, humans are artificially safe.

Jennie said, "I used law school to numb my mind."

"And margaritas," I suggested.

"Overwhelming myself with very demanding boredom just to keep from thinking."

"I needed to be with animals," I said. That morning, 9/11? I let out a cry and Molly ran to me. She climbed all over me, frantically sniffing, unable to figure out where I was injured. Her confusion comforted me, to be with an alert, intelligent being who couldn't comprehend the pain humans feel or the harm we inflict on one another.

"I have religious ideas," Jennie said.

"Don't," I said.

"I want to understand evil."

"Oh, call them evil, like that explains it."

"No," she said. "The point is, I want to know what spiritual path a human being must follow after doing what is unforgivable. It's not about redemption at the last moment—getting into heaven in spite of what you've done. It's how you live on earth after the worst of you has been made manifest."

"I'm not sure I get you."

"Everyone else is always the evildoer. It has nothing to do with us. We act like there's parts of history that never happened."

"No argument with you there," I said.

"Maybe it's because we'd have no idea of how to go on living once we face it."

"Cosmetic surgery," I said.

"You're the one with the plastic ear."

"To hold my glasses on!"

"I'm thinking of going to AA," she said.

'Wow," I said. "I know we've been drinking a lot, maybe too much, maybe irresponsibly—"

"I don't think I'm an alcoholic," she said. "I just want to go to meetings and be with people who admit they've done terrible things and then try to go on and live good lives in spite of it."

"I hear you," I said. I'd gone for a while, to keep Des company after his first DUI, when the judge let him off with restitution, community service and AA.

Jennie said, "Those rooms may be the only honest place in America."

But instead of going to AA, soon she would be reading history and sharing her research via email, e.g., As part of his campaign to round up, detain, and deport immigrants, J. Edgar Hoover predicted a Soviet-inspired revolution would break out on May 1, 1920 with a wave of assassinations, bombings, and general strikes and had the whole nation on high alert—hysterical, frightened, willing to suspend Constitutional guarantees—for nothing.

I found this reassuring, suggesting as it did that in America, rightwing racism, intolerance, and the impulse to dictatorship would always fester under the surface as a disease the country could never be cured of, but these occasional outbreaks didn't have to wreck your life. It was not much different, in the end, from having herpes.

I thanked Jennie for the information but advised her to stop the mailings. She herself was the one to tell me the FBI had begun monitoring private emails under a program called, coincidentally enough, CARNIVORE.

"I don't get you," she said. "You know how wrong everything is but you don't do anything."

"I've been diagnosed with a personality disorder," I said. "Violently oppositional apathy."

"Who diagnosed you?" she said.

"I did."

Jennie pulled the truck up and parked at the foot of Weezie's hill, but we sat there a moment without getting out.

She said, "If my parents hadn't escaped to this country, none of us would be alive."

"That's my family, too," I said.

It was weird. I grew up—and thought every Jewish kid grew up—hearing the vow of *Never again*. I thought it meant to never again tolerate genocide or persecution or discrimination of any kind against anyone. Then I found out to some, *Never again* applied only to Jews. Now there's people who've never heard *Never* at all. Who even say *I was just following orders* like it's a legitimate excuse.

"I love this country," Jennie said. "I'm grateful to this country. But—"

"When I was a kid, this boy confronted me on the playground," I said. "During recess. He wanted to know if there were a conflict between America and Israel, which side would I be on. I was American, utterly American, I couldn't imagine being anything other than American. But I said I'd be on the side of whichever country was right." I could hate my child-self for being so stupid, and I wished I could still be a child and believe a country could be right and that a citizen had any way of even knowing.

She said, "America is starting to look more and more like where my parents came from."

Her parents came from North Korea.

"Maybe that's an exaggeration," I said, though it was exactly the sort of thing I would have said for effect to David.

"Do I smell bad?" asked Weezie.

Was a truthful answer expected?

"I forget all about personal hygiene," she said. "I try to remind myself: My body is the small animal I must care for and comfort."

We had completed the task of removing the belongings that could be salvaged and taking them to storage. This was complicated by differing opinions over what needed to be saved. Weezie wanted us to store all the piles of sodden newspapers she hadn't yet gotten around to reading and Jennie was intent on finding the files, Marcia wanted a candlesnuffer named Willy—the only inheritance Weezie had asked for or received from her fabulously wealthy grandmother and which she now promised to Marcia "if you can find him." The bedroom closet door was guarded by a mean old feral tabby named Arthur, and Jennie was reluctant to open any closet doors on account of her fear of Hanta virus.

Nonetheless, after my body was raked by Arthur's claws, he himself spinning, spitting, fur electric with rage and sparks actually shooting from his eyes, and after Marcia took him from me and we watched him purring and cuddling in her arms, after we'd contemplated the mystery of how there's often nothing you can do to earn a cat's trust and often nothing you can do to lose it but one way or another, he makes up his mind, convincing proof—if any more were needed—that he has one, we did remove from Weezie's bedroom: two suitcases of clothing; shoe boxes full of receipts (some dating back as far as 1959); a beaver coat that moths had been at; pages of the Congressional Record that fell open to pressed flowers that disintegrated to dust; an

Ice Capades ballerina fixed atop a round mirror; twenty pairs of elbow-length gloves—a lucky find as Weezie's belongings were filthy and with her permission we each pulled on a pair; a box of classical and blues 78s; a jewelry box with a hank of hair inside and two more shoe boxes filled with jewelry; photos with faces cut out; high school and college (Wellesley, yes) yearbooks; report cards going back to first grade; a gold watch with initials not her own; hat boxes containing porcelain commemorative plates featuring portraits of First Ladies—"I have a complete set as far as Mamie"; high heels, all the same size and style and all black; stacks of canned cat food that we would open and leave out in the back field heading out to the foothills hoping this would encourage a transition to life in the wild.

I took a framed photo from the wall and brushed off the dust. There was Weezie, just as I'd imagined her, gloves and pearls, the sole female standing in a group of men behind President Eisenhower who was signing something. "I'm second from the left," she said.

We passed boxes and dresses on hangers and an improbable boudoir chair from one to another down the single file pathway left between trash piles and finally out the door. Before I took the bedside table Weezie snatched up the photo that stood upon it. A woman with short dark hair grinned into the camera, her arms around a very big dog. "Flori," she said.

In the linen closet, we found a dead cat lying amid congealed blood and vomit on a neatly folded pile of sheets. The towels on a higher shelf looked clean, but without removing anything, Jennie firmly shut the door.

In the kitchen, Marcia opened all the cabinets.

"Here he is!" Marcia cried.

"No dear," said Weezie, "that's an olive-pitter."

"There are good zephyrs and bad zephyrs," Marcia told me. "The bad ones make the flames flicker. Willy captures them, and then they can't do any mischief in the world."

"What happened with your DUI?" I asked her.

"Oh, they took away my license."

"Then how did you drive here today?"

"They took my license," she said, "not my car....Here he is! Willy!"

"No, dear, that looks like the thing I used to use to fix the garbage disposal when the garbage disposal still worked."

The refrigerator was full of cat food. From the freezer compartment Jennie carried off the small leather briefcase that Weezie identified as the repository of her files.

She smiled through her tears as we left the cats behind.

Marcia insisted on adopting Arthur, too old to hunt, too mean and ugly to find a new home. She carried him in his reeking basket. Weezie carried Nefertiti in her arms. Jennie chose Chessie for preferring French fries to meat-based pet food industry products while I, wanting every last one of them, was unable to choose and left the premises with none.

But as we transferred the last carton, last hat box, last winter coat to the storage facility I had rented, I felt the unmistakable sensation of young claws on my thigh. A black kitten clung there, then scrambled to my breast and hung on. In the dark depths of the truck he'd hidden, invisible until now. Even Weezie claimed never to have seen him before, and so I named him Ninja.

Chapter Eight

THIS IS PROBABLY A GOOD TIME to tell you a little more about the Church of Neoproctology. Seeing as how it and its members keep coming up, you might, wrongly, think this is unacceptable and unlikely coincidence, so I'll point out that in addition to The Castle where Marcia lived and Weezie was about to make her home, the Church owns countless square miles of prime Southern California real estate and casts its influence over millions of souls. And lest you think this is just another example of stereotypical California wackiness, I'll remind you that the Church extends its reach all over the United States and into many foreign countries, even those where its adherents suffer persecution for their faith, so that wherever you go you are likely to come across a devotee to the point where the odds are extremely good that you, reading this right now, are in fact a Church member or, in the language of the Church itself, a "host."

If you were to attend one of the free seminars offered, as Jennie and I did at David's urging, you would learn the difference between catabolic energy (created by the breakdown of complex molecules, contributing nothing to growth) and anabolic energy (which contributes everything), the difference between the hosts of angels (referred to in the Bible, a veiled reference to the god virus that enters your cell and duplicates itself without causing damage), and the demonic virus that kills.

The doctrine is spread, in fact, person to person, like a virus. No books, no junk mail solicitations, no television commercials or billboards or advertising on the back of bus benches, which should explain why you've never heard of Neoproctology if, in the unlikely event, you haven't.

If you were to pay the initiation fee (which we did not) or if you were to find someone willing to break a solemn oath and tell you secrets (as we did), you would learn that evolution was not, after all, a Darwinian matter of survival of the fittest, but driven by viral mutation, devised and executed by the true God in the form of the most complex organism in the universe.

Secret #1, which would ordinarily cost you $5,000, states: "Even the simplest virus is a helluva lot smarter and more adaptable than you are."

You would also learn the difference between virus and bacteria—bacterial action being what gives shit its stink, and how to maintain colonic and general health in order to make yourself the optimal host for viral godhead.

According to Axiom 1: "Nonbelievers run a fever. The true host is inflamed."

Later we'll explore whether a Neoproctologist can also be a deep ecologist, and what Neoproctology can reveal about the war in Iraq, but that's enough for now.

Let's just say we all smelled pretty bad when we arrived at The Castle, a great crafted wood and exposed beam building in the style of Greene & Greene—too much a recent knockoff to have made it into the Registry of Historic Places, but quite impressive all the same.

There was a heated discussion in progress. Someone said, "Charles Manson is not a Scientologist. That is so unfair." To Manson? I wondered, or Scientology? People broke off the argument to welcome us.

"Jennie Kim!" said a woman. "My daughter had you for third grade!"

Jennie sighed.

"We consider ourselves a family," Marcia said.

I'd grown up in a family and so did not consider this a recommendation.

Arthur quickly claimed a corner of the huge basement kitchen as his new domain. Weezie carried her suitcases into one of the women's dormitory rooms—four sets of bunk beds. We four filthy humans were treated to long hot baths, and offered use of the laundry room for our soiled clothes while several Neoproctologists more than willingly played with Ninja, Nefertiti and Chessie.

Portraits of the Church's founder, Dr. Jim, hung in every room, as well as—and there's no need to laugh—a crucifix-like caduceus with a healthy pink colon twined about it instead of the traditional snakes, but no one tried to proselytize except for a man who stared me down and said "You're avoiding life."

"It agrees with me," I said.

Then there was some talk about the virtues of a low-pyrine

non-skatole forming diet as we joined the hosts in the refectory for a tasty albeit vegetarian meal of jalapeños stuffed with cornmeal, broccoli au gratin, grapefruit and spring water by candlelight. We met some very intelligent people—urban planners, social workers, an acoustician, a particle physicist whose conversation I couldn't even begin to reproduce accurately—and they all got along in splendid good humor with the sprinkling of crazies, whose conversation about, for example, the eleven concentration camps being built in Glendale is more within my ability to report. There was also a former gang member—the Church had paid to have his tattoos removed—and a former Goth with two bare spots the size of quarters on his head.

"That's what they did to *me*!" said Weezie.

"No," I said. "Santa Cruz."

I guessed right. His parents had paid for his horns while he was in college and the Church had picked up the bill to have them removed.

Everyone already knew Weezie as it turned out the clinic where Marcia and Weezie first met had been the Neoproctologist Cleansing Tower. I would have liked to see the tower and the leadership bedroom suites, but instead, the tour offered to Jennie and me proved to be a tedious trek from "Here's our Xerox machine, this is where we eat lunch, this is the kitchen, this is a storage closet." The woman who led us didn't seem evasive, merely clueless. "My blood came back from the lab 1000 to one," she told me. "They said, Wow! Send us more! This person has the most amazing blood!"

Later, my mostly favorable impression of the church would

change because of what happened to David. Later, Jennie would ask, "Don't you see it's a total fraud? Some guy just sat down and made it up," and I figured, so what? How is that different from Plato? At one point I did tell David I was suspicious of their pseudo-science. "You're not a scientist," he said. "How would you know it's pseudo?"

Now because of the controversy surrounding the Church, some of which I myself was destined to stir up, I want to be clear and I want to be fair. Overall, that night at dinner, I had no sense that people's idiosyncrasies or individual natures were being suppressed. Our hosts were smart—even smart-alecky (as per style of Secret #1). I later learned of a significant overlap between Neoproctology and Mensa which may not prove much of anything. As Bobby was to point out, folks in Mensa may have high IQ's, but they are also ethnocentric with all the intellectual limitations that implies, having chosen for their organization's name the Mexican Spanish word for "foolish." We were in the midst of a guerrilla art action at the time, plastering LA with posters—stuff like: *Why does the U.S. have a better government than Mexico? In Mexico, two brothers rigged the presidential election and went on to loot the nation's wealth.*

Bobby was good at drawing cartoons and parallels. He thought the Mormon Church had made the same mistake as Mensa, receiving its revelation from the Angel Moroni. I disagreed: the name tends to prove the angel's legitimacy as what English-speaking mortal would have picked it?

"How does your Church address the evil in human nature?" Jennie asked the Neoproctologists. Basically by addressing toxins in the lower large intestine, and by extension, the catabolyzing of wrongheaded thinking.

I, myself, have studied the MoF (modulus of fineness of feces) in our primate relatives and can cite studies that correlate the texture of the fecal matrix to patterns of aggression and sociability and so I wanted to hear more, but once dinner and the social niceties were done, Jennie was in a hurry to leave. She wanted to open that briefcase and read those files.

I was sure I'd stowed it under the passenger seat, but when Jennie reached down to claim it, all she found was a copy of *Dr. Jim's Eat for Colon Health Cookbook*. The briefcase was gone.

Chapter Nine

I said to Bobby, "But here in the US, no one gets irony."

"Whaddaya mean? They get their news from the Daily Show."

I'm a teacher, so I explained the difference between irony and parody or lampoon. "And conservatives take everything literally. The Bible and all that. And anyway, it's not two Bush brothers, it's three." Everyone always forgets about Neil, but as a teacher I knew he was making a fortune selling the educational software mandated by his brother's No Child Left Behind scam.

During those weeks when I tried to ignore that war with Iraq was imminent and Jennie tried not to let me ignore either its imminence or its immorality, she and I returned to the Castle looking (unsuccessfully) for the briefcase and found out that Dr. Jim was not actually a proctologist but a renegade dentist, and I went back to where Weezie's house had stood to see the bulldozed site. (Weezie would get a bill for the demolition and cleanup.) Several cats scattered when they saw me. I wondered what would become of them. I thought of Angel, the sad little coati at the zoo who must once have been someone's—I have to use the word—pet. When the keeper came in to clean, she'd jump up on the human shoulder and cuddle. What really broke my heart was when children approached the fence. She'd extend her snout and gaze at them, quietly enraptured. I was sure she'd grown up in the company of children. She ran along the fence trying to follow them when they walked away and once they were out of sight, she'd pace in circles, coming up on her hind legs with a hop once on every turn. Stereotypy. I always wondered, What went wrong? Did she accidentally bite someone's kid? Was she confiscated? Whatever happened, the life she once knew could never be restored, not her wildness, and not the people who were her family, the human house that had been her home.

At the Castle, I learned Arthur's bad temper was traced to an abscess on his back. Following surgery, he kept scratching at the wound. One of the Neoproctologists knitted him a sweater so he'd leave the spot alone till it could heal. Weezie seemed happy but, with her smile, who could tell?

At the zoo, I monitored a sick siamang who vomited whenever she drank water until she herself hit on the idea of soaking a towel in the pool and gently sucking the moisture, and I watched as Lyle became increasingly more destructive—tearing limbs off trees, then uprooting the trees themselves, and doing things in the loft the keeper could describe only as "unspeakable."

At home, Ninja was not quite as clingy as the orphaned orangutan who was said to have clutched the body of primatologist Birute Galdikas so insistently for weeks on end she could not remove it even to shower, but still decisively staked his claim on me so that I had to mediate between him and Molly. I tried to overcome David's shyness by leaving phone messages, sending a series of humorous e-cards, and a weekly homemade cheesecake—OK, Jennie helped me bake them since she's much better at those things than I am, but I did send them—and I still made it my business to find time for art.

Just to give you an idea: Our Gorilla Theater homework was to study the balcony scene from *Romeo and Juliet*. We were also supposed to spend fifteen minutes a day exploring what it would feel like to have a tail.

"That's such a waste of time," I said.

"You're talking about time as we know it," said Bernice.

"Yeah."

"Anyway, you said you wanted one," she said. "Imagine the sensation. Bring your senses to life till you feel the blood flowing into the appendage. Feel the warmth. Feel where it connects to the base of your spine. If you really concentrate, you'll feel it twitch. You'll have the actual sensation of being able to knock valuable pieces of china off of tables and shelves."

"Sounds like psychosis," said Jennie.

"It's an adaptation of Lee Strasberg's famous coffee cup exercise," Bernice said. "You're not going to argue with The Method."

"No," Jennie said. "With the result."

"You've got to enter into dogginess," Bernice told us, "because we're going to play the scene as though Romeo and Juliet are two purebred dogs of different breeds who must not be allowed to mate. And they're in heat! Amory, you're Romeo. Devon, Juliet. Sara, be the Nurse."

"I resent the way my sexuality is routinely denied," said Sara.

"We're not doing this for you," said Bernice. "It's on behalf of Ruby."

"Who doesn't go into heat," Sara said. "She's been spayed."

Bernice dabbed at her eyes. "Talk about denying her sexuality!"

"Why can't I be Juliet?" Sara asked.

She loved her body. Sara was proud of the biceps she developed operating her manual chair. She visited the salon for Brazilian wax almost every week to remove body hair—all of it—so that her skin was always lustrous and soft as Weezie's kid gloves. She wore miniskirts because though her legs couldn't walk, they were as shapely as the rest of her and could be touched. People—even I—couldn't resist petting Ruby, proof she was not in fact a service dog which must not be touched or distracted. Ruby practically lived in Sara's lap. When people stroked her, she'd perk one ear up, let the other flop down, then wriggle and roll till your hands slipped onto Sara's silky flesh. ("And who," Sara said, "is to say that's not a service?")

"Someday," said Bernice, "—I should live that long—I'll get to work with actors who can take direction. Now, dogs take your places."

Even I would acknowledge there is no creature happier about being alive than a dog. Even I feel a quickening of hope when I see them—at a distance—tails wagging, ears flapping, leaping and bounding, ready to jump out of their very skins with joy. That was not the acting choice Amory and Devon made.

Amory whined and howled and scrabbled his paws against the wall. Devon, on all fours, whimpered and yowled.

"Here, girl, here!" said Sara.

Devon panted.

"Good dog!" Sara said.

Devon jumped and landed near Amory. Sara wheeled her chair in pursuit.

"Heel!" she screamed. "Sit!"

Amory jumped and slammed into Sara's chair. His teeth touched her neck, then he released her and Devon's whining grew more frantic as Amory mounted her from behind.

"Scene!" hollered Bernice who had failed to teach us—rinky-dink amateurs as she later told us we were—that *Scene*! means stop, "Scene!" while Amory dry humped Devon and I tried to pull him off her.

"This is the grunions all over again," I said.

"Oh, ick," said Devon. She pushed him away and stood.

"Look," said Sara, "if you really want to raise consciousness, let's go to my neighborhood. Here's the concept: Disability is a minority group that anyone can suddenly become a member of. Unlike race," she explained. "Like you can't just wake up one morning black."

A former boyfriend of mine did. Cyril's parents had emigrated from India to Trinidad. When he traveled to the US for college, he woke up one morning and was told he was a Negro. "No," he insisted, "I'm Indian." "Don't be a self-hating Negro," he was told and he lived as a black man in America for the rest of his life.

Brazilian Carnaval attire is how Sara dressed for our action, all feathers and yes, thong, with a beribboned Ruby providing modest cover to her lap. She was radiant. We paraded down every cul-de-sac in her gated community, though of course there was no one on the street to see us. Bobby designed and printed beautiful Award Certificates (though I think he gets too fussy with the different fonts) that we slipped under every neighbor's door.

YOU' RE A WINNER!

YOU MAY REDEEM THIS CERTIFICATE FOR

ONE WHEELCHAIR
upon proof of your becoming DISABLED due to
Sudden Unexpected Accident
or
Chronic Progressive Condition!

CONGRATULATIONS!!!

"What if they really try to redeem it?" Devon asked. Being David's daughter, she came by her literal thinking honestly.

Chapter Ten

She phoned and said she had a problem and needed to talk to me alone.

This was another part of my past I didn't want to revisit. I didn't want to be a nurturing adult figure in an adolescent's life. I used to be the kind of teacher who took an interest in her kids. Being an English teacher in particular, look, you're reading books with kids, you're having them write essays to express themselves, it opens things up. You don't just know their test scores. You know *them*.

They were Devon's age, give or take a year or two. You have to understand about the kids I taught. Since they hadn't dropped out before high school, they'd been overcoming obstacles all their young lives. They were the good kids, the smart ones, the determined kids. And some of them got shot, by gangs, by police, by family members, by one another and most of them weren't lucky with the bullet like I was. Some of them went to jail. I didn't mean to get so serious on you. I had stopped being serious myself. The last few years I taught?

I was just going through the motions, hoping to get through it all smiling like Weezie.

Devon thought I could make a difference in her life, when all I wanted to do was fuck her father. Still, her interest was flattering. I thought I was a stereotype. She called me a woman of mystery.

"I'm having a problem with Gorilla Theater," she said.

I was having a problem with it, too, having grown tired of holding hands and burning sage and rehearsals that consisted of bending and stretching and other forms of physical exercise which did not become more palatable to me just because we called it acting.

I met her at The Grove, her choice, not mine, the new shopping mall with its own little trolley where I was little more than two months later to risk arrest. I found her seated on a bench, clutching a bag from Victoria's Secret, and as the ornamental fountain spewed its jets in time to the piped sounds of *That's Amore*, she told me that Bobby was prejudiced against white people.

She'd been working with him on the poster series—the ironical posters no one was going to understand:

Why is the U.S. better than El Salvador?
Millions of Salvadoreans have no access to medical care.

Why is sharia law evil?
It doesn't separate church and state
And it's not Christian!

Bobby kept her busy taping up posters in neighborhoods where she could blend in and he could not, Brentwood being where she lived with her mother who owned a successful public relations business and accepted no spousal or child support from David—"All I'm asking is that you pay some attention to the children. Is that too much to ask?" Unlike her little brother who was devastated by David's neglect, Devon generously took her father's discomfort with fatherly affection to indicate that he needed to establish a normal healthy mutually satisfying relationship with an adult person before he could show any love or concern for his kids, and this was why she was so intent on making him a match with Jennie and, Jennie being unavailable, agreed with me that I would do.

It's also possible—and here I'm going to speculate in spite of my having said I would not—that her father's seeming indifference set her up to be extremely sensitive to any perceived hint of rejection by an adult male.

I suspected her problem with Bobby came about because instead of praising her work, he made speeches which she interpreted as dismissive, e.g., "Anybody can make art. Everybody *is* art, but not everyone is an artist, man," he said. "Some weekend day when you have nothing else to do you'll come out here and slap some paint on a wall and it's art. But that don't make you an artist. You don't live for your art and suffer for your art and sacrifice for your art. You may be poor all your life just like me, but you won't be poor for your *art.*"

"And I'm not that old!" she said to me.

"Old?"

"He keeps calling me Ma'am!"

"Oh, man, he's calling you *man*," I said.

"And I am not a man!"

Devon didn't have to earn a living yet. How could she understand? Bobby had a day job as a plasterer. When he and Bernice won themselves highly competitive Arts Council grants, he expected to be able to take time off and paint. Instead, by legislative mandate, he was required to enrich the lives of troubled youth—in this case, Devon and Amory—with socially affirmative participatory art projects.

"Bobby's pissed," I admitted to Devon. "But not because you're white."

The old clock chimed in the tower over at Farmers Market. Then above us, the decorative clock at Abercrombie and Fitch struck the hour a minute late, and I told Devon that development of the self is its own reward.

Ninja, for example. How he struggled to pull himself up into the litter pan. I took the top of a shoebox and left it on the floor upside down to give him a step up. He stepped up once, so it was clear he understood how to use the help I offered, but after that, he avoided the box top and preferred the struggle. Within a couple of days, his muscles were developed enough to make the short jump. He chose to work hard and grow strong instead of accepting help.

People walked by with ice cream cones. They sat under umbrellas with their lattes. I pointed out the sign in the window at Barnes & Noble, offering validated parking with a purchase of $150.

I told Devon that race was a very complicated issue.

"Slavery is so over," she said.

I told her race was more than black and white, though black and white was the conscious national trauma.

Devon sighed. "I don't know anyone black."

"Don't be ridiculous," I said. "Aren't there any kids at school?"

"I go to private school," she said. "But it's not like we're racist."

"The laws of probability kind of rule out it being random coincidence when everyone's white."

"*They're* racist," Devon said. "The four of them always sit together."

"Yes," I said, "white folks generally feel more secure when the color is dispersed."

Devon said, "But how am I supposed to learn about cultural difference?"

"I'll tell you. The uakari monkey in the Amazon basin? Peruvians eat them, Colombians and Brazilians won't. The Brazilians say because they look too human, the Colombians because they're too ugly."

I told her how when Cyril and I were together, people looked at him with his advanced degrees, good job, and white girlfriend and accused him of thinking he was white when the point was that the world thought he was black and had even talked him into thinking it too.

"When I was in kindergarten," I told her, "I ended up in counseling because my teacher called me Rachel. I knew she meant me, so I answered and they decided I had a troubled identity. So tell me this. If Rae was more than just a convenient label, if I was supposed to consider it me, how do you think I felt when I learned my mother had a different name before she married my father? I knew even then I wanted the right to choose my own destiny. The hell with classification. What I wanted was sovereignty. Self-sovereignty." She looked at me blankly. "So, Devon, what about your name? Have you been there?"

"Where?"

"Devon."

"Yeah. Where?"

She didn't know there was such a place and told me she'd been named for her grandparents, Debra and Kevin.

"Then it should be spelled Devin," I said. "D-e-v-i-n."

She looked at me blankly again, a probable victim of the education battle of whole language versus phonics.

"After '92 it just got harder," I said, realizing she had no idea what '92 meant. "Riot," I said. "Uprising. Civil unrest. Whatever name you put on it, things just got polarized. It got harder to cross the line, or what I really mean is, till then I wasn't so aware of there even being a line. And all these white people, holding onto all that unearned power. It's like they were asking for another riot, begging for it. Sock it to me!"

"Oh! *Sock it to me* means riot! I thought it was sex!" Devon said. "I guess I've got a dirty mind."

It was around that time I'd fallen into the arms of my alcoholic ex, a white man free of history, even his own, whose amnesia could be blamed on his disease.

"Did he sweat a lot?" she asked.

"What?"

"In bed," she said. "Cyril." And then she told me what her parents didn't know. "I had sex with this boy, like, three times, just to try it?" she said.

"Amory," I said.

"No! We're friends. I mean close friends, but..."

I shook my head. "It's hard for a girl to be friends with someone of the opposite sex."

"I don't think there is such a thing," she said.

"Friendship?"

"No," she said. "Opposite sex. I think it's more like overlapping."

She was smarter than I'd realized. I told her it was kind of like the drill baboon—they're classified with mandrills but their DNA puts them closer to macaques so they're hard to classify, but why should anyone care? The drill doesn't care.

"My best friends are always guys," she said. "I don't get along with females."

"It never works," I said. "You start to think you're part of the boys club and it always turns out you aren't."

"You become an object," she said.

"Actually, I like that part. When you're not you anymore, when you're a body, you're just two bodies, or, OK, if that's what you're into, three."

"Do you think Amory's gay?" she asked.

Ask him, not me, I thought. "I don't know how to tell," I said. "All these guys—gay, straight, it doesn't matter—they get their hair styled, they get manicures for godssakes, they all fuss with their clothes. All the white guys look the same, soft. Except," I had to admit, "for new immigrants. You go to that garage across from rehearsals? Then you know you're around men. Armenians, Russians, with real hair growing out of their ears."

"I guess I'd rather take my chances with someone soft," Devon said.

"Amory?"

"No," she said. "Alex." She rolled up her sleeve and caressed her tattoo. "This was for him."

"He's an anarchist?"

She rolled her eyes. "Like Alex begins with an A. I didn't know it meant something else."

"You're not an anarchist?"

"No." She grasped my wrist. "But don't tell my Dad. He thinks I am."

"I won't tell him about Alex either," I said.

"The first time wasn't so good," she said, "but that's what you expect, right?"

My first time... "I was so in love with that boy," I told her. "I had just given myself to him. That's what we called it then, and he said the words I most longed to hear, I love you. You know what I said? I said, That's OK. You don't have to."

"Omigod," said Devon. "No wonder people your age had to invent feminism. I don't think Alex loves me, but that's not the problem. The bad part is sweat. All that sliding around and your flesh sticks and makes gross sounds like body burps."

"Sweating just shows your body's excited," I said.

"Yuck."

"You don't always sweat," I said. "Sometimes."

"Alex said it was disgusting, and I basically had to agree, and that's why we stopped doing it."

"Oh, baby," I said.

"I bet my dad doesn't sweat."

I knew that kangaroo rats didn't. I couldn't say about her dad.

"It was kinda fun sliding around," she said. "I'm not sure the sweat would've bothered me if Alex hadn't been so grossed out." She sighed. "But you know I'm trying to be more multicultural?" She went to the Museum of Radio and Television and watched some old documentary about soul. "It was awesome," she said. "That's how I know about Aretha singing *sock it to me*. Did you see those shows when you were my age?" Devon thought it must have overwhelmed white girls like me to see all those black folks sweating. Chicks jumping on stage and grabbing at Smokey Robinson with sweat just rolling down his face.

"Back then it was soul," I told her. "Now it's nostalgia music for white folks. Black kids call it that tired old Motown shit."

"I guess African Americans think sweat is sexy," she said.

"Sweat is normal," I said. "People sweat."

"What do you see in him?" she said.

"Who?"

"My father."

I didn't know how to answer, so I asked her what her mother was like.

"Busy. Very busy. I wish I could think like a person of color," she said. "What's it like to go to bed with someone who doesn't make you feel disgusting? I just keep wondering how it would feel not to be ashamed."

Once again, I didn't know what to say.

So," she said, "if Cyril wasn't really a Negro, I'm wondering, did you ever make it with a black man?"

"Yes," I said, and surprised myself by grasping her wrist. "Don't tell Jennie."

Chapter Eleven

JENNIE DIDN'T NEED TO KNOW I found her husband attractive. Not that I'd ever do anything about it, and not that Loy would ever let me. She didn't need to know I didn't go to Loy for my dental care out of fear that his fingers in my mouth—even gloved in latex—would make me wet. I was careful, but it was really nice being around him. He was good to look at. He was a turn-on, but it wasn't like the deep troubling tug I felt toward David. Just as I felt with Molly, I felt David was leading me somewhere. I didn't know where.

I led him again to the drill enclosure. (Enclosure? Exhibit? Round house? We have lots of words to substitute for "cage.")

There was Lyle, still young enough to have the physique of a lifeguard, and Michael, with his big buffalo head and shoulders.

"Part of what I hate?" I said. "Each species gets put in a separate exhibit. No chance for interspecies bonding." This wasn't strictly true, as the pale-headed saki and the little pudu deer shared a home.

"Why would different species bond?" he asked.

"Familiarity," I said. "Affection."

"I see squirrels in there," David said. "Lizards, sparrows,

flies." He continued enumerating with that dogged insistence, that dogmatic unimaginative thinking that is so thrillingly, unmistakably male.

"Fleas," I agreed. "And humans."

David had been putting electrodes in baboon brains for years—or, rather, having it done; he never touched them himself—infecting the animals with disease, testing for cognitive ability-loss associated with drug addiction. Rosie's experiment was already pointless, there being no fetal development to monitor but the lab kept obtaining semen (inducing ejaculation through electroshock to each available baboon penis—a procedure I had to research on my own, David stuttering and then falling silent when I asked him where the semen came from). He continued restraining the girls and pumping them full of drugs while keeping physiological records referred to as "data" which might prove useful someday in the future the way junked cars on a lawn hold out the promise of parts.

David looked at Rosie and saw a thing, coextensive with the equipment that held her. If he could do that to her, just imagine what he could do to me.

Together we watched as Lyle jerked off. Michael watched too.

"Baboons learn through a mix of instinct and experience," I said. "Like humans. Showing them dirty movies might help."

Lyle's eyes were closed in concentration, his body thrusting and jerking. His prick, by the way, was very pink, and on the slender side, though the head was quite bulbous.

Michael was inspired enough to finger himself for a moment before he lost interest. David turned his head away.

Bernice thought it was time Gorilla Theater did an action on behalf of the drills. But first, we had to learn about Augusto Boal. "Any of you heard of him? I thought not."

We were meeting in my living room as my place was centrally located and Bernice could no longer afford rent on the storefront.

"This is where you live?" Devon had asked, and then, "Oh, I guess teachers are poor."

Is this how Americans became heartless and greedy? Imagining this is poverty?

"Teachers make four five times as much as artists," Bobby said. "Plus medical."

"I rent," I said, "because I'm opposed to the private ownership of property"—an impressive statement, but a lie. Marriage had left me with home and savings gone, credit ruined. My own fault because I'd known better. I'd known that living alone was vastly preferable to living with someone. Unlike what seems to be most women, who long for the married state and devote themselves to finding the right person to enter that state with, I'd let hormones and alcohol blind me to the fact that for a woman Marriage=Death.

This may lead you to wonder what sort of family I grew up in. This is all I'm going to say: My father once asked how long a cat is expected to live. When I told him twenty years would be a very long life, he said, "Just when you're starting to get attached to it, it dies!"

Now the cats distracted us from Augusto Boal. We watched

Ninja wriggle over the tops of books in the bookcase to hide. Molly patiently pulled the books one by one off the shelf to corner him. He darted past her and fled under the sofa, then darted out to untie Bobby's shoelaces. Molly stalked around snarling.

Sara was snarling too because I'd assured her my apartment was accessible. It was ground floor, after all, but I'd forgotten the two steps up to the front door. Amory had ended the stalemate by lifting her from her wheelchair and carrying her over the threshold, a romantic notion to some, an undignified event to Sara.

She narrowed her eyes at Molly. "Before John Ashcroft goes anywhere," she said, "his security team sweeps the area for cats. He thinks calico cats are of Satan."

Maybe the Attorney General was right. I didn't know how else to explain what had happened to my cat. I had infantilized her, stuck that passionate creature with a name suited to a milkmaid or a rag doll. Molly, Mollycoddle, Mollycuddle, Mollycat, my gentle Victorian darling, ornamental, respected, desexed. Now, in her senior years, she was trying to kill Ninja and though I worried for his safety, her new monstrousness thrilled me.

This, too, was my fault. I knew from the zoo that animals must be introduced to one another carefully, gradually, and under observation. Instead, I'd brought Ninja home, thrown them together, and faced the consequences: bleak afternoons when he and I retreated to my bedroom where we'd cling together on the bed, trembling, listening to the thump thump of Molly throwing herself against the closed door. There were heartstopping moments when she hung from the knob until the door swung open and she lunged at us, mouth open, teeth bared, hissing.

I wanted to blame Weezie. Surely she hadn't introduced her cats carefully and scientifically, and they had more or less formed a tribe. She'd set a bad example.

We did it the right way at the zoo with Michael and Lyle and they had learned to get along. They spent months off-exhibit, in separate enclosures near one another.

They could see each other, smell each other, hear their vocalizations, but without direct contact. Only once they'd more or less come to accept the other's existence did we put them together, at first just for an hour or two, under observation.

Lyle had been born in the zoo to a mother who rejected him and a father who got violent. That's why he was raised in human foster care. He'd never been around an adult male. Now given the chance, he couldn't take his eyes off Michael. He'd walk over, make a friendly gesture, then a series of head bob threats. Who says only humans give mixed signals? Michael stayed mellow but time and again Lyle would make a threat and then run for it. He'd climb someplace high and stay there, an hour, sometimes more, just staring at Michael and sucking on his thumb or big toe.

Only when it became clear they weren't going to kill each other did we allow them to join Becky, Leona, and Melissa. Lyle had to be tranquilized to make it safe to transport him. He arrived back home in such disoriented condition that little Leona threatened and attacked him with impunity and even after the drug wore off and even after his long sharp canines grew in, she retained the confidence to harass him.

We waited to see Lyle and Michael compete for sex. They didn't.

Michael used his authority to keep things calm, break up

fights, not start them. He kept Leona from attacking Lyle. He was the patriarch in the positive sense, the right kind of goddamn alpha male. And a lot of good it did him.

Now the issue was what to do with Michael and Melissa. The zoo was threatening to ship her to Columbus, the idea being that with Melissa gone, Michael would get down to business and impregnate Becky. I remembered the way Melissa used to drag herself around, how painfully she moved her arthritic limbs, how little interest she showed in life, and how lively and limber she became once she met Michael. Now, just because she couldn't produce offspring—separate them?

"They sleep in each other's arms," I said. "Nothing comes between them except for trucks."

"We can do something about it," said Bernice, if we would just sit still long enough to hear her lecture on Augusto Boal. "This is a very famous story, but you've apparently never heard it."

Boal, she told us, was known all over the world, except to us—a Brazilian theater artist who committed himself to the struggle for social justice, and not just to get a grant.

In the late 60's, his theater company traveled to northeast Brazil where poverty was widespread and land ownership had been concentrated through fraud and violence in a few hands. They performed an agitprop drama which ended with the actors raising their rifles and calling on the peasants to spill their blood for the land. The peasants were impressed and invited the actors to join the fight.

"These aren't real rifles, these are props," Boal explained.

"That's OK," they said, "we have enough guns to go around."

"But we're not peasants or revolutionaries, we're actors."

The peasants said, "We thought you were sincere."

"Yes, we're very sincere. We're sincere actors..." etc.

"Oh, I get it," said the peasant leader. "When you say, Let's spill our blood, you mean *our* blood, not *your* blood."

That's when Boal realized you don't instigate action you aren't willing to take yourself and he decided theater should help you articulate your own desires or stimulate public debate instead of telling you what to feel and what to do. He developed a whole philosophy of turning passive spectators into participating spect-actors and a grab bag ("arsenal") of theatrical techniques that became known as Theater of the Oppressed.

I was thrilled. "Right now," I said, "who is as oppressed as Michael and Melissa?"

I was less thrilled that Bernice had a different take on it. "What's great about their situation is you can argue both sides."

Like Indian sovereignty, a subject on which Jennie and I disagreed. I, of course, supported tribal self-determination. It was bad enough we'd tried to exterminate the Indians, suppressed their cultures and stolen their lands. At least on the reservations, Native peoples should be indisputably in charge.

"Why should they live under corrupt regimes that deny the rights we enjoy?" Jennie said. "Why should corrupt tribal chairmen be able to ignore labor laws and environmental protection and civil liberties and civil rights?"

"Why should the BIA rip them off?" I said. The worst tribal chairman just did on a small scale what the white boys in the White House did on a large scale. When Republicans did it, business was business. When Indians followed their lead, it was savagery.

My critique of bad tribal government—not that it was any of my business—was the same as my ultimate objection to Neoproctology: both had conformed to turn-of-the-21st-century American culture in which everything—government, education, social services, health care, and art—must follow the business model which is a model of greed, inefficiency, inequality, and corruption, powered by the profit motive in the face of which no ethical system can stand.

"Even if you believe in progress," I said, "especially if you believe in progress, it's clear that capitalism has outlived its usefulness as an engine of innovation. The only thing left to it is the generation of ever more ingenious, ever more socially and economically destructive scams."

"I thought you weren't political," Jennie said.

"I'm post-political. I just talk the talk to annoy people."

"But you used to be political, right?" she said. "You used to be an activist."

My past was catching up with me.

Chapter Twelve

JENNIE CONTINUED SENDING EMAILS: the entire text of the Patriot Act, for example, which I found much too long to read.

"That's OK," she said, "the people in Congress who voted for it didn't read it either."

When she summarized its provisions, its belief-system struck me as being not unlike species conservation in zoos—the only way to promote survival is to embrace captivity.

She sent me an exposé about accounting practices at the Bureau of Indian Affairs—how Washington was cheating tribal members out of billions of dollars.

She sent estimates of how much money Bechtel and Halliburton stood to make if we went to war in Iraq, and names of who in the Administration would profit.

She sent links to the website of The Project for the New American Century in which Bush's current advisors back in the '90's had laid out plans for US world domination.

"Stop with the emails, please," I said.

She said, "I've got to do something."

"We—Gorilla Theater—we are doing something."

For weeks, Bernice had been moving us day by day, step by step, closer and closer to the zoo.

In Griffith Park, we lay on the grass with our eyes closed.

"You are a single cell in the soup of creation," she intoned. "You divide, and divide again. Light barely reaches you, and you have no eyes to see it."

I was not alone in the soup. There were bugs crawling on my legs, gnats buzzing around my hair.

"Keep your eyes closed till I say so!" said Bernice. "All creatures begin at the same place. Back at the beginning, when we are one. Soon you will emerge from the primordial sea. It's the first morning. For the first time ever in history, you open your eyes. You see the world. You see it by the light of the sun." The light was blinding. "Feel the sun's warmth." I stretched. I tingled. "And for the first time, you see others like yourself."

We crawled out on dry land and I pulled myself through the grass toward Jennie.

"You differentiate into species. Now you see others not like you."

From crawling on our bellies, we began to rise on all fours. We stretched our necks and looked around. We raised ourselves like lizards doing push-ups on a fence post. Devon slowly plodded her quadripedal way over to me and Jennie.

"You search for food."

We converged as though somehow the very same single blade of grass had become the only food in the world and each one of us wanted it. Amory bared his teeth and advanced toward Devon. Bobby's back went up.

"Scene!"

I saw their shapes, like demons, like the Furies, I had no mental functioning except for the most visceral rage and fear.

"Scene!"

Sara, who'd been left on the sidelines, shrieked like a banshee as she scooted her chair toward Amory to protect Devon. Her wheels caught in the grass and Jennie, breaking character, jumped up and caught her as Sara pitched forward.

"Stop! Stop!" Bernice was screaming. "That's enough! Scene! Stop!"

We stopped. We sat and caught our breaths.

"Take a moment to return to neutral," she said. "Return to yourselves."

I looked and saw Sara, Devon, Amory, Bobby, Jennie.

"It's clear you're all infected with the culture of war," said Bernice. "Before we deal with evolution, we're going to need an exorcism."

Jennie said, "Rae and I know a shaman."

"She's not a shaman. She's a crazy person," I said, but a day later, we were gathered in the zoo parking lot with Marcia asking us to name our power animal.

"If you don't already have one, I'll give you one," she said.

Of course I said *cat*.

"No, no, no. Your companion animal is very different from your animal companion." She stared at me. "Turtle," she pronounced.

"Turtle?"

She pointed around our circle. "Eagle, bear, jaguar..."

"Turtle?" I repeated.

"Yes, turtle."

Sara and Bobby didn't get animals. Marcia gave them African drums. They drummed. We lay down, forming a wheel, our feet aimed towards the center. Bernice stood sentry like a meerkat, but instead of watching out to warn of predators as meerkats do, she made sure no one ran us over while trying to park.

"From the sacred direction of Doo-Dah, from the equally sacred direction of Hoo-Hah," said Marcia, or something like that. "We evoke the serpent and the eagle and the exploding star. From the north and south and from the golden thread, we evoke the ancestors and the elders...I am the seer of visions. I am the specialist of the soul!"

We rose and stretched our hands into the center, and one hand on top of the other, we closed our eyes and hummed *Om*, sort of like a basketball team at prayer.

"The time has come," said Bernice, and we paid our admission (except for me, I have a badge) and entered, at last, the zoo.

Our stage set was the drill exhibit and the public area around it. There were two gates, one that kept me from the baboons, one that kept the public a little further away, to afford the animals a modicum of privacy.

Marcia took Jennie by the arm. "Do you know how to get medical records? They won't give me the results of my brain scam."

I twirled the combination lock and stepped up to the enclosure, costumed with my zoo ID, clipboard, stopwatch/timer set to go off every 60 seconds, and the same data collection forms

I used when I was observing them for real: a grid to enter scan sampling and proximity codes with blank space below to record bouts of behavior.

Enter Devon and Amory, walking up to the gate, hand in hand.

Stage directions: Rae writes on forms.

Not in the stage directions: Marcia asks if she can have a piece of paper and borrow a pencil.

Sky code: 3 (Partially cloudy, less than ½ the sky filled with clouds)

Temperature: 68 F.

Precipitation code: 0

For your information, some of our abbreviations: AP=Approach; G=Groom Another (so ME G MI means Melissa grooms Michael); PR=Present (so B PR MI is Becky presents to Michael even if he ignores her); FZ=Frenzy; AI=Examine Anogenital Region; MO=Mount; TH=Thrust; IN=Intromission; EJ=Ejaculate, (the latter two, alas, had never been recorded as we were instructed not to score EJ if in the context of masturbation); EC=Explore Feces/Coprophagy (which alas was scored often due to Leona's lamentable habit of eating her own shit).

During real observations, my role was to be quiet and unobtrusive so that my presence wouldn't affect their behavior. But now I found myself gasping and crying out when Lyle tore at his own hair (LY FZ), I sighed when Michael and Melissa kissed, muzzle to muzzle (ME MM MI; MI MM ME), I muttered You little bitch at Becky. It was awful to discover I ham it up even playing myself.

A small crowd had gathered to gape at Lyle who was throwing branches, bobbing his head, and slamming at the bars. (L SS

OHU; L HBx5 OHU; L SS OHU). He was enraged by the teenage boys who knew too much for their own good. Someone had told them about head bobs, and they were threatening Lyle in his own language. Marcia hollered "Stop it!" Becky snarled at people (B SN OHU). Leona kept her distance. Michael and Melissa stayed up on their ledge and only had eyes for each another.

Bernice and Bobby entered from different directions, playing Amory and Devon's parents.

Bernice: You promised me you wouldn't see her!

Bobby: You're coming home with me right now, young lady.

There followed a lot of I love her! I love him! You're a child! What the hell do you know about love? The father/daughter tension between Devon and Bobby was convincingly real.

Sara and Jennie were our plants in the audience, ready to instigate discussion if the zoo patrons (OHU, or Other Humans) were too shy.

It worked. We heard a lot of arguments about puppy love and respecting parents and respecting young people and the psychological damage caused by smothering Moms. OHUs argued the relative merits of going steady and playing the field.

Marcia said, "I wouldn't mind having an orgasm right about now."

"Well, guess what," Bernice said to Amory. "You might as well say goodbye, because I'm moving us back to Cleveland."

Amory and Devon embraced. So did Michael and Melissa, who touched muzzle to muzzle and gazed into each other's eyes.

"Look at them!" said Sara. Melissa groomed Michael and he gently placed a hand against her cheek.

“They look like they’re in love,” said someone.

Devon laid her head on Amory’s shoulder. Melissa lay on her side, and Michael stroked her fur. Becky chattered angrily below them.

“Melissa’s going to the Columbus Zoo,” I said.

“Without him?” asked an OHU.

“That’s the point. They’ll forget each other soon enough once they’re not seeing each other every day.” I explained that in order to save the species, it was necessary for Michael to turn his attention to Becky.

Lots of people expressed themselves on the subjects of artificial insemination, and the better solution of having Lyle impregnate Becky, and whether the species needed to be saved. Marcia suggested that Melissa and Michael—who were adults—had more rights than Devon and Amory who were not. From my clipboard I pulled out envelopes, stamped and addressed to the director of the zoo, so people could mail in their comments.

I also had to give everyone a survey as Bernice was required to supply quantitative data for her grant report.

> Date you attended Gorilla Theater:___________;
> BEFORE seeing the presentation were you ___ likely or ___ unlikely to hurt or kill a non-human primate in cold blood;
> AFTER seeing the presentation were you ____ more likely or ___ less likely to hurt or kill a non-human primate in cold blood;
> I ___ do/____don’t believe animals have feelings.

Later, Bernice called it a very successful example of Invisible Theater. I disagreed. It was still the opinions of people that got expressed, not the opinions of drills.

That afternoon, though, everyone along the fence watched as Michael and Melissa wrapped their arms around each other, stretched out on their platform and, nestled together, fell asleep.

"Isn't that what everyone wants?" said Bernice. "Don't they have what we all wish for?"

Chapter Thirteen

Jennie wasn't drinking, but when I got in the car, she handed me a flask.

"Loy says lots of people flunk the first time." She hadn't yet told him she had no intention of ever practising law or taking the bar exam again. We were celebrating her failure. "It's Irish whiskey," she said. "Jameson's."

The good stuff, but when I unscrewed the cap, the smell alone was enough to turn me off. My joylessness had been in remission, but this was a sign it was coming back. Toward the end and in the aftermath of my marriage, see, when you love someone who's a drunk, all kinds of things happen to your life. It goes beyond the ravages of the disease, beyond the grief and shame over the terrible thing he's done—which you surely feel more keenly than he does. It's how you stop going out, because you know the sight of someone with a drink in his hand will make you stiffen. You see six-packs stacked in the supermarket and you find it hard to breathe. The smell of alcohol on someone's breath turns you to stone. There's the hurt and helplessness you feel all the time.

You ask yourself questions: Isn't the drunk driver who makes it home by sheer luck without a fatal accident just as guilty as the one who kills someone? Isn't the passenger who gets in the car without protest just as guilty as the drunk behind the wheel? You turn life into a perpetual ethics seminar and turn everybody off.

Who has clean hands?

You turn down invitations. You lose your friends. You'd rather stay home New Years Eve and that makes you a morality-imposing fucked-up Puritan. No one understands it just hurts. You become a withdrawn and bitter person.

David sent me an email once, I'm losing my daughter. Only I misread it on the screen, I'm losing my laughter. Until I met Jennie, I had lost mine.

"I don't want any," I said.

We were finally going to Basoba, but the powwow was long past. Some celebration this was going to be. Jennie had the radio tuned to KPFK. People were reading poetry for peace. I zoned out and stared at traffic, railroad sidings, gravel pits, spools and pallets, freight containers placed among the mobile homes as if—was it possible?—people were living in them.

At the casino, huge American flags were flying. The chains and pulleys on the flagpole jingled in the wind, ringing like the bells on ice cream trucks. We trudged across the parking lot.

Yes, liquor was served, in abundance, and the cigarette smoke made Jennie feel sick. We didn't see any Indians.

We wandered over to the blackjack tables.

"You know how to play?" she asked.

"No. You?"

"No."

We wandered over to the slot machines. They looked very complicated too.

"You know how these work?"

"No."

"No."

But we threw some dollars away anyway.

We wandered outside to the grandstand.

"The powwow must've been huge," Jennie said.

We sat on the bleachers and looked out on the field where nothing was happening but high winds.

"It's flat," said Jennie. "I thought we'd be in the mountains, like in *Ramona*."

"The mountains was where Ramona and Alessandro fled to," I said. "The land stolen from the tribe was pretty flat."

"She wrote nonfiction, too," Jennie said.

"Ramona did?"

"No. Helen Hunt Jackson. I've been reading *A Century of Dishonor*—that's her nonfiction exposé of all the US government's crimes against Indian nations."

"When did she write it?"

"I don't remember. 18-something."

"So it's been more than a century of dishonor now."

"She did all the research in the New York Public Library," said Jennie. "She came out to California later and met Mission Indians, including some Basoba people, before she wrote the novel. But all the broken treaties and all the slaughter? It was all part of the public record. No one even tried to hide it."

"No one cared."

"When it was published, she paid to have a copy sent to every member of Congress."

"Any of them read it?"

Jennie shrugged. "Her correspondence is the best stuff. Full of invective. She called the Secretary of the Interior a false-souled unprincipled liar, a pitiful, audacious, wicked, insincere blockhead and arch-hypocrite."

We got back in her big car.

"Maybe there's a tribal office or a museum or something," I said. "As long as we're here."

The road got narrower and turned to dirt. We drove down narrow streets, past neat yards that housed trailers and modular homes. Not bad looking. Modest, but more than OK. There were lots of American flags and lots of dogs. The flags flapped, the dogs barked, and the wind clicked and rattled in the half-bare trees. Occasionally a child peeked out from behind the bumper of a car in a yard, but aside from that we didn't see any people.

"Do you feel like we're trespassing?" said Jennie.

A circular drive led to the official buildings, all locked up and dark. It was the weekend after all. We parked by the tribal office and looked in the window. Nothing resembling a museum. It was a private place, not trying to attract tourists or seekers, bearing no outward sign of spirituality or genocide.

"If we stand out here, maybe someone will come by," Jennie said. And then, "If someone comes by, what do we say?"

"Here she comes," I said.

A woman in jeans and a red sweatshirt was slowly walking toward us. I smiled but couldn't hold it as it was taking her a long time to reach us. We started walking in her direction, to meet her halfway.

"Well, I suppose you're from the church," she said.

I wanted to nudge Jennie. See? no question!

"No," I said.

"I guess the EPA's finally paying us a visit. And I'll say it's about time."

"We're not from the EPA," said Jennie.

"You're with the DNA."

The what? "No," I said.

"Then you better come with me," she said.

Months later we would meet again, and I would learn her name was Cheryl and she would help me learn a whole lot more.

"Come along," she said.

We started to follow her, but instead of walking the road, she went over to Jennie's big car and got into the backseat.

"Lucky thing I found you," Cheryl said. "I need someone with a car."

I tried to figure out how to say Why? in other than question form while Jennie drove and the woman gave directions. We drove past manure-colored knolls laced with dirt roads. A couple of large cinderblock homes in the process of being covered with adobe. A running fence—live ocotillo with barbed wire strung branch to branch, and a padlocked gate standing by itself in the middle of a field, no fencing on either side so anyone could walk or drive around it, guarding nothing.

"Still wish you were the EPA," she said. "I keep thinking they've got to send someone now, since those sons-of-bitches shot my nephew."

Now, that was a statement that called for a question, but I'd prepared Jennie well. "He's all right, I hope," she said.

"Dead," said Cheryl.

"I'm sorry," I said.

"And here I am, getting help for others, when I can't get help for my own."

"We're glad to help," Jennie said, "I think. But it would help to know what we're helping with."

"There's a white girl in my house needs a ride out of town," she said, "and not the first one, either. I don't know who signs these leases, but I guess you wouldn't know either. I guess the EPA stuff i'nt none of your business."

"I'm wondering if it's a matter of jurisdiction," Jennie said. "Of sovereignty."

"You a lawyer?"

What was this? An Indian asking questions?

"I just flunked the bar," Jennie said.

"When a moron like Pete Wilson could pass it?" Cheryl shook her head. "They said my nephew was running a meth lab," she told us. "They said he got crazy with drugs and killed hisself, but you tell me how a young man who never did a dishonest act in his short life manages to shoot hisself in the back. Three times. Johnny was clever, but still. You been to the casino?"

"Yes," I said.

"West of town. That's what people see. They trucked in all that sludge and dumped it out east. We had a tribal meeting in that very office you was standing in front of, that place where I saw you. The BIA man telling us what a good deal it would be. But we voted no. Next we know, there's trucks coming in at night. Three four trucks almost every night. We got us a mountain hill east side of the reservation now where it used to be plain flat. So my nephew calls the BIA. He calls the EPA. They say 'cause the company doing the dumping didn't get a federal lease, the US government can't stop 'em. Figure that out."

"My God," I said. "Why doesn't anyone know about this?"

The woman said, "It was in the news. Old photo of my nephew, from his high school graduation. We had more recent, he was 28."

You show a teenager, I thought, and people think the death is normal. They assume gangbanger. They think he deserved it.

"The tribe has no enforcement. The sheriff says it's not the county, it's the state, the state says it's the feds. No one does a damn thing. And a neighbor I could name is driving a new SUV and his wife buying up a lot of turquoise. So you tell me."

"That doesn't sound right," said Jennie.

"Person don't need a bar exam to know that," the woman said. "We're here. I'd invite you in, except it's a mess."

The house was surrounded by a fence made of some kind of desert plant. The white woman was very thin and very pale except for a welt visible at the neckline of her cotton shirt. The shirt was short sleeved and very light and she was shivering.

"I don't have any money," she said. "I can't pay you."

"No problem," said Jennie.

She climbed into the back seat. Jennie and I said our names. She nodded and said nothing.

What we didn't know then was that the Church of Neoproctology leased a plot of land deep inside the reservation, reached by dirt road and surrounded by razor wire. Some people still say the site is a church retreat and it's a special privilege to be invited there. Some say it's a prison where people are tortured, cleverly located on tribal land where no legal authority has clear jurisdiction.

I reached over the back of the seat with the flask. "Whiskey?"

"No," she said. Then, "yes."

She gulped some down and handed it back.

"You know anything about the toxic dumping?" Jennie asked.

"Why are you asking me that? Do I look like someone who needs to be detoxified?" and we got nothing more out of her till well after we hit a roadblock on the county road and the sheriff's deputy drew us a quick map for the detour.

We drove a narrow road through a canyon and along a shallow river, little more than a creek, but water enough to support a border of willow trees. We came out into flatlands of dry waving grass and a sky where hawks circled and the sun hurt my eyes through the windshield.

When we came upon a subdivision in the making—foundations being dug, rebar sticking out of concrete blocks, neat grid of streets with already occupied homes—Jennie pointed out the unmistakable pink colon coiled around each mailbox post. There it was again at the entrance to the golf course. On the awning of the café. On the billboard for the assisted living center.

I said, "The Church must own this whole town." I turned to look at our passenger to see if she was amused. She was holding a newspaper up, covering her face. Staring out at me from the first page were the dull eyes of a baboon captive in restraints. "My God, is that Rosie?"

"Oh, you found the Animal Liberation stuff?" Jennie said. "They were leafletting in front of the zoo."

She'd gone over to them because of one of their posters: REMEMBER THE BANGKOK SIX. She thought it referred to political prisoners.

"Smuggled orangutans," I had to tell her. "They were rescued, but they died."

Jennie's connection to Animal Liberation was just that casual and simple, though it would end up meaning a helluva lot more than that.

"Let me see that," I said to our passenger. "Does it give the baboon's name? Does it name the lab?"

She remained hidden behind the pages. "Are you church members?" she asked.

"Not me," Jennie said. "Brought up Methodist, but today? If I were going to be anything, I guess it would be Unitarian. One third of them don't believe in God, one third do, and one third think the question is irrelevant."

"I meant Neoproctology," said the woman. She said the word in a hush, the way people used to say "cancer," the way Devon, in embarrassed sympathy repeated my age after she asked and I told her.

"Oh," Jennie said. "Sorry. I just didn't think of it as a church."

"We've been to the Castle," I said.

"I'm not saying anything bad about the Church," said the woman. "Or the people."

Once we reached the freeway, she had us leave her at the first rest stop.

"You have no money," Jennie said.

"I'll call a friend collect."

We never learned her name or her story but I hold onto the idea that whatever happens at that secret reservation site, some people do find a way to get out.

We weren't finished with Basoba.

"Someone needs to look into that toxic dumping," Jennie said.

"Not someone who's hoping to be pregnant," I said.

In stressful situations, I had the habit of tugging at my silicone ear. I tugged, and focused, trying to pinpoint the boundary between feeling and not.

Chapter Fourteen

IF YOU'VE BEEN KEEPING TRACK of the passage of time, and it's no surprise if you haven't as I admit the chronology here has not been linear the way people of David's ilk would like it, you may have realized we were headed towards the end of November, but don't worry, you're not going to have to sit through a Thanksgiving dinner. Jennie and Loy spent the holiday with her parents and then invited our crowd for Saturday instead of Thursday and served a (mostly) vegetarian meal.

"Hitler was a vegetarian," I said to Jennie, as I often did, to provoke her.

"And he loved animals," she said.

"He loved dogs. That doesn't mean he loved animals," I said. "Even Bush sleeps with his dogs. That's why I don't like them. A dog will go with anyone."

Devon was invited as a courtesy to David who was invited for me, and that meant inviting Amory to keep Devon company. Bernice wasn't invited because the presence of the boss wrecks the camaraderie and neither was Sara because the house was built on an Echo Park hillside. To get to it, you had to park below and climb two flights of stairs. Over my objections, Jennie had included Weezie and Marcia—"She's been to Basoba. Maybe she knows something." Bobby was there because she wanted him to meet her neighbor Mirady. Jennie still had this picture of the world as an operetta where everyone gets paired off happily in the end.

Ninja was invited not just to visit, but to stay, and though there was no attempt at the careful introduction I at this point believed essential, he easily relinquished his hold on me and scampered over to the other cats. Monk sniffed at him, Chessie groomed him, and soon the three were rolling around in ecstasy treating each other like catnip toys.

Amazing. I was even more amazed that everyone invited had shown up.

"Well, yeah," Loy pointed out. "They all said they would," as though he'd never noticed that in LA, no means no, and yes means nothing.

Weezie was washed and brushed and smelled okay. She sat down at the piano and smiled at the keys. Marcia latched onto David and was socially inappropriate enough to ask immediately, "So what went wrong in your marriage?"

"I wasn't attracted to my wife," he answered. "I'm interested in young blonde women with..with..."

"Big tits?" she suggested and led him out to the deck.

I wanted to call him back and point out that Marcia was mentally disturbed and middleaged and her hair was bleached, but he was looking at her tits, not at her. I wanted to tell him she believed her grandfather ate Amish children. I wanted to say, I know I'm not a young blonde woman with big tits: that's why I set my sights low enough that you came into view.

"I'm so sorry," said Jennie.

"I don't know what I was thinking," I said.

Now we were stuck with Devon for nothing, and with Amory, who expressed himself primarily through his T-shirts—today's read *What good is your religion if you can't hate me?*—and always acted like he was doing us a big favor by joining us, which tended to piss the Gorilla Theater people off though I'd taught high school long enough to figure he was merely shy and that, most likely, aside from Devon and us, he had no friends.

I made them follow me out onto the deck where Loy had charcoal glowing in the grill and I could keep an eye on David.

"What's that supposed to mean?" David pointed to Amory's slogan. "Do you even know any Muslims?"

"It's not referring to Islam," Amory said.

"As far as I know," I said, "the main difference between Islam and the Judeo-Christian tradition is that they believe animals have immortal souls."

"Put a person on a par with a donkey," David said. "No respect for human life." So he was a bigot, too. "Can I get you a drink?" he asked Marcia and I followed him back inside where Mirady was leaning over Weezie at the piano.

"Do you play?"

"I used to," said Weezie.

"Who plays? Jennie, do you play?"

"Loy plays," said Jennie.

"Play something!" Mirady called to him, but he had been cornered by Devon who wanted to know if she should get braces.

He said, "I'm not an orthodontist."

"Get her away from him," Jennie said to me.

"You're wanted at the piano," I said.

Bobby coaxed Weezie away so Loy could take the seat.

"I'm a singer," said Mirady. "You want to try something?"

"Billie Holiday?"

"No."

"Astrud Gilberto?"

"No."

I joined Jennie in the kitchen. David was on his way out again with two glasses of wine and Jennie tugged at my shirt to keep me from following. I found bowls for the hummus and olives and marinated artichoke hearts and mushrooms while she got the spanakopita and vegetarian lasagna into the oven. I am not desperate, I told myself. He tortures baboons and I don't even like him.

Bobby came in for a beer.

"Mirady's a lovely woman," Jennie said.

Mirady was big and very impressive in her caftan and dozens of strings of beads. We could still hear them at the piano.

"You know any Cole Porter?"

"No."

"Mercedes Sosa?"

"No."

"Where is Mirady from?" I asked.

Jennie shrugged. "She always just says *in my country*. She never names it so it seems impolite to ask."

"Ella Fitzgerald?"

"No."

"Billy Joel?"

"No."

"J-Lo?"

"How can she not know Ella?" Bobby asked.

"Either of you remember the name of the auto garage across from Gorilla Theater?" I said. "David needs a good mechanic."

"Give up on him," she said.

"Piaf?"

"Patsy Cline?"

"Sondheim?"

"I don't do cover songs," Mirady said. "Don't you know anything that's unknown?"

She joined us in the kitchen. "This looks great," she said. "I'm a vegetarian."

"Beer?" Bobby offered.

Jennie picked up the bottle of white wine and poured a glass for me. I left it on the counter. For herself, sparkling water. I looked from her drink to the excitement in her eyes, and I knew. She nodded yes.

She was happy. I hoped she was really ready for this. The birth of a baby disrupts everything. When Cici the gelada baboon had hers, all the other females fought for the chance to hold it. When Mindy the cottontop tamarin had hers, she was so wrapped up in the baby she couldn't be bothered protecting her wimpish mate who was then attacked over and over again by his angry adolescent daughter and left with dangerously festering wounds. When the baby Speke's gazelle was born, her father tried to sniff and examine her but, terrified, she fled. He chased her. She caught a hoof in a hole and fell. He ran to her and scooped her onto his back with his big horns. She rode a moment then went flying through the air, and landed apparently unharmed but leaving a tuft of white baby hair on the rocks. An agitated female ran into the barn and threw herself against the wall, injuring herself, and the whole herd ended up in lockdown.

I hugged my best friend. I expected the worst, but I said, "That's the best news I've heard in a long time."

WE FILLED OUR PLATES and draped ourselves over chairs and sofas. Mirady chanted something microtonal. Ninja clawed at upholstery. Chessie ate lasagna off Weezie's plate and Mirady and I both accepted hamburgers off the grill from Loy.

"I thought you were a vegetarian," I said.

"You've crossed the border to Mexico, yes?" she said. "You're still an American."

"I'm proud to be an American," David said.

"How can you be proud of something you did nothing to earn?" Amory said.

Jennie said, "I'm ashamed."

"That's a terrible thing to say!" Marcia said.

"Why?" I said. "You can't feel shame for something separate from you. You can only feel shame for yourself, or for something you're responsible for or something—someone—you love."

“Patriotism is so disagreeable,” said Weezie, “when it takes hold in someone else’s country.”

If you suspect I’ve fallen for another romantic cliché here—that crazy people are the only ones free to speak the truth—please keep in mind that all this really happened and that it’s Marcia who was crazy and Weezie merely surgically impaired.

Ninja scrambled back up to my lap, and Chessie and Monk went on playing. Watching them made my heart clutch to think of the fellowship Molly was missing though she’d made it clear she didn’t see it that way.

Jennie said, “Helen Hunt Jackson had this great line. Something like, I have never suspected in myself any tendency to patriotism.”

“I’ve never heard of Helen Hunt Jackson,” David said, “and I don’t care to.”

THINK: THE SMELL OF GARLIC. Think: the clatter of forks on plates. Shreds of spinach from the spanakopita caught in people’s teeth. People getting up to serve themselves. Pouring drinks. Sitting down. Finding awkward places to set their glasses and someone of course spilling.

“That was a delicious meal,” said Marcia. “We don’t get to drink at The Castle.”

People starting to clear away the dishes and being told thanks, but just leave them, and Monk caught on the kitchen counter licking plates clean.

"That was delicious!" "Great dinner!" "Oh, that was good!"

David smirked and said, "Pleasurable sensations exist so that animals will do what they need to do to survive. Intelligent humans know you have to eat and drink. We don't have to enjoy it."

This was the man I'd baked cheesecake for, sort of.

We took our after-dinner drinks to the living room. David claimed the armchair so that, I thought, no one could sit beside him, but Marcia plopped herself down on the carpet, her head by his knees.

"No one really likes turkey anyway, all that dry white meat," Loy said, getting Devon upset and flustered, though I'm sure he meant nothing by it.

"Thanksgiving is a Native tradition," said Marcia. "The Natives thanked the animals for giving up their lives so they could eat them. That's where the Pilgrims learned it except they thanked the Indians for letting themselves be killed."

"Speaking of Indians," Jennie said, "you've been to Basoba..."

Marcia stood and spoke to the four corners of the room: "Thank you, thank you, thank you, thank you."

Mirady said, "I came to this country as a terrorist."

No one reacted, probably because I was not alone in thinking she said *tourist.*

"What are we listening to?" Amory asked.

"That's *Central Avenue Sounds*," Jennie said. "LA jazz."

"I hated Americans," said Mirady. She twisted her fingers through her beads. "I hated you for what you did in my country. I came here to kill people."

"With what?" David said. "Voodoo?"

"Guns," said Mirady. "Bombs. What else? Till I discovered how nice you all are."

"Except for David," I said.

"Generous, openhearted, warm," Mirady said. "I never knew till I came here, you people have no idea what your government does."

"Yes, we do. Now," said Loy. "It's all out in the open."

"Democrats," David said. "You're just bitter about the election. Get over it."

"I'm not a Democrat," said Loy. "Ninety thousand black citizens not allowed to vote? Except for the Black Caucus, not a peep out of Congress or the Democratic Party."

"In our lifetime," I said, "I bet we'll see a black president."

"And he or she will be an American president," said Mirady. "Which means nothing will change."

"There'll be threats of armed insurrection," said Loy. "They'll have him running so scared, he'll do the master's bidding."

"Oh, ho!" said David. "I wondered how long we'd have to wait till you brought up slavery. Will you people ever—"

Devon rolled her eyes. "Someone give him a whiskey sour and he'll fall asleep."

"But this is great," I said. "When in LA do you ever hear anyone express an opinion? This is so exhilarating. So open."

"We ended up with His Fraudulency," Weezie said.

Jennie said, "I can't bear to look at him."

"Not me," I said. "I'm glued to the screen, hoping for a Jack Ruby moment."

"That is treason," David said.

"No," I said. "It's a one-liner."

"No more Gorilla Theater for you, young lady," said David. "I don't like the company you keep."

"D-a-a-d. I'm a capitalist," said Devon.

"No," he said, "you get an allowance."

"I'm a fugitive from justice," said Marcia.

"The point is," I said, "that my instinctive visceral reaction to evil is every bit as violent as Mr. Bush's. I want to kill," I said. "I want to destroy. Where I'm different from Bush is I know not to act on that primitive impulse."

Weezie said, "When I was a girl, you never left a flag out in the rain. I can't quite cotton to flags made of plastic. It's a disgrace to see a tattered flag flying from a car antenna. When you took it down, there was a special way to fold it up—"

"I remember that," I said. "In triangles."

"—and if even the tiniest bit of fabric brushed the ground, the flag was defiled and had to be burned in a special ceremony. The flag was sacred."

Bobby said, "Here's a theater action: we stand on a street corner and burn copies of the defiled Constitution."

Loy said, "That frat boy in the White House would wipe his ass with the flag if it would put a dollar in his pocket."

"That's our Commander-in-Chief you're talking about," David said.

"He's going to cut taxes," said Devon.

"If you look at Western history," Bobby said, "Protestantism and greed are the same thing. He smells of it—the old Calvinist theology."

"I assume your people are all Catholic," David said.

"Feed the hungry, clothe the naked," Bobby said. "You got a problem with that? But Calvinists? You don't get to heaven with good works. If you're one of the elect—and it's all been decided in advance, called predestination—it doesn't matter what you do. And the way you can tell who's been saved is God has already marked them on earth—with money and power."

"Let's change the subject," said Jennie.

"Why?" Weezie said. "I grew up in a very political home. We always discussed the issues of the day at table."

Jennie said. "Who wants coffee?"

"Decaf?" I asked.

"We don't get coffee at The Castle," said Marcia.

LOY NOODLED AT THE KEYBOARD. He could have put himself through school playing in piano bars, I thought, instead of enlisting.

"Bush demands freedom for Iraq," Mirady said, "while taking it away at home."

"Boo hoo," said David. "No one's taking anything away."

"Secret tribunals?" said Mirady. "People held for months without charges filed against them? In secret so no one even knows where they are. Not their families, not their lawyers."

"Innocent people don't need lawyers," David said.

"Or families," I said.

David said, "Good people have nothing to worry about."

"I'm worried," Mirady said.

"Yes," said David, "and you're a terrorist."

"Terrorism is one solution to overpopulation," said Marcia.

Weezie said, "We should have a yearlong bacchanal of worry-free sex followed by mass suicide."

"What's a bacchanal?" asked Devon.

"Time to go home," said David. But they stayed.

WEEZIE SLUMPED OVER on the couch and snored.

Jennie said, "Have you noticed that Brian Williams looks just like Tom Brokaw and they both look just like Bush? All we care about owning is the oil."

"Look who's talking! Look what you drive! There are SUVs smaller than your big car."

"There'll be looting and cholera and typhoid," Loy said, "and we'll have done Al-Qaeda's recruiting job for them."

David said, "Don't you think the White House knows more about the situation than you do?"

"Man, have I ever heard that before," I said. "During the war in Vietnam, and it turned out the only thing LBJ knew that we didn't know was that he was lying."

Devon said, "I am like so not interested in the Johnson Administration."

"Neither am I," I said. "It's old news."

Jennie said, "Just because something's old doesn't mean it's wrong. Helen Hunt Jackson said the poisons of baseness and treachery and cruelty could build up in a nation's character with a cumulative and toxic effect, and I think that's exactly what we're seeing."

I didn't want to see it. There was nothing I wanted to watch but animals.

Mirady said, "Wake up," and Weezie did.

YOU OUT THERE READING these words may have sat through many a conversation just like this when all of this was going on, so maybe there's no reason to repeat it. Of course a lot of things got even worse once Bush was gone, but I'll keep going just in case you've forgotten or didn't give a damn at the time or hadn't yet been born.

David said, "If Iraq doesn't pose a direct and imminent threat, why are they blocking inspections?"

"National sovereignty," said Jennie.

"It's about bad, needing to look bad," Loy said. "Iraq's got a neighbor, Iran, and the world's only superpower, us, threatening to destroy the country. Suppose Saddam has no weapons of mass destruction. He knows damn well if word gets out, he's toast."

"He used chemical weapons against his own people," David said.

"We sold him those weapons," Loy said. "We told him to use them. And even after he gassed the Kurds, we sent him more."

"What do you mean by *we*?" said Devon.

"OK," said Loy. "You're right. It's the government, not the people."

"You're wrong," Jennie said. "I do blame Americans. I'm ashamed of Americans. We let this happen."

Amory said, "I read it was Iran that used the chemical weapons against the Kurds."

Loy laughed. "Yeah, yeah, I remember that. The CIA put out a false report covering up for Saddam. See where that leaves us? Who can you believe?"

"I believe in revolution," said Mirady.

"A revolution in consciousness," Jennie said.

"No," said Mirady. "Revolution. The real thing."

I said, "What we used to say? We each contribute to the revolution in our own way. The cobbler needs to make revolutionary shoes, though I was never sure what a revolutionary shoe would be."

"Ask the shoe bomber," said David. "You sound like a Communist."

"What's a Communist?" asked Devon.

"Something from the Fifties." I said. "They're extinct."

"North Korea?" David said.

"I'd rather not see the peninsula blown up," said Jennie.

"I'm a Communist," said Mirady.

I said, "What's the good of violent overthrow? Take out Bush and you'd still have Cheney and Rumsfeld."

"No denizen of the White House is going to dismantle your Empire, " said Mirady. "That's why you have to—"

Marcia said, "After World War II, the US occupying army turned Sicily over to the Mafia."

Strangely enough, I'd heard that before. Marcia might actually be right.

"Elections don't bring change," Mirady said. "We learned that in my country. One of these days you'll—"

"Killing breaks the moral spine," I said. "If you overthrow tyranny by any means necessary, that's how you'll rule. Have you ever seen a revolution lead to a just state?"

"The American Revolution," David said.

Amory said, "Canadians have as many guns as we do, but

they don't use them to kill people. See, they didn't go to war for their freedom."

"Why don't we just vote the way they do in Canada?" Jennie said. "Paper and pencil."

"Why don't you try living under Saddam Hussein if you think he's so great," said David.

Jennie said, "Let the weapons inspectors do their job."

"We have to protect ourselves," Devon said.

"How does dropping bombs on Iraq protect us?" Amory said.

"So they can't do another 9/11."

"They didn't do the first one," he said.

"But they're evil," she said.

"You know what was remarkable about the Founding Fathers?" I said. "They recognized their own capacity for evil. That's what you were looking for, Jennie, weren't you?"

Bobby said, "They didn't know the president's family would buy the Supreme Court and that Congress would just roll over."

"Why don't you go back to Mexico?" David said.

Wouldn't the world be more complex and therefore more interesting if the man who tortured baboons was, at the same time, a gentle person, an open-minded person, a man committed to human rights? Believing as I did in complexity, it hadn't occurred to me that David might be, simply, hateful.

"I was born here," Bobby said. "My parents, my grandparents, my—"

"Mirady's the only honest person here," said David.

"We're all guilty," said Jennie. "Rae here keeps animals under constant surveillance."

"Observation," I corrected her. "For their own good."

"Tell me." David smirked at Mirady. "What would Lenin drive?"

"An SUV," Weezie said. "To sharpen the contradictions and bring on the revolution that much sooner."

"Maybe now that we know Mirady's a terrorist," Amory said, "the government should drop a bomb on this house, kill everyone here. I mean that's what we do."

"Puerile liberals," said David. "You'll sing kumbaya while Rome burns."

"Maybe American democracy is over," Amory said. "Nations get the government they deserve."

"Your sound bite doesn't work," Jennie said. "What happens here affects people beyond our borders who didn't choose it and don't deserve it."

"It doesn't rankle Romans that they don't run the world anymore," I said.

"It bothered Mussolini," Bobby said. "Don't forget that. Fascism."

David said, "You liberals use that word so loosely. Do you have any idea what it actually means."

"Well, the way Mussolini defined it," Bobby said, "Fascism affirms that inequality is immutable, beneficial, and fruitful. The Fascist believes war alone brings up to its highest tension all human energy and puts the stamp of nobility upon the peoples who have courage to meet it. He said the Fascist repudiates democracy, that the State must deprive the individual of useless and possibly harmful freedom."

"You've read Mussolini?" Jennie asked.

"Back in the old days, every time I called someone a Fascist I got told I didn't know what the word meant. So yeah, I looked it up."

"If you ask me," I said, "Romans are perfectly content eating well and wearing good clothes. Rome is not burning."

Weezie said, "If you ask me, it's fair to call this administration Fascist."

"You'll hand over the matches," David said.

"The capitalist will sell the rope we use to hang him," said Mirady.

"Satan!" Marcia cried. "I command you to leave this man!"

David reached for her outstretched hand and she sat down quietly again at his feet.

Loy said, "Okay, okay, okay. David, please just listen. I have a confession to make. I have shut a lot of people out of my life. People who hurt me, people I didn't agree with, people who stood for everything I think is wrong. Like what's the point of arguing? What's the point of trading insults? You don't get anywhere."

"So don't argue with him," I said. "Just pull out his teeth without Novocaine."

"Take it easy, Rae. The point is, what I have to remember is, keep the lines of communication open. With respect."

I said, "We're going to end up like that generation of Germans. We're going to have to explain to our children and our grandchildren how we let this happen."

"Don't worry about it," David said. "You'll never have children. Or grandchildren."

"That's not helpful," said Jennie.

Devon rolled her eyes. "Do we have to do history? It just gives people reasons to hate each other."

She was a foolish ignorant American girl and I thought she was right.

Jennie said, "Let's think like Augusto Boal. Let's not tell each other how to think or how to act. What we can do is imaginatively explore the consequences of our beliefs and our actions."

"I couldn't love George Bush," I said. "Pull out my fingernails one by one, I still couldn't."

"If you were a real re-earther, you would," said Jennie. "You'd send your love out even to him."

"What about that doctor he appointed?" said Mirady. "The one who tells women with gynecological problems to read the Bible."

"I feel sorry for the president," said Jennie. "There's no joy in his life. He should never have quit drinking."

"Maybe he does have an AA sponsor," said Mirady. "Dubya phones the guy late at night, and his sponsor tells him, Don't internalize your anger. Bomb Iraq."

"So what you're saying," I said, "if we can't love and respect David in spite of his appalling opinions and unforgivably bad behavior, there's no hope for the world. So instead of putting him to sleep with that whiskey sour or asking him to leave, what are we supposed to do? Go around the room and one by one, say I love you, David?"

"Don't do me any favors," David said. "You convinced me that nonhuman primates feel love. Love: leave it to the baboons."

"That's the beauty of biodiversity," I said. "There's room in the universe even for you."

"That's not helpful either," said Jennie.

"I love you, David," said Marcia.

"I love you, David," said Weezie.

Jennie said, "Devon, if it's more comfortable, you can say I love you, Dad."

There were tears in David's eyes. I didn't know if this was due to Marcia and Weezie's words or because Devon said nothing.

The rest of us mumbled our I love you's. This was not the way I'd hoped to tell him. I wasn't feeling what I'd hoped to feel.

"And now let's change the subject," said Jennie.

"What do you pay for cable?" Mirady asked. "Or do you have a dish?"

"About 80 a month. Loy, how much do we pay?"

"I don't know."

"I was brought up it's rude to talk about money," Weezie said.

"Money's only important if you don't have any," said Bobby. "If you got a roof over your head and you're getting enough to eat, my God, give it a rest."

"$83, 89, something like that."

"For how many channels?" David asked.

"I don't know. We don't watch them."

"I don't watch them either," David said. "I pay 60 and get more than 400."

So this was normal. We were back to normal.

"Anyone see *West Wing* this week?" I asked. "I mean *ER*. I mean *Gilmore Girls*. Why can't we all just get along?" I kept talking. I couldn't stop. I talked about Lyle, how he ate raw onion, fennel, roses with the thorns removed, oranges, chunks of bark, basil leaves and lettuce, peanuts and worms. Everyone stared at me. I tried to include them: "Anyone on a new diet? Do you have a good nutritionist? A 24-hour health club?" Maybe I'd had too much to drink. Maybe I was losing my mind. "Do you have a personal trainer? Are you writing a screenplay? Is Michael Jackson a pedophile? Will Robert Blake be convicted? Is Nicole Kidman dating?" I didn't want to be up on a soapbox. I wanted my bare feet on the earth. I didn't want to be angry and shrill. I wanted to hear the birds and the crickets. I didn't want to bore people. "Is bottled water really safe? How about them LakersDodgersAngelsTrojans-BruinsSparksClippersDucks." I didn't want to be political. "Should Oprah restart her book club? What's the best new vodka?"

I had many more questions but Jennie led me to the guest room. I was face-to-face with the print above the bed, *Sunrise on Mt. Cook*.

"Where's Mt. Cook?"

Jennie tucked me into bed. Ninja scampered in and wriggled under the covers. Jennie propped up pillows behind me so I could sit.

"I've got to get home and feed Molly." God knows I wasn't upset about David. I didn't really want a man in my life, though it would be good to live with someone who could feed the cat when I was gone.

"It's OK," Jennie said. "You're going to be all right."

But I didn't know where Mt. Cook was and I used to know everything. I was trembling.

She handed me the remote control.

Jennie and Loy were good people, nice people, even if she used to drink and drive which, in any event, she had stopped doing.

I was surfing through hundreds of channels when Weezie came in.

"Good night, dear," she said, and handed me a briefcase. "I found it."

I didn't want it. Secrets, government scandals. The hell with it. I listened to the good nights and the closing of the front door and waited till all the guests were gone. Then I came out and gave Ninja and the briefcase to Jennie. Let her be the activist. Let her make the world a better place for her unborn child.

I hugged her and Loy and went home to my cat.

Chapter Fifteen

About this time, I began to suspect Becky had been seduced and abandoned. She didn't try to get Michael's attention anymore and once when he did trot over for a sniff, I saw her wheel around and slap his face.

David hadn't seduced me, but I wanted to slap him silly. Though why blame him? It was my own damn fault. I'd looked at a man who was too repressed to enjoy the taste of food, a man who months later would stop shaving to avoid the possibly pleasant sensation of his own fingers on his face. That's who David was, but what I imagined was so much pent-up passion, it would have to be explosive once released. The potential made me shiver, along with the megalomaniacal thrill of believing I had the power to tap everything that was hot and smouldering and locked up inside him.

He made excuses, too busy to see me, but he was always home when I phoned and we talked—or rather I did—for hours.

"You've got to stop blocking primary emotion," I said.

He grunted, but was he listening?

"Sensory input stimulates the limbic system," I said, though he was the one with the Ph.D. and who was I to lecture him?

"There's a release of hormones and neurotransmitters and that's why we feel emotion right in the body."

"A primitive response," he said, "from the most primitive part of the brain."

I pictured him holding the phone and smirking.

"Secondary emotion is when your frontal cortex reacts to a thought." I pictured him wandering room to room. "If the frontal cortex sends the right signal to the limbic system, a thought can make you feel. That's in a healthy brain, a healthy person, but if there's a block, a broken signal, a disconnect, an area that's ravaged or numb..."

The thought occurred to me that in telling him what was wrong with him I was diagnosing myself. This then would account for the jolt that ran through me the first time I saw him, though I liked it better when I was sure he was the not-me. I waited for the thought to jolt me, but it didn't.

I pictured him opening the refrigerator door and letting the cold air out, playing with a pencil, picking up a scientific journal, pissing into the toilet, his cock in his hand. All I had to do was get his clothes off. Then he'd be set free and my own desire would be unleashed—all the feeling that had once flowed and poured from me and now was gone, used up like a well run dry. Worse. Before it ran dry, it was poisoned.

And I couldn't count on Jennie for fun anymore. She was too busy humming to her fetus and saving the world. Since she wasn't going to be a lawyer, she'd decided to work fulltime for the peace movement and every other movement that would have her.

"The enemies of freedom are never idle," she said.

It was the week when Iranian-born men in the US were required to register with INS to prove they weren't terrorists. Thousands were locked up and thrown into cold cells to sleep on the floor, not allowed to contact their families, some abused by Muslim-hating guards, all because INS was slow in checking paperwork. A customs agent was bitten while confiscating seven Exuma Island iguanas that subsequently ended up at the zoo. Devon had her tattoo modified with a red slash over the A, thereby renouncing anarchy, Alex, or both, and the little markhor got pregnant with the big ram's baby. I watched Molly play with a spider, touching it so gently not a single delicate leg was harmed. If she found a baby rabbit or squirrel, I was sure she'd raise it as her own, happy to share her world with any creature as long as it wasn't another cat.

It was the week the homeless shelter phoned. According to Jennie, 13% of the population of Los Angeles had no idea where their next meal was coming from and she said the statistic was official—direct from the Department of Health. As I'd had no place to go for Thanksgiving, I'd tried to volunteer but on holidays so many celebrities showed up the shelter didn't need me. Now they did.

Four volunteers plus several homeless men on kitchen duty joined hands in prayer. Faith-based charity. The men took turns thanking God and Jesus and George Bush and then they thanked the volunteers for volunteering. Every time the word *volunteer* was said the guy on my left squeezed my hand. We prayed in English and then we prayed in Spanish and the praying and the squeezing went on and on and on till I all but gave up hope the chaplain would ever say Amen.

The food was already prepared. The first volunteer in line slapped a scoop of noodles on a plate and then I glopped on some tuna gravy and I passed it along for the fried rice and the old guy at the end poured on dessert which was some thin applesauce that looked like gruel. When we ran out of tuna gravy, I got a tray of macaroni from the day before and we served that with the fried rice and then the fried rice ran out and we had cold leftover steamed rice but there was still plenty of thin apple gruel to go around.

I tried not to look at the tables because I didn't want to see the men eating. I didn't want to see their faces while they ate this slop.

Next they put me out front by the trash cans and said one of the residents would show me what to do.

We worked side by side. The homeless men brought up their plates and water glasses and we took them and emptied leftover water into plastic pails and dumped the leftover glop into the trash. You tossed the empty glasses back through the window behind you where the dishwashers caught them. The guy beside me could do it without even looking.

He said, "You'll get the hang of it, Barbara."

I said, "I'm Rae."

Everyone at the shelter called me either Judy or Barbara.

He said, "There's a lot of things I didn't know before I came here. Like that I didn't have to be a criminal and a drunk."

The men kept coming with their plates. The Anglos said God bless you, and I answered God bless you, too. The Latinos said Gracias, and I answered Buen provecho.

The guy said, "I'm new here so I'm on Helping Hands. That means I got my regular work assignment during the day and the rest of the time they rotate me to offer my helping hands where I'm needed, and tonight I'm needed right here scraping plates with you."

Out on the street I'd seen men who didn't look like they could say a sentence. They looked as though they had no names. They wouldn't know how to use a fork or say God bless you and I'd found myself reciting in my head: *A dog starved at his master's gate, Predicts the ruin of the state.* I was an English teacher after all, not that I'd ever read William Blake with my students many of whom were headed to the streets, or prison, if not already there, or to prison first and then the streets. At the shelter, I thought that glopping slop on plates meant nothing. What mattered was that this man was having a conversation, so as not to lose the habit of being—and being regarded as—human.

"I don't see it as punishment," he said. "I like being Helping Hands. Even when I've done my time, I want to do it more. I've learned it feels good to be useful."

A very big man came by without a plate and out of the corner of his mouth said, "Ten seconds."

"Says who?"

"Chaplain."

The man I was working beside told me, "It's the rule. We're only allowed to talk to a female for ten seconds."

Barely time enough for God bless you and God bless you, too.

The chaplain came over and sent the guy behind the wall.

To me he said, "We don't need women here with bad judgment. You'd better leave."

At the zoo I never got in trouble though I'd once held Lulu's hand which was strictly speaking against the rules.

Sometimes I helped with food prep. The colobus monkeys got their yams cooked, the lemurs and sifakas got it raw, and I sprinkled slippery elm bark powder and Missing Link on their collard greens and kale. The ringtails got lettuce, the blue-eyed lemurs didn't. Some of them got monkey chow that smelled of citrus and some got Old World monkey pellets and there was always enough so they could enjoy their meal and never have to fight for food.

I always hoped to see Michael offer a treat to Melissa, but much as he loved her, I never observed them to share.

Lyle still tore at himself in his frenzies but everyone else was doing well. Kelly, the silverback gorilla, grew bigger and more muscular. His sagittal crest seemed to be bursting with thought. The orangutans lay above the world, hanging in the canopy of nets, then Higgins climbed slowly down the wall like a huge and mutant henna-dyed tarantula. The red uakaris locomoted in their various ways: brachiating, walking, pacing, leaping, whirling, swinging, richocheting and bouncing, running, sliding, seesawing on branches, doing handsprings, rocking and rolling on their backs while trying to grab their own feet. I didn't understand how anyone anywhere could eat them, looking as they did like old sunburned people in fur coats, their faces the color of boiled lobster and their red ears sticking up above their little bald heads.

I was in the middle of a drill observation when Sara wheeled herself over.

"I can't talk now," I said. "I don't mean to be rude, but don't distract me."

"They're not doing anything," she said.

Sometimes hours passed and nothing happened, just Lyle in the loft out of sight (NV—not visible), Leona clutching her burlap, Becky sitting with her legs crossed like Buddha, Melissa watching the sky, Michael asleep beside her, but as soon as you turned your head away, all hell would break loose and you'd have no idea who even started it.

Sara said, "I've met someone who knows you."

I'd rather not go into that, at least not yet. So instead, let me tell you about Sara.

She was once an international surfing champ and parlayed her fame into a career writing features for glossy lifestyle magazines. "The usual crap," she said. "How to tell if he's cheating. How to tell if he's lying. How to be his best friend." The cheating article was the start of her downfall. "I happened to see the piece in galleys before it went to print. The writers never saw the galleys, though they let the advertisers read them in advance. One of my stories got killed because of what the editor called a conflict with Maybelline. I was so naive back then, I thought she meant the Chuck Berry tune. That it was copyright infringement or something. No, they thought the piece wasn't cosmetics-friendly. Anyway, the editor had added this opening paragraph to my infidelity piece. It now started I never considered myself a jealous person, until the day I came home to find my boyfriend in bed with my best friend. That had never happened."

She went to her editor who told her the article needed to be more personal and entertaining.

"But it isn't true," Sara said. "It impugns my integrity as a journalist. It impugns the morals of my boyfriend, and my best friend."

"We needed a more colorful opening," the editor said. "And we don't name them."

"*My* name is on it."

No one at the magazine understood why she was making such a fuss. She had to hire a lawyer to prevent the publication.

"Last time I ever got an assignment from that magazine," she said.

But she had a reputation and she continued to sell stories elsewhere, until—and here's the reason I've wanted to avoid her—she was run down by a drunk driver.

"After the obligatory personal essay, heavy on grit and determination, the work dried up," she said. "They all said they didn't need the disability point of view. What point of view? There wasn't any reason I couldn't keep churning out crap on Why do you procrastinate? and What to Ask Your Doctor about Facelifts and Planning the Traditional Second Wedding. But they felt disability was now the only subject I could write about. OK, I'll write about it. I mean, think about the demographics—how many readers live with a disability or have a family member or partner who's disabled."

"Yes, of course," said the editor. "But we don't want the advertisers to know that. Let me tell you a secret," the editor said. "Cripples aren't big spenders and we're not really about journalism."

"We're about entertainment," Sara said.

"Actually, we're about marketing."

Once upon a time, I'd hoped to become a journalist.

"Once upon a time," said Sara, "it was worth doing."

"But you still—"

"I'm just a copy editor. I have to make a living and it's what I know how to do."

But she was working on a feature story. "Something meaningful for a change," which meant she wasn't being paid and it might never be published. "It's something I need to do."

Fine, but I didn't need to hear it.

So instead I stood on one leg and touched the green leaves. I watched the drills. I drove to David's to confront him—not about Marcia, but about the lab.

Since his ex (and Devon) got the Brentwood house, David had moved into corporate housing down by the marina—a temporary situation that had lasted almost three years. To phone him, you had to go through a switchboard and now, showing up live, I had to get past the front desk.

I gave his name and was told there was no such person in residence.

"But he's been here for years," I said.

The young woman shrugged.

"I know he's here," I said. "I've been sending a cheesecake every week," though of course I'd stopped that after Thanksgiving.

My timing at least was right. Through the glass office doors I saw him—David, with a suitcase in each hand.

"There he is!"

"He is not in residence," said the woman. "He checked out fifteen minutes ago."

I caught up to him in the patio.

"Vacation?" I asked.

"Not exactly."

"I have to talk to you," I said.

He put the suitcases down. "Strangely enough," he said, "I owe you a great deal."

He gestured and we took two chairs poolside.

The woman from the front desk came running out. "Facilities are for guests only."

For once, David and I were on the same wavelength. We ignored her.

"My daughter started it," he said, "but you get much of the credit, too. You've made me reassess beliefs that were so ingrained, I have to admit I never examined them. I had ways of thinking so fixed, I took them for granted. My behavior was controlled by precepts you forced me to question."

I couldn't believe what I was hearing. I put my hand on his, and he didn't pull away. The woman stood with her hands on hips, then shook a finger at us.

"I'd offer you a cup of coffee," David said, "but obviously I can't get back into my room."

There was a Starbucks across the street, but I decided not to mention it.

"You have to understand," he said. "I worked with design and data, not with baboons. I didn't come into direct contact with the animals—ever. My office wasn't even in the same building. Oh, go away," he said to the woman, and she did. "I'd been in once at the start to inspect," he said. "Then, after you took me to the zoo, I went back. In a way I can't forgive you for that, but if you completely upset my equilibrium, you also helped me find new balance. But you were wrong, you know. They do have names though it's not a matter of respect. Have you ever heard someone say your name—? You've heard *Rae* haven't you, said with such contempt and mockery, even disbelief that a thing like you could even have a name—that's how I heard her name pronounced. I heard *Rosie*, I heard her taunted with that name, two mocking syllables to underline how degraded she had become."

"What are you going to do?" I asked.

"If we end the experiment, the baboons will simply be euthanized," he said. "I don't know what to do about the animals. What I'm doing for myself is, I'm moving into The Castle."

"With Marcia."

"She introduced me, but not with her."

Of course not. They weren't allowed to have sex in The Castle. Convenient for you, I thought, you impotent worm.

"Only on a trial basis," he said. "It's not a commitment to Neoproctology. At least not yet. It's just a source of more information. Their method of analysis is helping me make sense of what I've done and how I've been living and what I should do next and I have to say the colonic irrigation did me a world of good."

"Enjoyed it, did you?"

"I wouldn't say that," he said. "If the body is full of toxins, the brain matter is contaminated, too. No wonder a person's thinking can be toxic. They're very careful with the cleansing. The, uh, naturally pleasurable sensations induced in the, uh, posterior nether regions are always distinguished from, uh, penetration aberrations, and minimized to avoid their elaboration into, uh, sexual arousal."

He assured me he'd maintained his personal dignity throughout.

No believer like a convert. But I couldn't have guessed he'd even take to heart that loony theory about concentration camps in Glendale, that he'd take me hiking in Brand Park to prove it and end up crying in my arms. All that was in the cards, but back in the marina, I didn't expect to see him ever again.

He stood and shook my hand and asked me where that auto mechanic was that Jennie and I liked so much.

"Well, we'd better leave before that woman throws us into the pool," he said. "Carry on."

He hoisted his suitcases and left me.

Chapter Sixteen

Sometimes you just fall in love. It can't be explained. Actually, it's only the intensity I can't explain. Consider Melissa's calm and gentle nature, her gratefulness, the way Michael's attention made her glow. Of course he would choose her over Becky (the bitch) and strange little burlap-loving Leona. He showed the good taste that's so often unaccountably lacking in human males and females.

On Valentines Day, Bernice, Jennie, and I chained ourselves to the gate at the drill exhibit to protest the impending separation of Michael and Melissa while at USC, students handed out Valentines to passersby, cards that said *I miss you* and named just a small number of the hundreds of thousands of people disappeared by INS. I didn't know then that soon I would be missing Jennie Kim.

Was there anyone I missed?

Sara said, "I've met someone who knows you."

I said, "I can't talk now."

"You were married to him," she said.

Knew me, I thought. Doesn't know me.

She said, “He’s a remarkable man.”

You’re in love with him, I thought. Everyone always was. And you don’t have a clue.

How did I love him? Let me count the ways.

The mildness in his eyes, warm with affection, the way his voice caressed their names when he spoke of his friends.

I loved the crooked teeth he never got fixed. Such a handsome man devoid of vanity.

I loved the way you could be in a room with him and not feel he took up all the air and space.

The times he’d quietly touch my arm and point so that I’d see a redtailed hawk, a hummingbird nest, a raccoon up in a tree, silvery in the moonlight.

I loved him worth three totaled cars, $25,000 in property damage, a craftsman bungalow lost to foreclosure, sleepless nights, terror, tears, guilt, despair.

“He’s a drunk,” I wanted to tell Sara. What on earth could someone confined to a wheelchair—sorry, who *uses* a wheelchair—because of a drunk driver have to say to a drunk? As it turned out, plenty. I’m sure he was gracious to her. He always is, flirtatious and kind. “He’ll hurt you,” I wanted to say, but I didn’t say anything.

We sat under the umbrellas at the snack bar. I was thinking about alpha males. Among chimps, if success means impregnating as many females as possible to ensure the continuation of your genetic material, being alpha isn’t the best thing to be. He gets his way now and then through intimidation or force, but the females consider him a bully and avoid him. They prefer to mate with friendly, generous, easygoing chimps.

With Des, there was no coercion, no imposition. No infringing on or canceling out my will.

When I laughed, Des didn't think I was laughing at him.

It was a time when most of the men I met had problems with cocaine. Des's heavy drinking seemed like fun, harmless, even old-fashioned, part of his anachronistic charm.

I loved it that he was a carpenter, that he spent the day building things that were real, and didn't all carpenters have a finger missing or two?

He never talked about the wonderful things he was going to do for me. He made me no promises (except about getting sober). He just did things without waiting to be asked.

I love to be right and he always said I was. You're right, I have a problem. You're right I have to quit, and I was supposed to be satisfied with being right.

I didn't tell Sara any of that.

"1964," I said. "Freedom Summer. He went South to encourage black folks to join the Mississippi Freedom Democrats and register to vote. He walked the back roads, all those dirt country roads, and one afternoon, he came to the usual shack, and a woman came to the door and she was beautiful. Just beautiful. He tried to talk to her but she wasn't really listening. Nothing but resentment in her face and fear. Resignation. She didn't even want to look at him. So she cuts off his spiel and says her husband will be home soon. And he's thinking, you know, she's inviting him to wait, to talk to the man of the house, another potential voter. Till she says to him in this awful voice, Get it over with. That's when he got it: she thought he was there for sex. What other reason would bring a white man to her door in the middle of a summer's day? No, he said. It's not like that. I'm not here to hurt you, which wasn't exactly true because if she tried to demand her rights, he knew they might kill her."

And people did get killed. People risked their lives to go to the polls and a mere thirty-something years later, yours truly didn't bother voting anymore and a corrupted Supreme Court would install George W. Bush in the White House, ruling the individual citizen has no federal constitutional right to vote for electors for the President of the United States—none of which bore thinking about.

"He left and the woman shut the door but he was sure she stayed at the window, behind that curtain made from a flour sack, watching him as he sat on the broken porch and cried."

"Yes," said Sara. "He told me that."

It was a story that was safe to tell. "I've got to go enter data in the Tandy," I said. "I can't talk now." I wondered why I was still protecting him.

JENNIE SAID, "We've got to stop appointment of this awful judge. We've got to protest against the Bush tax cuts—just welfare for the rich and cutbacks on everything else."

"And I've got to stay away from politics the way my ex needed to stay away from booze."

"We've got to stop FCC deregulation—look what's happening to the airwaves. Nothing but rightwing lies. We've got to repeal the Patriot Act. We've got to stop clear-cutting in the national forests. We've got to block drilling in Alaska for oil. We've got to insist the UN inspectors be allowed to do their jobs."

"You may not realize it, but you've got a problem," I said. "One protest leads to another. You're probably telling yourself, just one more cause, one more won't hurt, I can stop any time I want to."

"At least send an email," she said. "No, emails aren't taken seriously. Send a fax. No, show you're serious with a real letter. Oh, God, I just don't know. You write a long articulate letter and what for? It gets delayed while they screen for anthrax. When it's finally delivered, the staff just classifies it pro or con and tosses it into what may or may not be the right pile. Letters don't help. You have to phone. The lines are always busy, that's how outraged people are. The only way to make your point is to visit the office. The local field office. Or better yet, maybe we should go to Washington."

"Oh, Jennie," I said. "People like us don't get heard."

"We've got to stop this war before it starts," she said. She had that stunned drugged soft-eyed look of pregnant women and the stereotyped non-negotiable craving, the difference being that Jennie's craving was not for pickles. "I had this idea. We get five cars, five drivers. Each car has a letter in its back window. P-E-A-C-E. We drive side by side on the 10 Freeway and then we all brake and come to a stop and block traffic with the message."

"Think about road rage," I said. "You'll get shot. Think about the baby."

She smiled. "Touch my belly," she said. "Touch it if you want to."

I said thank you but kept my hands to myself. "What does Loy say?"

"Loy said not to."

He gave her another idea. Recruit everyone on her email list. We'd each wear signs, front and back, reading NO WAR IN MY NAME. We'd each choose a different spot in LA, and at noon on the same day, we'd all lie down on the ground and stay there for fifteen minutes.

"Instead of a mass demonstration," she said, "it will be dissent popping up all over, unstoppable. We'll be everywhere."

"Not me," I said. "Loy gonna do it?"

"He can't," she said. "I've got to act and speak not just for myself."

"For the baby," I said.

"And for Loy. Don't you realize, he's silenced because of his position."

Shit. It was so easy to forget Loy was still in the Guard.

"OK. I'll do it," I said.

When the Abercrombie & Fitch clock struck noon, I was back at The Grove, this time without Devon, dressed in black, wearing my signs. I took a quick look around at the people I would be trying to reach:

A man in a business suit talked into his cell phone: "It's noon and I'm at The Grove. Now I'm walking past the pretzels..." as though he needed to believe someone cared about his whereabouts as passionately as his mother presumably once did.

A muscled young man in baggy pants instructed his less developed friend, "Always rewind your video, man. It's like flushing the toilet after you use it, OK?"

I wanted to lie down on the grass but chains were up to keep people off. I lay down on the walkway. Happy music rose from the flowerbeds. I had to close my eyes against the sun.

Within seconds, a voice: "Ma'am, I'm the head of security and I have to ask you to leave."

His head and hat and uniform blocked the light. I could look into his face without even squinting.

I said, "I can't leave."

He said I was trespassing on private property. I said I was exercising free speech. He said there was no free speech at The Grove.

I gave him what I was sure must have been a strong and forthright look as I told him that in order to prevent a war I was committed to staying until 12:15. I told him I had an alarm clock in my pocket and as soon as it sounded, I would leave.

"Is that an alarm clock or a bomb?"

Me, a suicide bomber?

"Are you alone?"

"All over the city at this very moment," I said, "hundreds of people, maybe thousands, are lying down just like this." Well, I really thought so.

"Are you alone here? Or are there others?"

Even Jennie, I later learned, had stayed home, due to morning sickness. If she lay down at all, it was on the tiles of her own bathroom floor. "Each of us was free to choose an individual location. I don't know for a fact that anyone else is here, but there may be more. Many more."

There was some whispered consultation. I closed my eyes.

"OK, since you say you'll leave peacefully, I'm giving you till 12:15. I'm going to establish a perimeter around you until then."

As the guards took their positions, I didn't let on I was grateful. I'd felt vulnerable lying there, expecting Republicans to step on or spit on me. The perimeter attracted attention.

People walked over to see what was going on.

"I'm going to need a copy of your sign."

I said at 12:15 I would give him the signs I was wearing.

Shoppers stared down at me. No one said anything in support or agreement or opposition or surprise. I squinted up from time to time to see them: gawking, talking on their phones as they walked away.

The security chief was still there when my pocket beeped.

"Do you need help in rising from the ground?" he asked. "Can I give you a hand."

"I'm fine," I said. I rose and I took off both my signs and gave them to him. It was all very solemn. We shook hands as if we had just signed a treaty. I thanked him for being considerate. He gave me his business card and a package of info in English and Spanish with, among other things, The Grove's code of conduct that prohibits "non-commercial expressive activity without the prior written permission of the management" and pages of Supreme Court decisions that allow shopping centers to exclude people from their property who engage in purposes other than shopping.

When I got home and read the pages, I learned I'd got in just under the wire. More than fifteen minutes and they could have had me arrested.

I was arrested once, in 1968. I waited for Des the first time he went to jail. But now? Getting busted was, to use Devon's turn of phrase, so over.

Sara stalked me. "Tell me about Kenny Desmond."

"I was at an open house for teachers a few years ago," I told her. "They had artists and performers demonstrating the programs they could bring into the classroom. And there was a storyteller, named Judy Witters. I don't know, I thought storytelling, how corny, it could hardly be anything I could care about. But she was magical. She told the story of a knight who, with his very life at stake, was given one year to go out into the world and come back with the answer to the question: What do women want? In the woods he met an old woman, the most hideous misshapen loathsome creature he had ever seen. She told him she could give him the answer if he would marry her. Desperate, he agreed. And she put her hideous lips up to his well formed ear and whispered a single word which he carried back to the castle and spoke before the queen. "A woman wants sovereignty."

"That's Chaucer, isn't it?" Sara said. "The Wife of Bath's tale. What does it have to do with Kenny?"

"The knight kept his word and married the hag. And on their wedding night, she told him another secret. She said, I, your old and ugly wife can be a true wife, always faithful and a constant helpmeet and support. Or, your kiss can transform me to a beautiful maiden, one who will bring ruin and despair to you and your house. And what does he do? He gives her her sovereignty. It's her body. He lets her choose, and when he says that, she becomes both beautiful and good. And it made me think of Kenny," I said. Sara didn't have to know his friends called him Des. "Because he was the kind of man, you just knew that if he loved you, that would be his answer: the choice is yours."

I knew she wanted more. I said, "I've got to go."

Chapter Seventeen

GORILLA THEATER WAS MOBILE. We didn't need sets, so Bobby made costumes and masks.

The elastic was too tight. The cardboard pressed against my nose and so hard against my glasses I thought they'd break at the bridge.

"I can't wear this," I said.

"I'm not a mask-maker," Bobby said. "I'm an artist."

"Wear it!" said Bernice. "Creatures are suffering!"

Slinking and bounding, meowing, bowwowing, we descended on the Federal Building where INS was registering Muslim men. Amory slobbered, Devon rubbed up against the legs of strangers, and Bernice hollered through a bullhorn: "When men are detained without notice, what provision is made for their pets? Dogs and cats are starving because of INS!" We chanted "What about the pets! Down with INS!"

I had objected to the word *pets*, but had to admit it was a near rhyme.

A man approached me. "My boss let me go early and told me to get over here. He said I must report."

"Where are you from?" I asked.

"Palestine."

Oh boy. Far be it from me to tell him his country wasn't a country.

"What passport do you travel on?" Bobby asked.

"Jordanian."

"I don't think Jordan's on the list," Jennie said. "Which is kinda weird. Neither is Saudi Arabia. And they only make men register, not women. Like a woman can't be a terrorist. Obviously, there's another agenda. This has nothing to do with preventing terrorism."

"Are they going to take my parrot?" said the man.

The INS security guard picked a fight with Bobby. "What are you doing here, helping these people? My own cousin got deported. When it's Mexicans, no one gives a damn."

"Hey, you work for these people," said Bobby.

"It's a job. And one that pays shit. I know how bad they're treated in there. Why haven't you been out here fighting for your own?"

"We have no interest in race, religion, creed, or national origin," I said. "We're here for the animals."

Bernice led us away and promised, "More anon."

Six of us piled into Jennie's big car—"the family car," she said—for a protest out in San Bernardino, Raymond Chandler's San Berdoo, where the airport was expanding and leasing land that was critical habitat for the kangaroo rat, a mammal that, as I pointed out to Devon, does not sweat.

"You're sitting on my tail," said Devon.

We crossed the railroad tracks and drove past fenced-in fields with flags and flowers stuck in the chain link. A surveyor was setting up his equipment under a small striped orange tent. Jennie honked and we all booed. Everywhere, signs said No Parking, No Stopping Anytime.

"There's got to be airport parking," Jennie said.

"We do not pay for parking," said Bernice. "And you are driving awfully fast."

"You can drop us off somewhere and circle for a while," I said.

"Why didn't Sara come?" Bobby asked.

"She was nervous," Bernice said, "because it's a Superfund site."

"What?" I said.

"This used to be Norton Air Force base. When they turned the land over to the city, it was pretty contaminated. Highly radioactive."

"Then it's not gonna do the kangaroo rats much good," Bobby said.

"Well, they've cleaned it up," Bernice said. "I think."

"I'm not getting out of the car," Devon said.

"Let's get out of here," said Amory.

"But we're already in costume!" said Bernice.

"I'll go down the 215 to March Air Reserve. There's rats there too," Jennie said.

"Those are Stephens kangaroo rats," Bernice said. "Not San Bernardinos."

"We discriminate against subspecies now?" I asked.

"Of course not," said Bernice. "I mourn the passing of the Neanderthal."

Amory said, “It might be inconvenient to have them around.”

Devon said, “I know quite a few.”

“They’ve got a fighter jet museum there at March,” Bobby said. “Perfect place to protest. And a sculpture honoring war dogs. We can protest sending canines into battle.”

“Absolutely not,” said Bernice. “We’re trying to win hearts and minds. You don’t do that by demonizing people just because they’ve dropped bombs.”

“You have wasted my whole morning,” I said. “You have got to stop wasting my time.”

“What else would you do with it?” asked Bernice.

To tell the truth, I didn’t know.

WE WERE FIGHTING on too many fronts. Though I worked at the zoo, I didn’t know they’d shipped Junie the elephant off to Knoxville till I saw the news on TV.

Junie the African elephant and Gita the Asian elephant were supposed to grow old together, two ancient ladies, companions for more than sixteen years, taking the sun and eating their feed.

Bernice was outraged. “There are other African elephants in Knoxville. They say she’ll be happier with her own kind. How do they know? Who asked her?”

And what about Gita, left all alone? But humans, as usual, thought they knew best.

“Melissa will be next,” Bernice said. “Time for preemptive action.”

That’s when we chained ourselves to the fence at the drill exhibit. How were we to know there would be consequences?

It seemed so simple. Lyle did a bipedal waddle in my direction, erection in hand. I got a reprimand and both Jennie and Bernice were searched by security and asked to leave. We thought, big deal, that was all.

SOMETIMES YOU JUST CAN'T do what you mean to. For instance, I had every intention of watching the State of the Union address but Molly jumped on the remote control, first hitting mute, then off.

The next day, Bernice confronted me—"What am I doing wrong?"—cloaking her aggression in self-pity. "I'm working round the clock for Gorilla Theater and—"

"Round the clock? What are you doing? How much can there be to do?"

"See! No one understands. Paperwork, bookkeeping, grant reporting, and look at this bullshit. I wrote about the budget cuts, and look what I get." She waved a letter from the California Assembly. *The types of funding choices we face at this time are cuts for health care funding for the poor versus funding for the arts.* "That is not the choice. The budget for health care and for the arts is so minuscule to begin with. Put a tiny tax on SUVs—it would more than cover it. How about the choice to make billionaires and corporations pay their fair share? Oh, they say, they'll leave the state. Really? Where they going to go? Someplace with winter? And the phone keeps ringing, I'm copying scripts, finding venues, doing the website—do you have any idea how hard it is to write code—getting the costumes and the worst of it, trying to get and keep you folks together. Call a rehearsal and someone can't make it. And some of you say you will and don't show up. And arranging transportation for the kids and a lot of gratitude I get for that. I hear you had a party without me."

I wondered who told her. "It wasn't without you," I said. "Jennie likes to mix and match," I lied. "Introduce people who've never met. It's not like everyone from Gorilla Theater was there. I didn't see Sara."

"I'll bet you didn't," said Bernice. "I'll bet you can't get a wheelchair into Jennie's house."

"If you're going to criticize where someone lives," I said, "how about Sara? What kind of person lives in a gated community?"

"A woman who can't run from predators," Bernice said. She sniffled and there followed much wiping of the nose and all that goes with it. "I don't understand how you could have a party completely unbeknownst to my knowledge. Look," she said, "I know you don't like taking direction from me because I'm younger than you are."

"Not by much." Wrong thing to say. "Uh, where did you get your glasses? I love the frames."

"A great little place in Leimert Park," she said. "I do not understand how Jennie could schedule her party to conflict with Chanukah. I am a deep listener. I have learned to empathize without condoning. I have a course certificate from UCLA Extension in the non-authoritarian leadership style."

"I'm sorry," I said. What else could I say?

"Will she invite me to the next one?" Bernice said. "Introduce me to new people?"

"Jennie's so busy with politics right now, I don't think there's gonna be any more parties."

"That figures," said Bernice. "Programs always get discontinued just when it's my turn."

Listening to Bernice complain was like being stuck in traffic when you have to change a tampon. (Yes, I still bleed every month and my face still breaks out, too.)

"I've known too much disappointment," she said.

"When you're disappointed again and again, you just have to stop feeling it."

"You have never once asked about my personal life," she said. "You have shown zero interest. You have never once asked if I'm seeing anyone."

"I tend to afford people privacy."

"Don't you know how to interact?"

"OK, OK," I said. "Are you seeing someone?"

"No," she said. "And I'm tired. Everything's out of control. I can't keep up at home. Can you recommend a good cleaning lady?"

"No," I said.

"Well, who cleans your place?"

"I do," I said. "Or to be more honest, I don't."

"And as if I didn't have enough trouble from you all, Devon quit. She says she just wants to have fun and make money. She says Gorilla Theater isn't what she expected. Do you want to know how many times I've heard that? You're not what I expected. I'm not having as much fun as I expected. I expected you to be this or that or the other thing. Anything other than what I am. Amory was absolutely right. If we get people to treat animals like people, that's the worst disservice we could ever do them."

Gorilla Theater wasn't what I expected either. I, too, wanted to quit, but Bernice was in despair so I didn't have the heart.

"Do you take pills?" she asked. "I mean, what gets you through the day? You have nothing."

"Once upon a time," I said, "we respected people who had nothing."

"Who's this we?" she asked. "You're over fifty and you don't even have air conditioning in your car."

"I do have A/C," I said. "It just doesn't work when it's very hot out."

"You don't believe in God," she said. "No comfort for you there."

"My cat comforts me."

"Your cat!"

"Oh, Bernice," I said. "Sometimes I think the world is doing its damndest to make me miserable and I refuse to be—out of spite. When you've got enough spite, you don't need Paxil. Anyway, you're the one who taught me about deep ecology. I believe in my place in Nature. Small amid the immensity. Respecting my place and doing as little harm as I can."

She said, "Don't you ever wish you could believe in God?"

"I'm just trying to survive," I said. "Maybe you're not aware of this but women feel stress and anger 30% more than the average man and this results in damage to the blood vessels, inefficiency of the immune system, and an increased risk of cancer. For your own sake, just stop complaining. Let go of it!"

“You don’t believe in anything,” she said.

“Sometimes I wish I could be like Mirady. To believe that after all the violence and suffering, history is inevitably moving towards a golden age. I wish I believed it.”

“But you don’t,” Bernice said, “and I don’t know what gets you up in the morning.”

“Molly does. She drags the covers off and jumps on me.”

If I may speculate here, I believe it was Bernice herself who was having trouble getting out of bed.

She said, “According to Devon, knowledge makes a person unhappy.” Now Devon was the authority? “She says curiosity killed the cat.”

To give Bernice her due, she did love animals and she began to weep at the very thought of a cat being dead.

“What would a cat be without curiosity?” I said. “It’s instinct, it’s an integral part of the cat’s life. Without it, can you even say a cat is alive? That it’s a cat? We have to know, even though I wish I didn’t know most of what I do. Ignorance is bliss,” I said. “But it’s unnatural. It means killing yourself in order to live.”

Chapter Eighteen

I REALLY DIDN'T WANT TO KNOW about US military aid to Colombia and its probable impact on the endangered cottontop tamarin.

An exile who'd been arrested and tortured told us that Colombia received the most US military aid behind Israel and Egypt. It was supposed to be for the War on Drugs, what a joke. We defund prevention and treatment in this country where the demand is, and spray toxic defoliants all over a South American country, even in places where coca was never grown.

"How would Americans like it," he said, "if Colombians decided to spray the killer tobacco fields in Kentucky?"

In Congress, the only debate was who would get the contract for helicopters—Sikorksy in Connecticut or Bell Helicopter in Texas.

"It's happening under the radar," he said, "just like the nightmare of Afghanistan. Is anyone paying attention to Afghanistan now?"

It was true. If the little markhor was airlifted from a war zone, that meant the war was still going on, and it was a war involving people, but since we'd invaded Iraq, no one talked about Afghanistan. The markhor herself wasn't so little anymore but she still craned her neck and twisted it back. She was still watching the sky.

"Did you know your tax dollars pay for armed protection for Occidental Petroleum?"

How can I know everything?

The cottontops at the zoo stretched and arched their bodies like cats. They had clawed little feet, faces like African masks with thinly furred white stripes, tufted headdresses and tails that sometimes coiled up like cinnamon buns.

In Colombia three million people had been driven from their homes. Internal refugees. The cottontop's days were numbered. All of this was connected.

What would it be like to see your entire family slaughtered before your eyes, to be the one survivor, to take a few possessions in a sack and flee?

"That's the story of my life," said Mirady. "The story of my country. Your government destroyed so many lives in my country and got away with it. That gave them the confidence to do it here."

I DIDN'T MEAN FOR THIS to get so serious. It was just data. I was just keeping tabs on what life was like, what we said, what we did, maybe because I was wondering about myself, about who I'd become, or maybe thinking this might be useful someday, just the way all the records we keep on the drills will maybe mean something at some point to someone.

No one was supposed to suffer in this narrative except for

Rosie, and after all, to most of you she's just an ape and you're not even right about that, since baboons are monkeys. I could have started this before the planes went into the Towers, instead of afterwards, when we were getting used to a world in which that could happen. When I started this, people were dying in Afghanistan, but we had saved them, right? I could have shown you a family out in the street and homeless, but instead I showed you Weezie who could keep on smiling and be happy enough finding a home with a wacko cult. I wanted to share the word about re-earthing, in the spirit of American optimism. If you wanted violence, I figured you could go to the movies. I wasn't trying to reach your conscience or your heart.

My own heart, as I've mentioned, had turned nice and hard. But then Sara caught up with me again. "You have to listen to me," she said. "I looked up Chaucer. The Wife of Bath. You left out part of the story. The knight was exiled and sent on his quest because of his crime. He raped a young girl," she said. "You left out the girl who was raped. What happens to her?"

"The story doesn't say."

"The knight is redeemed. The evil spell cast on his bride is broken. They live happily ever after. But the girl who survived his violence...what becomes of her?"

"I don't know."

"I'll tell you," said Sara. "She's forever changed. Something has been taken from her. And she's just supposed to get on with it. So she smiles, she reassures people that she's fine, so they don't know about the rage, and the fear, the bitterness in her heart because she feels so alone. Always, entirely alone because everyone else is just living as though nothing has happened to her." She said, "Kenny at least doesn't get to live happily ever after."

Unbelievable. I said, "If you're trying to tell me that Des raped someone, I am telling you it's not possible."

"He's in prison," she said. "But not—of course not, for that."

I was silenced for a moment by the inevitability of it all.

"Twenty-five to life," she said. "He killed a child."

"Goddamn him. Driving drunk," I said.

"No," she said. "He shot her. A six-year-old girl, his girlfriend's daughter. He shot and killed her."

"Des would never own a gun," I said.

"Just sit down and let me tell you," Sara said.

So I listened.

SARA HAD NEVER HAD THE CHANCE to confront the drunk who hit her, and she got the idea that if she could just come face to face with someone like him, it would help her. "I kept asking myself how could he do it? What does he feel like now?"

Convicted drunk drivers turned out to be harder to track down than she'd expected. "I said I was working on a story. And I am—though I'm not sure I'll ever write it." She posted her search on a prison message board. "The guys don't have access to computers, but a family member told a prisoner and he didn't want to talk to me, but he told Kenny Desmond and one day I got a letter." A few letters went back and forth. He sent her the form to get on the approved prison visitors list. As soon as they met, "He got a hold on me."

He always did.

When we were married, I got used to women giving him the eye and me the once-over—You think you've got him? Who are you kidding?—before gazing up, smiling, at my husband.

"I think," she said, "though he hasn't said so, maybe it eases his mind just a little to see that a person who uses a wheelchair can lead a full life."

"What about the woman he ran down?" I asked. "Do you know how *she* is doing?"

She was a 54-year-old woman who walked three miles every day, rain or shine, for her health. She worked in Lakewood City Hall. She walked nowhere in particular. She walked through her neighborhood. She clocked her distance with an odometer on her wrist. There were sidewalks. She always walked in parks or safely on sidewalks. And it was ten in the morning. Who expects a drunk driver at ten in the morning? Well, it was a Saturday morning meaning Des was still out since Friday night. You don't expect anything to happen, not just around the corner from home, your keys already out of your pocket and in your hand. You don't expect my husband taking a corner too fast, losing control, the car flying up onto the sidewalk to crush you and pin you beneath its wheels. I suspect it would have been a hit and run if Des hadn't passed out behind the wheel, not a goddamn scratch on him.

She survived. He got two-and-a-half years, served less than two. The judge seemed to think a woman her age hadn't got much activity left in her anyway.

I wanted to call her, her family. I wanted to do something, anything to help, but the lawyer told me not to, and I listened.

What is in the heart of someone who survives violence?

"Something lifted from my heart after I met Kenny," said Sara. "Maybe that's what I really needed. To see this reckless, guilty, awful human being and focus on the last part, the human being part. Kenny turns out to be—"

"Tell me about the child," I said.

It turned out to be a kind of 9/11 story. Des never had trouble getting women to fall for him and this time the girlfriend was Persian. Ana. Anahita. They lived in a town near Lake Shasta and while it wasn't the most welcoming place to begin with, after the terrorist attack, the real trouble started. Ana got spat on. The phone rang with threatening calls. Des bought a gun.

"She'll never forgive him," Sara said.

Or herself, I thought.

Sara said, "He got paranoid when he was drinking."

Yes, I remembered that. Drunk was the only way he could express anger. Though it never exploded against me, I began to fear it was only a matter of time.

"The phone rang," said Sara. "The caller hung up, and Kenny took it as a threat. He thought it was this neighbor they'd had trouble with. He got the gun."

"He was gonna go for the neighbor?"

"Ana says—"

"You've met her?"

"She wouldn't see me."

"So Des says that Ana says—"

"He started raving about the KKK. She got scared—of him. And tried to take the gun. It went off."

They were fighting over the gun the way I used to fight him for the keys.

"Daria—the little girl. Daria got shot."

According to Sara, he never tried to deny it or escape responsibility. He pled guilty. He was in prison for life, trying to make sense of what he'd done.

It's not like there were no signs. It's not like no one could see where it was heading. But you get to where there's just nothing you can do.

"The conditions he lives in," she said. "Our prisons are horrific."

"He'll love it," I said. "He'll organize a hunger strike."

"No," she said. "Protest never enters his mind. He does nothing, because nothing the State can do to him is as bad as the guilt."

It was a page I had turned, a book I had closed, but the world is too small, the web is too tight. Sara told him about Gorilla Theater. She mentioned me.

Sara said, "He wants to see you."

Chapter Nineteen

I believe I am a good person even though I do eat meat and have cut out of my life the people who've hurt me.

And I haven't told you everything. I've left out quite a few things. I've tried to keep it light. Or you could say, I stuck within the protocol of behaviors we've chosen to recognize. For example, if one of the drills were to kill another, there's no code on my chart to report it. I didn't tell you that leaving Des brought me to the brink of wanting to die. I was guilty for facilitating his drunkenness. I was impotent to stop it. I hated him and loved him and when I left I wanted him beside me and inside me in a desperate gnawing way that went on and on with no relief and made love a cancer.

I tried and tried till finally there's a disconnect between knowing and acting. Finally you get your life under control in this neat little way, harming no one, and thinking that should be enough.

I didn't tell you that my former colleagues got in touch much more often than I would have liked to let me know each time a former student was killed. There were so many funerals, we used to work on a designated mourner system, so that every teacher wouldn't have to go to every one. Not employed any more, I wasn't designated. I was informed. But I stayed home. I couldn't bear to go.

I didn't tell you how scared I was once troops were deployed to Kuwait, just in case, though their being there surely made the case more likely. And how terrified we were once Loy's unit received a mobilization alert.

"Don't worry," he said. "My time's up on May 1. Then I'm out."

"What if they mobilize before that?" I asked. "What will you do?"

"I don't know," he said.

Kids were enlisting like crazy. Idealistic, seeking revenge for 9/11, fresh meat eager to be battle-tested.

Preemptive war. What was that but a euphemism for war of aggression? Damn my English degree. Why did I have to pay attention to word use? Des had been a conscientious objector, but once you were already in the military, like Loy, you didn't have that choice anymore, did you? All you could be was a deserter, a traitor. "What are you going to do?" I asked.

"I told you. I don't know."

I didn't tell what happened when we tried to recapture old times, the three of us at Taylor's Steak House in Koreatown. Same red booths, same clubby dim lighting. Same tough blonde waitresses and Korean clientele and me, as usual, trying to notice if people were staring at Loy while hoping no one noticed me looking. Same wait for a table that left us standing half an hour at the bar. But Jennie wasn't drinking. Instead she was trying to read us her latest letter to the editor. I wanted to, but didn't, say Give it a rest.

Once we were seated, she ordered her usual lettuce and a baked potato, but this time Loy tried to talk her into eating meat again, protein and iron "for the baby."

Jennie said, "I don't know that we should bring up a child in the city of LA."

"Los Angeles isn't a city," I said.

"Of course it's a city," said Loy. We were all in a testy mood. "What else could it be? Where do you get this crap, anyway? From the New York Times? More American cities are built like Los Angeles than like New York."

Our food came and he sliced into his steak. "Try it."

I wanted to, but didn't, warn him Don't, and there it was, the bit of red meat on his fork, moving, moving in front of Jennie's face.

At first I thought it was Jennie who'd screamed.

Have you ever been out eating dinner, enjoying it or not, and suddenly had the restaurant invaded by what seems to be dozens of armed men? If not, and if Jennie was right, it's a scenario you had better get used to. I don't know if they were cops or FBI or INS or some new Homeland Security goons. They pushed cooks and dishwashers out of the kitchen. Grabbed the waiters from in-between the crowded tables. Made the workers lie on their bellies while the feds searched for green cards and ID. I'd thought being shot once had purged me of fear but it wasn't like that. At the sight of the guns, my ear began to burn and sting. It wasn't the bullet I was afraid of, but the power behind it.

"What the hell is going on here?" Jennie stood up.

"Keep your head down," I warned while Loy tugged at her shirt.

"I'm an attorney and I demand—"

"Things are getting kinda crazy," I said. "Don't push it."

"Someone has to push it."

"Sit down," said Loy.

I said, "We'll all get through this."

"You're all going to have to sit tight for a while," said one of the agents. "You might as well relax and enjoy your meals."

We didn't touch our food. Jennie was crying. I couldn't. I couldn't even breathe. The agent said, "This is for your own protection."

I looked at the red meat and the blood congealing around it and wondered if I would finally turn vegetarian after all.

YOU START TO BELIEVE the worst. Everyone did, but some people believed that Iraq posed an imminent direct threat to the United States while others believed the US government was the greatest threat ever to our existence as citizens of a democratic republic not to mention the continued existence of the planet. And while even I was beginning to take Jennie's warnings seriously, the only reason I went looking for concentration camps in Glendale with David is I was sure we wouldn't find any.

I drove through winding streets, past houses with façades so stately they looked like movie sets against a backdrop of mountain, then through a gauntlet of palms, through a white Moorish arch into Brand Park and up to what a sign identified as a library: an Arabian Nights fantasy of minarets and domes, the stained glass fanlight above the entrance spreading colors like a peacock's tail. Was there a palace somewhere in Baghdad that looked like this? The scenes on television—boxy buildings, flat roofs, palms—looked just like LA which meant the war-planners in Washington couldn't possibly be Angelenos. You can't want to drop bombs on a place that looks like home.

Big old crows perched on the big blue trash cans in the parking lot and a harem began to emerge from station wagons and SUVs—women of all sizes and shapes, dark ones, blonde ones, hennaed ones and gray ones, red silk fluttering, coin necklaces jangling along with ankle bells and finger cymbals. Some had bare bellies, flaunting jewels. Others wore black corsets over their harem pants. It had to be a movie set, unless David was right, and somewhere in this park, Arab men were held behind barbed wire and these, their wives, had come to find them.

I stopped a big blonde with glitter on her eyelids. "Can you tell me what this is about?"

"Belly dancing lessons in the Japanese garden," she said, and the alcohol on her breath made me think of the old days with Jennie. "Can you be objective?"

"I have opinions..."

She called a friend over. "Should she be Johara or Jumanah?" she asked.

Her friend slowly raised thin arms above her head till one hand rested behind the other, both thumbs extended horizontal to the ground. "The Hands of Fatima!" she announced.

"She's been dancing for months now and she still doesn't have a stage name. I'm Samira. That means entertaining companion.

Belinda wants to be Jumanah which means silver pearl but think she should be Johara. That means jewel."

Ana. Anahita, I thought and I didn't know what her name meant other than terrible loss and terrible pain.

"Silver pearl," said Samira. "It makes me think of those sugar balls you put on top of birthday cakes."

"Belinda's a nice name," I said. "Even if it's not Arabic."

"Arabic!" said Samira. "We're American!"

Belinda said, "There are no Arabs here!"

Just north of the parking lot, I found David being crucified on a green plus-sign.

When he saw me, he stepped down revealing what his body had hidden: a goddess figure, arms outstretched, with broken logs piled at her feet, or rather where her feet should have been. They were missing, as though she'd survived a landmine or as though her legs had been treated like timber and chopped.

The plaque read: HELP SAVE OUR TREES - The Forest is the Mother of the Rivers - 1928

Technically it was winter, but it was winter in Southern California, and we hadn't even had rain, and David was wearing a decent enough looking sweater, but he was shivering.

"It's disguised as a water treatment facility. Or a reservoir. Something like that," he said. "They're preparing it to house thousands of dissidents. House them and maybe...dispose of them."

"What's happened to you?" I asked.

"No more Paxil," he said. "They're right. I've been poisoning myself."

Paxil could account for the nonexistent sex drive, I thought.

But it should have mellowed him out. Without it, was he going to be even meaner?

"Come on. Come on," he led me uphill. "Look. Why are there earthmoving machines? Why all that rubble? Why is there a pit in a public park?" The air smelled of eucalyptus and creosote. He stopped to stare at a sign. "Disposal. Solid Waste Disposal...Just what kind of disposal do you think...?"

The man was having a nervous breakdown. I reached for his arm and he turned, held my shoulders and looked into my eyes and I felt it was only my looking back into his that kept him steady.

"We never got to see the grunion, did we?" he said and then he started talking about information molecules in cells and energy transducers, about people who chewed their own fingers and lips to bloody ribbons.

"Don't you get it?" he said. "Illogics must be catabolized to release energy, though only logics can be anabolized for growth. Bush omits his data source markers. There's three kinds. Common or traditional knowledge; what you've witnessed personally; what you've been told by another person or read. His information comes from nowhere and when he repeats it the second time he starts to mark it common knowledge. That's a deceptive practice, otherwise known as a lie."

He stopped and stared at a motorboat surrounded by a fence. I couldn't explain what it was doing here either, many miles from any water.

"You take this toxic catabolic—that Iraq supports Al-Qaeda—for which there is no evidence, only the President's words, and put it into anabolic disguise. That's an analysis that leads to the conclusion he's lying. He says Al-Qaeda's in Northern Iraq but he omits that they're in the area in open rebellion against Saddam since the last war. He doesn't mention that those Al-Qaeda fighters are Saddam's sworn enemies. It's like saying because the airplane terrorists trained here, the US is a terrorist state—which of course it is, but not for that reason."

"What's gotten into you?" I said.

"Lies. My mind is being polluted, intoxicated—have you noticed? intoxicate, toxic—poisoned by the President. He's bringing the world to the brink of war. I didn't know we were the ones to supply Iraq with the chemical weapons. I didn't know that when Iraq shoots at American planes, it's planes that are dropping bombs on Iraq. Why didn't I know this? Oh my God. Look!"

Up on the mountain, we could see some hikers, their white shirts moving up the trail.

"Why would anyone climb a steep trail like that UNLESS ORDERED TO DO SO? And what the hell is that?" he said.

I hadn't hiked in the mountains since Des. One more thing I used to love that I had stopped doing because it reminded me of him.

"That's a debris basin." Oleander—not in bloom this time of year—grew along the fence and we looked down at the broad concrete runoff channel, the flat area like a basketball court, and a cinderblock structure 11-stories high.

"That's an incinerator," he said.

Maybe it was.

"And look at this," he said. Three strands of barbed wire on top of the chain link.

"So kids don't climb in and get hurt."

"Really?" he said. "Why are the barbs facing in instead of out?"

"What's the difference?"

"It's not keeping people out. It's there to keep people in. How many do you think they can fit in there? Ten thousand? Twenty thousand?"

"David! No one is putting people in there! And it doesn't matter which direction. You're still going to tumble onto it if you're not careful. And really, anyone—even I—can get over barbed wire if you're careful. You use razor wire when you're serious."

"Nothing is the way I thought it was," he said.

He held up a finger as if testing the wind or asking for silence. We heard: a trickle of water down rock, footsteps approaching at a run, heavy breathing. A man jogged by with a Doberman. The dog was panting.

"Animals. Vectors of disease," David said. "That's what they are. We'd all be better off in the world without them. My God, Rae. Why didn't I know all this? When we mined the harbors of Nicaragua—did you know that?—and when the World Court found us guilty, we said the US wasn't bound by international law."

"That was a long time ago. That happened under Reagan."

"It doesn't matter who's in office," he said. "It doesn't change. We run the School of the Americas, to train death squads. We have weapons of mass destruction and we're willing to use them."

"Yeah, I know that," I said.

"What's that?"

I could hear quail calling in the sagebrush on the other side of the fence.

"Cries for help!" said David.

Two pretty birds among the sage. Why couldn't he just stop and enjoy this?—the clear winter sky, the yucca and squash vines and sagebrush, the cliffs of crumbling rock faces exposed amid the chaparral. "Quail," I said.

"Are they native," he said, "or have they been loosed here to mask other sounds? The eucalyptus isn't native. So why are these trees there? Eucalyptus goes up like a torch. Lock people in and set the woods afire and it's an accident, right?"

He reached into his shirt and pulled out a map. "See, over there!"

He took off running and I followed.

"OK," he said. "Tell me. What the hell is that?"

The sign said Reservoir 968, but there was no water, and the space was filled by a low chicken coop-like structure with narrow slit windows covered in mesh.

"David," I said. "These men are turning this country into something almost unrecognizable as America. But even they can't go this far. It's impossible. I don't believe it will ever go as far as you're saying. It can't."

David knelt and hollered, "Are you in there? Hello! We're here to help!"

The flat roof looked snow-covered, painted white, and there were small stones scattered over the surface, the way you leave little rocks on Jewish graves. Eight chimney-like vents rose up from the roof, three of them had yellow structures on top, about the size of the Yellow Pages of major cities.

I was just observing, and drawing no conclusions.

"Hello!" David called. "Buenos días. Salaam!"

"Did you see those women?" I asked.

"Answer me!" he hollered. "Please! I come in peace!"

I knelt beside him. "David. There's no one there."

He turned to face me and I noticed how smudged his glasses were. He used to be so fastidious. He said, "Have you ever noticed the similarity between feces and fasces?"

"There's no concentration camp," I said.

He put his hands beneath my elbows and urged me to stand. "Have you ever noticed," he said, "when Southern California is green, it's so many different kinds of green. The dusty green, the shiny green, the faint shy green, the green-gray sage, the dark green pine. When you talk about loving your country, isn't this what you're really talking about?" he said. "I'll admit Nature used to make me uncomfortable. Nice to look at from a distance, but up close, it's just dirty. But look—I can see it now. The landscape. Even if you live in the worst dictatorship, don't you love your mountains and your valleys? You can't possibly want them pocked with bomb craters, strewn with bodies of the dead, dark with blood. You want your old trails and pathways free of land mines. And there's people out there who will destroy it all because the only green that matters is the goddamn dollar bill."

I couldn't believe this was coming from David.

His shoulders began to shake. "Nothing nothing nothing is the way I thought it was. Will you forgive me?" he said.

"Yes," I said. "Of course."

"I reported Mirady," he said. "She said she was a terrorist so I called the tip line."

"You what?" I said.

"Maybe I shouldn't have," he said, "but you all got me upset. America's under attack, right? I didn't name you, Rae. Mirady and Jennie were the only foreigners."

"You dropped a dime on Jennie?"

"What did you expect me to do?" he said. "I am so scared."

I was so angry and this was so insane, but then he started crying and the map crinkled inside his shirt as I put my arms around him.

I had held Des just this way so many times. I remembered each bout of drunken bitter remorse after which, each time, he'd sober up and forget. Sara hadn't been around him long enough. She didn't know the hope and the letdown and she didn't know that no, I would not comfort Des again. I would not go to his prison and sit in some visiting room and let him work his Twelve Steps on me, making amends for what could never now be mended. Believe me, during those days, I went to AA to try and understand. I also went to Al Anon where they told me I had no power over him, which was true. I could no more stop his drinking than poor Jennie could stop the war. At Al Anon they told me that if alcoholism was his disease, empathy was mine. I had to think of myself, stop thinking of him. Impossible. Loving him had become so integral to who I was, it could no longer be separated out. I would have to die first or have a stroke that would destroy all the parts of my brain that knew and loved him. And when I left, of course it was hoping he would sober up and win me back, hoping that my exit would finally make him hit bottom. I suffered for him day and night, and suffered for me, missing him, wanting him, enraged with him, wishing there were a way out of this misery, and day after day and week after week at some point the feelings were exhausted. I hardly remembered why it all mattered. I hardly remembered struggling to be free. One day I realized weeks had gone by without my thinking of him. I said his name out loud and there was no response from inside me. No desire. No anger. If there was still a heart at my center it would love the green leaves and the earth and the cats and the drills and even this pathetic creature crying in my arms who was no longer David. His face was simply the face of suffering, and suffering must be relieved, so I held him.

Chapter Twenty

MIRADY DISAPPEARED of her own volition.

Mirady, at least, said goodbye. She told me she knew I liked Bobby, that she was sleeping with him, but it was OK, I could have him since she was a lesbian and anyway she was leaving town, "going to ground."

"You really are a revolutionary," I said.

She shook her head. "I do believe we'll have a better world someday, but I'm not doing a damn thing to bring it. I'm just talk and I talk too much, and things have gotten too hot for me here."

"What happened?"

"Surveillance. Being followed. Called in by the FBI." I didn't have the heart to tell her it was because of David. "I'll leave town and keep a low profile till the war hysteria blows over."

After she offered me Bobby, she offered me Tijuana.

"I was supposed to go on a work project with the Unitarian Church," she said. "But I'm out of here. You speak any Spanish?"

"Well, yeah. I taught for LAUSD," I said as though it were a reasonable assumption that an LA public school teacher would speak some Spanish, as though I'd never heard anyone in the teacher's lounge ask, "What's the polite word for Mexican?" as though the nationality itself were a pejorative.

"That's why they wanted me. Take my place if you'd like."

Is there anything more constructive than construction? By which I don't mean another luxury subdivision on what was supposed to be protected wetlands or a nature preserve. I mean I leave days' worth of cat food and water for Molly, drive south, cross the border and head inland into the broken ravines past hillsides blooming with trash and wildflowers and down steep rutted streets and up again and down, and find a family where both husband and wife work fulltime in a maquiladora plus grow flowers to sell in the marketplace and imagine that even so, the only housing they can afford is a shelter put together of discarded panels from abandoned trailers, covered with wood grain contact paper. No electric. No plumbing. And imagine that for 18 months, they've been setting aside 18% of their income to buy materials and in their ample leisure time they and their kids have been making cinderblocks and roof tiles. And that we would work with them side by side and put up a two-room house in about two days and they would feed us and after we left, they'd go on contributing money so that their neighbors, one family at a time, could eventually have real houses, too.

It was great to get away from Jennie's nagging about politics, to work at physical labor for hours, to lose myself as completely as I did when watching animals, to be so exhausted I could push away the memories of the house we once restored, me and Des. Only days before, it would have been hard to imagine myself digging a trench for a septic tank. Harder to imagine myself with a church group, even this one.

A lot of us weren't members of the congregation. "I really wanted to start the morning with a prayer," a woman confided, "but you know how funny Unitarians get about praying."

We formed lines to pass cinder blocks down to where they were added to the walls and I didn't even scream when the pile turned out to be infested with black widow spiders. Two of the Mexican guys were considerate enough to stand nearest the pile and shake out and kill the spiders before handing the blocks off down the line. We extended rebar, tied it off, knocked tiles out of the molds and trimmed the edges with hammers (what we called roof-whacking), braced walls, put in temporary frames for doors and windows, trued the walls and poured them, filling buckets with sand and gravel to pour with cement into the mixer. Then heavy buckets had to be swung on down the line and up to the people on the scaffold doing the pouring.

"North Americans are so strange," said a woman in a Bruins sweatshirt. "You're here building a house and helping people have a better life while other Americans are destroying homes and killing people."

We broke for lunch and the family set out picnic tables, tied oil cloth to the trees for shade, and gave us rice, beans, tortillas, a pork and chile stew, and juice made of crushed fresh strawberries.

Before we got back to work, local people came to greet us, including a woman who gave me a big hug. "You built my house two years ago," she said.

"I wasn't here two years ago. I didn't earn that hug."

In answer, she embraced me again. "You're helping my neighbor, so you deserve lots of hugs."

I didn't want to return to my real life, ever. Better to be a happy roof-whacker, I thought, for the rest of my days.

I RETURNED TO LA in time for the Hollywood Peace March.

Jennie was going to meet me. I took the Red Line to Hollywood and Vine. Who knew there would be tens of thousands of people, and the cops would be cheering us on, and even the Metro conductor would call out over the intercom "Who's going to the peace march? Now squeeze on in! We want to get as many people to the march as we can fit!"

All over the world, people were marching for peace. No one wanted this war. Though Bush and Perle and Wolfowitz had been planning it for years, we still thought we could keep it from happening.

I saw a few vegetarian teachers from my former life. I kept an eye out for Sara, to avoid her. I ran into Amory and we walked together.

"This is awesome!" he said. "This is so great! I finally know what it was like for people like you, what it must have felt like in the early days of the civil rights movement. It must have been so great!"

In those days, the police and the crowds on the sidewalk weren't cheering you on, they were trying to kill you, but I refrained from telling that to Amory.

"Holy shit! I don't believe it!" he said. There, marching alongside the clergy with the Interfaith Council banner, there was

David, carrying a placard that read Flush the Fascists against a background of that now-familiar pink coiled colon.

Around the world, people were marching in cold and rain and snow. We surged down Hollywood Boulevard under a perfect Los Angeles blue sky. I didn't see any of the celebrities or the Butoh dancers in white shrouds and I couldn't find Jennie, but I saw people who had never raised a voice in protest ever before and I saw David, and that was plenty.

"Wow," Amory said. "I can't believe it. We're a rainbow of colors. A whole penelope of protest!"

An older couple walking near us clucked. They looked like they'd been around forever, and they were still marching. I was marching again too, but their hearts were in it and mine wasn't anywhere in particular.

The woman took Amory's arm. "I think you mean panoply."

"That's the fall of Communism for you," said the man.

The woman said, "Marxists read books. Marxists had some serious vocabulary."

"So, if Bush gets away with bombing Iraq," said the man, "who you think will be next?"

"Iran," said Amory, "Syria."

"Good guess," said the man, "though I put my money on Venezuela, Colombia, or our former colony, the Philippines."

"The US doesn't have colonies," Amory said.

"Former, he said," said the man's wife. "The Philippines are a former colony. The current ones are Puerto Rico, Guam, Samoa, Virgin Islands...Am I forgetting any?"

"Those aren't colonies," said Amory.

"OK, Mr. Smart Boy. What are they?"

"I don't know, but the US doesn't have colonies."

A young mother scooted between us, pushing a stroller decorated with balloons. She passed us and I kept pace with the couple and told them about my trip to Tijuana.

"Good work," said the man. "As long as people like you provide the housing, the maquiladora owners don't have to pay a living wage."

They moved on and I lost them in the crowd.

At the rally, I listened to a woman whose name I never caught and whose face I couldn't see: "Look, if I've left out what you consider the worst abuse committed by this administration, I'm sorry. But if I were to list all the crimes of the Bush regime, we'd be here till next week."

It seemed we might be there for hours as she shouted through the megaphone about every law we needed to repeal, and every executive order, and every gutted regulation that had to be restored.

"We can do it!" she shouted. The crowd of course responded with *Sí se puede!* We could hire investigators and impeach every corrupt judge, she said. We could vote the bastards out and take our country back.

I thought she was dreaming.

I PHONED JENNIE as soon as I got home. Loy answered. "Isn't she with you?"

"No," I said.

"Can you get over here right away."

First time I'd ever seen Loy when he didn't look freshly laundered. Miles was blasting out of the stereo.

"I could use a whiskey. You?"

No, but he'd already reached for a second glass. I tried to guess how long I'd be staying, and whether the booze would be out of my system by then according to the California legal limit, but he looked like he needed the company, and bad, so I gave up calculating and said "Yes."

The music was awfully loud.

"It needs to be," he said. He poured two shots and then took the pad near the kitchen phone and wrote *Wiretap*. Was he as paranoid as David? *Jennie. Not with you, not with parents. Afraid the feds have her.*

I just looked at him and he stared me down.

"They already took her computer." I didn't get it, or didn't want to. "While you were gallivanting around Mexico, we had a visit."

He was pacing. I didn't know whether to stand still, or try to keep up with him. He was already pouring himself another drink.

"What happened at the zoo? The day she was searched."

He offered me the bottle. My glass was still full. "I'm good," I said. "We were protesting for Michael and Melissa."

"That part I know," he said. "Did the police get involved?"

"Just zoo security."

It was no big deal. Like my lying-down at the Grove. It was nothing.

"She said they searched her."

"Not her. I mean, not a strip search or anything. They went through her backpack. And Bernice's."

The cats were playing as if nothing had changed. Chessie scratched at the climbing tree I'd brought over for Christmas. The same pictures hung on the living room wall. Watercolors of the neighborhood. An old poster of mine that Jennie had liked—colobus monkeys at the Makerere Biological Field Station. Loy's recent find: A poster from Vichy France assuring children the German soldiers were their friends. The bookcases, the fireplace, family photos on the mantel, the piano. Normal, I told myself. Everything is normal.

"I'm not blaming you," he said. "Don't get defensive. Just tell me. Was there anything in her backpack?"

What had she been carrying? The usual. A bottle of water. Wallet. They went through her ID and credit cards. Brush. Cosmetics. Tissues. A notepad. "They made a big show of going through everything. But it was all simple. I got a reprimand. Jennie—they confiscated some Animal Liberation leaflets."

"Shit," he said.

Jennie on her own would have had no interest in Gorilla Theater. The first time I'd dragged her to the zoo, the only question she asked about each animal was "Do they bite?"

Loy poured me another. "The Animal Liberation Front is on the government list of terrorist organizations."

"That's crazy," I said. "What do they do? Throw blood on fur coats? And if all Jennie did was pick up a leaflet..."

"If they saw her pay for it, that's financial support of a terrorist organization. It means they can do whatever they want with her. Haven't you read the Patriot Act?"

"It was too long to read," I said.

"Even if they don't accuse her of terrorism, they can hold her as a material witness—in secret for as long as they want to. People have been locked up incommunicado for months. It could be years."

"That's impossible." It had to be. If the FBI was busy chasing people like Jennie, when did they have time to find terrorists?

I thought of David saying good people had nothing to worry about.

Loy wiped his face. First time I'd ever seen him sweat. "You know she was born in North Korea."

"Her parents escaped. Jennie was born in the South."

"Axis of evil," he said. "You know they found a lot of anger on her hard drive."

"A lot of people are angry," I said.

But this wasn't another case of concentration camps in Glendale. This might—insane as it seemed—be for real.

He said, "Whether you believe me or not...Can I count on you?"

I hadn't felt her pregnant belly when she asked me to. She told me she'd dreamed of a child. That's my child, she thought in the dream and felt the greatest joy she'd ever known. How did I answer? With my own motherhood dream: I was carrying a child on my back, a child who weighed more and more and more until it crushed me. And I told her about the child Des should have nurtured but instead had shot and killed. I ate bloody meat in front of her and I lusted, albeit secretly, discreetly, diplomatically, for Loy.

He said, "Jennie was going to hold down the fort while I'm gone."

"Gone where?"

"I've been called up."

I didn't want to believe any of it.

"They're mobilizing the Guard and my enlistment has been involuntarily extended. They call it stop-loss," he said. "We're being deployed and I'm now enlisted through—get this, baby—according to Mr. Bush, I get to serve my country right through the year 2029."

It made no sense. "You're not going to go. You can't."

"If I desert, I won't be tried by a civilian court. They could do anything to me. And in the meantime, where's Jennie? I can't help her from the brig. I can't help her from Kuwait. I can't help her from Iraq. And I'm supposed to go wage an illegal immoral war under the flag of the hijacked country that's locked up my wife?"

I couldn't say anything.

"I'm not a coward," he said. "But I can't go over there to destroy. How did we let this happen? Something like this doesn't just happen. It doesn't happen overnight."

"It's like the Hemingway line," I said. "It happened gradually, then all at once."

He shook his head. "Maybe it's time to start kicking ass and taking names," he said. "And I don't mean Iraqi ass. I don't mean Iraqi names."

This was the man who wanted to keep the lines of communication open. Who wasn't going to cut off the people he disagreed with. Who wanted to stick with reason, and compassion.

"I'm a coward," I said. "I am really scared."

"I'll need you to feed Chessie and Monk and Ninja. I'll give you power of attorney. Attorney—yeah, I'll have to get a lawyer, for Jennie. If anything can be done. But you'll have access to our accounts."

"Your office?"

"My receptionist is already calling to reschedule patients. I'm having our bills sent to the office. She'll pay them from there. Mortgage and all that. But just in case, I want you as backup. And...I'm not sure how to ask this... If they freeze our accounts. If they confiscate..."

"That won't happen."

"I don't know," he said. "I have to plan for it. Can we borrow from you? Can you cover us for a while?"

It would mean going back to work sooner than I'd planned, but I said, "Of course." Who else could he ask? His father died young—asthma attack. His mother passed away a few years ago. There were brothers and sisters scattered around the country, but no one near. "Then you're really going," I said.

"Going somewhere," he said. "But as far as you're concerned, I'm reporting to my unit."

"Loy," I said. "You've got camping stuff, right?" I drew him a map, the best I could remember, and wrote down the name of the family. "We just helped build them a house. Tell them the house people sent you. These people are poor. It's practically a shanty town, no tourists or anything like that but I bet they could use a dentist." I knew they would feed him and they wouldn't give him up. "The Army won't think to look for you there."

He left the map on the kitchen table and paced. "I haven't made up my mind," he said. "I probably won't know what I'm doing till I do it."

"Loy—"

"Going into hiding. What does that solve?" he said. "I should be doing something to make this stop. This has to stop."

Then he opened the freezer. He took out Weezie's briefcase. "I don't know why Jennie kept it in here. This stuff drove her crazy," he said. "You might as well take it."

"You," I said. "Take the map."

He folded it up. "Thank you," he said. "I'm with my unit. Got it?"

"They can't tap journalists' phones, can they?"

"Not yet. Not legally, anyway, I think," he said. "But who cares?"

I wrote down the number of Sara's direct line. "Please. Use this to stay in touch." I must have seen a lot of movies, it all came to me so fast. "Identify yourself only by saying it's about Lyle."

"Who's Lyle?"

"An ex."

Loy said, "I'll walk you to your car."

There was a full moon and the crickets were stridulating to beat the band. I wished I didn't know that a male cricket calling for a mate will copulate with anyone or anything: female, male, inanimate object. I didn't like what I was thinking and knew it was a bad idea to have Loy beside me in the dark.

"I'm fine," I said.

He said, "You'll meet me at the bank tomorrow? Signature cards and all that?" He put his arms around me and I held him. I let my head rest on the broad strong chest that waitresses reached out to touch and I had never dared to.

Chapter Twenty-One

ONCE YOU'RE PAST FIFTY, you shouldn't sleep in your car. Everything ached, but I'd been much too drunk, confused, and scared to drive, and I hadn't really slept much, not with Weezie's still cold briefcase as my pillow and thoughts of Loy filling my head.

If something happened, would it really be so wrong?

I respected Jennie's marriage, but to be really adult about all this, it's possible, it occurred to me, you're not really married until you've committed adultery. It can be a rite of passage, into what's serious about marriage. Into being adult. Though I'd never cheated on Des—cheated, didn't the word itself reveal how conventional I was at heart?—I'd never held his adventures against him. He never remembered them, and as for me, I hit the reset button and went on. None of it counted. Lots of people engaged in spouse swapping, threesomes. This fidelity thing was more concept than practice. Everyone knew that. Of course I didn't know Jennie's point of view on monogamy. She and Loy were so together, it had never come up in conversation. So she might well feel betrayed, but on the other hand, she wouldn't necessarily disapprove. She might be gone a long time. Surely it would be better for her if someone like me put the moves on Loy because unlike whatever other women he might come across, I would always recognize Jennie's prior claim, and I'd get out of the way as soon as she returned. I'd be doing her a favor. Having sex with me wouldn't make Loy not a good person. So having sex with Loy wouldn't make me a bad person either.

This kind of thinking was just human nature—unfortunately. Chimps can reason, I reasoned. They can lie. They're probably capable of this sort of rationalization. Self-justification is not beyond them, but it's surely beneath them.

It was a good thing Loy was leaving town. All I wanted was to get home to Molly. I should have driven right off. Instead, I opened the briefcase.

Inside there were folders and inside the folders there were yellowed pages that crumbled at the edges though someone—Jennie, I guessed—had used a lot of transparent tape on the clippings trying to preserve them and she'd made photocopies, too. There weren't any transcripts of secret White House meetings. No suppressed documents. No confidential notes in the Senator's hand. Nothing but newspaper stories, various dates half a century ago. The sun stabbed at my eyes through the windshield and the print was small. I read about a woman named Martha Laird who lived in Nevada near a nuclear test site. In the article, she was quoted as saying that her husband and son both had leukemia, that their cows had white spots and "cancer eyes." She told the reporter she'd been threatened and called un-American, told her complaint was "communistically inspired." Here were European leaders, warning that the US in the post WWII era was moving in the direction of Fascism. Ralph Bunche warning that the UN's effectiveness in preventing war was compromised by the Big Power politics of the US. Abe Feller, chief counsel at the UN, expresses shame at cooperating with US attempts to investigate and weed out dissenters as security risks. He goes to his window, and jumps. A B-29 carrying nuclear weapons is believed to have crashed on takeoff in California. The government floats the idea of reorganizing the American Protective League—amateur spies who would report on disloyal neighbors. Lots more, but my eyes hurt.

Everything was falling apart and I was sitting in my car with old clippings. Weezie's presumed secrets had all been reported by the press. Forgive me, Molly, I thought, and drove to The Castle.

Palm fronds cracked beneath my wheels like bones. Gas on the right. Brake on the left. I was exhausted and had to keep reminding myself. Parallel parking? Forget about it. I found plenty of open space on a steep hill nearby and pulled up, trying to remember which way you turn your wheels in case of earthquake.

My heart was pounding so hard, it was as though the whole world was fractured by a strobe—Weezie in the garden feeding cats, lots of cats. My words tunneled back at me. "I-don't-get-it." And hers: "Of-course-you-do."

It was public information, and no one cared.

"Then why did you save these?"

She said, "I save everything."

I stepped through an aperture into the Sunday morning service, over a threshold outsiders were not supposed to cross. A man in white asking if I'd had a BM.

Dr. Jim. No, someone said, he's in veil, or was it in Vail.

The man said, "This is a basic scientific fact beyond dispute."

The man in white droned on. I nodded off. And then there was David, standing alone before the assembled hosts while the man pointed at him.

"Brother David says the US government has systemically deceived us. What's wrong with that statement?"

"Self-canceling redundancy!"

"Why?"

"Dr. Jim says the primary purpose of government is to lie."

"Does that mean we are anarchists?"

"NO!"

"World peace is achievable through the Word. Let's face it: This church has enough money to buy any election anywhere in the world. But do we?"

"NO!

"Instead of reforming government, we must reform ourselves. Instead of marching in protest, we must reach out to our fellow humans who have not yet become hosts. Brother David has already been to the Cleansing Tower." The man laid a hand on David's shoulder. "Do you want to go to PVM?"

The hosts roared Go! Go!

"I don't know," said David. He was trembling.

"It has to be your own free choice."

Go! Go!

His shoulders slumped. His mouth turned down. His chest caved in. His whole body seemed to say Don't hurt me.

And then we were in my car. I was so exhausted, I'm not even sure how we got there. I didn't know how to be angry at him now, though I started to say, "Jennie..." The car's nose pointed to the sky and gravity pulled us back as if tilted in a dentist's chair. He tried to move towards me but the parking brake was in the way. He released it, the car began to roll, I jerked it back up. David hollered as the back of my hand hit him in the balls and I thought of Devon's scream of pain the first time we met and I thought of everything I didn't want to think about, everything that had happened since then.

David fell against the seat, then turned my head and kissed me. I hadn't even brushed my teeth and I had David's tongue in my mouth. "Please," he said, and unzipped his pants and took my hand. "Please," and he placed my hand on his limp cock. "Please." I stroked it. Nothing happened. "Please," he said. He put his hand on top of mine and kept it there, Please, on this soft little mouselike thing, Please.

"We don't have to do this," I said.

"I do," he said, "please." He whimpered. "Please." Then he sat in the passenger seat staring at the car's roof. "I wish I wanted you," he said.

"It's OK," I said. "You want Marcia."

"No. That's a charade. I can't do this."

"We don't have to," I said.

"I have to." He put on his seat belt as though we were going somewhere. "Remember you told me that story about your grandmother. Nye boyitsa, nye boyitsa." He played with his zipper. Up and down. Open closed. "Don't be afraid. That's what Dmitri said."

Dmitri?

"I met him at the garage when I took my car in. I'd never known anyone like him before. I was so scared, but he said nye boyitsa when he kissed me and he repeated it over and over and I wasn't afraid."

And now he would love, I thought, and he would value life, and he would be a real father to his children, and he wouldn't torture monkeys and—

"...and Rae, I've been hiding all my life, even from myself, and finally, for the moment I was happy and free. But..."

"But...?"

"I HAVE TO KEEP THE EXIT PURE!"

"Nye boyitsa," I said.

"But it's wrong. Dr. Jim teaches it's wrong."

"Dr. Jim is full of shit."

"Don't say that!" he said.

"You have to leave The Castle."

"That's what I'm thinking," he said. "I'm going to let them send me to PVM."

"What the hell is PVM?"

"The Program for Viral Maximalization. It's a rehab center."

"No," I said. I turned the key in the ignition. "Come with me."

"Nyet," he said.

The engine caught, coughed, died.

"I'll take you to Dmitri."

"Dmitri's not the answer."

"If he's not, you'll meet someone else."

I floored the gas.

"You're flooding the engine," David said. "Let up gradually."

"I know that's what you're supposed to do," I said, "but it doesn't work."

"What if they're right?" he said.

"They're not," I said. "They're just playing on your old guilt. The guilt that's kept you locked up for years."

"I'm so afraid they may be right."

The engine stuttered, grated, growled. Then nothing.

"I'm tired, David," I said. "I'm very very tired."

"Toxins, probably." He unlocked the door but gravity held it closed.

"David," I said. "Think about me and Molly. People better not make fun of my love for her. Or, actually, I don't care. Let them say what they want. What do they matter? I love her."

"Your situation hardly compares to mine," he said.

"That's true," I said. "I'm not ashamed of loving."

The car started with a roar. At the first stop sign on level ground, David flung open his door. He slumped away without looking back.

The son-of-a-bitch was responsible for what had happened to Jennie. Go to hell, I thought, and hollered after him, "Go to PVM!"

Chapter Twenty-Two

MARCH 3RD, ALL AROUND THE WORLD, actors presented simultaneous performances of the antiwar play, *Lysistrata*. Gorilla Theater did not participate.

I wasn't up for anything. Jennie. Loy. I felt the kind of pain and rage that make you want to blow something up, that can send you to the hospital begging for the mercy of lobotomy.

Bernice thought *Lysistrata* was anthropocentric bullshit. "If they have to do Aristophanes, why not *The Birds*?"

"It's bullshit," I agreed. "The whole conceit of the play, that you can end war by withholding sex." Women get raped in wartime. It's the most common awful war crime. Doesn't everyone know that? And wasn't it common knowledge that a lot of men would rather fight than fuck?

To distract and cheer us both, I invited her to the zoo, to the aviary, but it was closed due to fear of Newcastle disease.

"I've been sending thank you notes to foreign governments," she said. "Do you think I'll get in trouble? Turkey, not for allowing US military. France and Germany for trying to stop us from going to war. Germany. Can you believe I sent a thank you note to Germany?"

The gorillas were gone. I hadn't even realized, but Bernice had her sources and knew all about it. "We traded them to San Diego, Cincinnati, and Atlanta." When did zoos become like baseball? "But they'll be back," she said, "once their new habitat is built."

We paid our respects to Toto and Bonnie, patriarch and matriarch of the chimpanzees, born wild and free in 1954 and '56, same years as my younger brother and sister. These chimps were the closest things I had these days to contemporaries. What did they remember? Growing up in the '50's, discipline yes, conformity, yes, and Communists under every bed, but still it wasn't like this. This is not the United States I grew up with.

"They're an inspiration to me," I said. The chimps used to have the worst exhibit in the zoo. No privacy. Just stuck out there all the time on an awful bit of concrete, freezing in the winter, burning their butts in the summer. Just a little trickle of water down the rock face. They should have turned depressed and angry, psychotic even. "Look at them," I said. "Do you see any PTSD?"

Unplanned pregnancies, yes, and various delinquencies, but that was normal. We'd raised enough funds to give them a decent home. Most of the family was sprawled out now on the rock ledge beneath the waterfall. They made a pretty picture, relaxing in comfort amid lush greenery, and rocks and termite mounds.

Delia, the juvenile, played near us in the hammock. She shredded the fastening rope till she could stick her head through it like a noose which got me nervous but she gaily threaded the needle with her whole body and came out the other end laughing.

"They survived as healthy individuals, their personalities

intact," I said. Watching them gave me hope, as I tried to see their success as proof of all that blah blah resiliency of the human spirit, though few captives do as well under these conditions and we couldn't have put them in this beautiful new habitat if they were human and you know damn well Des in prison had no waterfall.

Delia ran up to the window to greet us but turned her head away when Bernice pressed her lips against the glass in a kiss.

We didn't go to the drills. Too many memories and too much loss. Melissa had already been shipped to Columbus. Instead we stopped by the uakaris and watched the female with ratty coat and big breasts whirl at high speed like a top. Her name was Flo but I had started calling her Marcia. Inti, the male, peed into his hand and slapped the urine into his fur.

"Disgusting," said Bernice. "I don't have the patience for that kind of thing today," so I led her to the gibbons. Luke and Lulu could lift anyone's heart and ours certainly needed lifting. We watched them swing, gliding through air the way a diver slices clean through water.

Though, yes, I'd been here with David, I didn't often watch them with a fellow person standing beside me. It's a different experience when you're alone with the animals. There's a blurring of species identity. When all you see is Them, they become the standard for what a living thing looks like and how it behaves. There were wonderful moments when I often forgot I was human. With Bernice beside me, I couldn't forget.

"We're learning a lot of new stuff about gibbons," I said. "They're monogamous all right, but turns out they do engage in extra-pair copulation. And they're not as stupid as we used to think."

Luke ran a few upright steps, arms outstretched in a V. Then he hoisted himself into the air, one hand on an overhanging branch. Lulu swung on a rope, holding on with two feet and one hand, the other arm extended like an aerialist taking applause.

"Look!"

The two naked calluses on her buttocks began to move.

"Look look look look look!" I grabbed Bernice by the arm. "She's got a new baby clinging to her, wrapped around her. Those are its feet!"

Even Bernice cheered up. "Good news for the species!"

"Congratulations, Luke! Are you a proud papa?"

Bernice said, "That's not Luke."

"Of course it is." I said.

"Luke had diabetes."

"I know," I said.

She said, "He died."

I couldn't believe it.

"I have my inside sources," she said. "Last year."

"Lulu?"

"I don't know what became of her," said Bernice.

I'd held Lulu's hand, but the cream-colored gibbon swinging in front of me now was a stranger and I hadn't even noticed the difference.

The legal word is *fungible*. A thing that substitutes for another thing with no difference in quality or value. I'd learned that when Jennie was studying for the bar. Human beings are not considered fungible, except maybe in the Book of Job—wife and kids dead, no problem, God'll give you new ones—and in the minds of those who plan war, who figure casualties in numbers not in lives.

At the zoo I stepped into the middle of stories and sometimes heard how they started and almost never learned the story's end. Lulu, Luke—two individuals who loved each other, who might indulge in casual sex but for whom no other gibbon would ever, could ever substitute.

The female came up to the chain link, the baby clinging to her breast. She studied me. Her fingers grasped the fence, looking just like the hand I'd once held.

I believed no living creature could be replaced but I'd been visiting the gibbons all year and had never recognized who or what I was seeing.

On March 15th, I marched downtown in the pouring rain. I did it for Jennie even though I was trying not to think about her. That ache, that wrenching sense of sudden loss, is what you feel when someone's dead and I had to believe she wasn't. Sometimes a picture flashed in my mind like the updated images they create of missing children—Jennie smiling, her eyes shining, her belly larger and rounder, ready to pop.

A few days later, the US began dropping bombs on Iraq.

People dressed in ghostly white walked slowly and solemnly through downtown streets.

At the Federal Building, protesters massed on the sidewalks while volunteers knelt, blocking traffic and waiting to be arrested. The police stood in formation, quantities of plastic handcuffs hanging like key rings from their belts. It was arrest as ritual. A group of officers approached a single kneeling volunteer and spoke, fixed the handcuffs. The man stood to applause from the demonstrators on the sidelines and walked peacefully with police escort to the waiting wire-windowed bus. Then three officers approached a kneeling woman and carried out the next arrest. Applause. Someone cried out "Thank you!"

Someone began to sing. At the very first word, we all knew what was coming. *We...* My voice caught.

Was it just that sound waves make the neurotransmitters fire? Was it just the release of chemicals in the brain? *We shall overcome...* and I was crying. Is it just that songs do that to you, melt you, songs from your past? It couldn't just be my youth I was remembering. I thought, I'm crying for the belief we could change the world and had to. I'm crying for the dead. All the dead. I couldn't stop crying and couldn't say if it was for then or for now, almost forty years later, to be in the street again. The song reminded me that people putting their bodies on the line had changed the nation. It reminded me of everything that hadn't—and still needed to be—changed. I couldn't say whether I was crying from despair or from the joy of standing with others again for justice.

We are not afraid...

Come and get me, I thought. Take me to wherever it is you've taken Jennie.

Demonstrators filled the street, another surge of confident exhilaration. I was lifted way beyond myself to something glorious and embracing, something demanding I be better and more.

You have to feel it in your body and I did. I hadn't realized how dead I'd been till now, coming back to life.

A man on the sidewalk held up a sign: *CHRISTIANS for GEORGE BUSH.*

For a change I didn't look at him and think You moron. I didn't laugh or feel outrage because for once I felt stronger. Whatever They had done, we would prevail. I was as transfigured with righteousness as a Neoproctologist or a patriot. That thought almost stopped me, but I couldn't be stopped, not with this intimation of something strong that wasn't either rage or despair.

Though I hadn't planned to go to jail, I walked into the middle of the street and knelt. Three cops came up behind me. "Ma'am," one of them said. "I don't want to do this."

Did I look like his mother, his grandmother? I couldn't see his face.

"Is there anything I can say or do," he said, "to make you change your mind?"

It sounded like a folksong. It sounded like a love song. He leaned closer and I smelled his cologne.

"Please," he said. "What can I do?"

And I found myself singing out. "Stop the war. Stop the killing."

"Ma'am," he said. "Don't you see, I have no power."

I cried out, "Stop the war!"

"All I'm allowed to do," he said, "is this."

The cuffs cut into my wrists, but his hands were gentle.

FINGERPRINTING, BOOKING, overcrowded holding cell, overflowing toilets. Bail, desk appearance ticket, and release. It was a ritual without malice, very different from the last time I was arrested, which was also the first.

Picture me—a much younger me—as a criminal, trying to look casual in the supermarket, heart pounding, wondering if the growers also felt this way: as sick to the stomach at their behavior and as excited. 1968. I was a good girl. If I weren't good, I wouldn't have taken the semester off from college to volunteer with the Farm Workers, right? I had a past. It was called 1950's conformity. It was an elementary school— public—with badge-wearing patrols stationed every few yards to make sure we walked in orderly military fashion. The terror of being threatened with a demerit. The anxiety-producing drive to have a successful life, when success meant getting through without a stain.

Is there always such terror and joy when you cross the line?

And looking back, what a piddling little penny ante line to cross. No pipe bomb, no guns, just a straight pin concealed in my pocket. Pricking my finger, stabbing it, to distract myself, stay centered and calm.

The man who called himself Alberto said picketing wasn't getting us anywhere. We were fighting for the mere right to picket and in the meantime supermarkets were still carrying grapes. "Cesar says the new strategy is sabotage."

Surely someone argued that Cesar Chávez would never have said that.

"Are you calling me a liar?" said Alberto.

That's exactly what he turned out to be—paid by the growers to set us up, discredit the movement, and land us in jail.

So I became a criminal for La Causa.

The pin concealed in my hand. The pin jabbed fast into the bottom of a milk carton, the pin tearing a quick narrow rip in a bag of flour. The pin dropping to the floor when the security guard grabbed my wrists, opened my hands.

The guards and, outside, the police were waiting.

We were booked. I remember being stripped and told to wash myself in a bathtub with an inch or two of water. I've never understood why the water was there. If they wanted to humiliate me, if that woman wanted to stick her jagged fingernails inside me, why not just do it? Why bother with the water?

I believed my life was ruined. I thought, Now I can never join the Peace Corps, I'll never pass the FBI background check. I thought, Now I am a criminal. I won't be allowed to save the world.

Was it the world we lived in then, or was it me, that I thought I'd die of shame?

A month later, I was back in college and life went on and nothing was ruined and I hadn't thought about it for years, but after my release from the holding cell after the peace march, I found myself at Bobby's house, telling Bobby.

"Yeesh, man," he said, "I was arrested a few times before I got involved with the union. Of course in those days, man, if you were brown they'd arrest you for breathing. But I'll admit to you I did a bit more than breathe."

Bobby lived in South-Central in a stucco box, four columns supporting the peaked roof with its tarpaper shingles. There was a mockingbird singing out front atop a No Parking sign.

"It was fashionable those days to support the Farm Workers," he said.

I felt dismissed.

"Anyway," he said, "you forgot Marvin."

"Marvin?"

"There are four Bush brothers, not three. Marvin was in business with Kuwaiti investors. They had the contract for security for the Twin Towers before 9/11."

He was pasting twists of old newspaper onto a canvas, creating a desert floor which seemed to be rising, its color gradually transmuting from sand to blue.

"You really shouldn't use oils," I said. "At least not without better ventilation. You probably shouldn't be breathing those fumes, though I guess acrylics won't let you do as much with texture."

I picked up a page of newspaper. More stuff I didn't want to know.

"Old news," Bobby said. He pointed to a figure. "What does this look like? A cactus? But see, if I do this, it has wings. A tail. But it stands upright. Are we talking animal, vegetable, mineral? Does it stand or float or fly?"

"I don't know," I said. What do you say when you don't understand art? I like the colors?

"It's the mutability of existence," he said. "A slight modification in your DNA and you could have fins or gills. You could be a cat."

"I wish," I said. "I like the colors."

"There's angularity there," he said, "but it's not harsh. It's modified by cellular curves. Both masculine and feminine if you insist on applying outmoded terms."

He pulled some canvases away from the wall. "Look at these." Canvases with slightly raised magical figures, flying on carpets or simply levitating in air, creatures composed of intricate dots and whirls with hair or tentacles or contrails drifting behind them, standing, dancing, hovering, leaping, walking, through fields and deserts and offices and the halls of Congress and temples and houses and spinning in air.

"I'm Chicano, man, so I'm supposed to paint murals. I'm supposed to do political art. Not supposed to do anything else."

"So, like, is this how you see the world?"

"I don't see it till it's on the canvas," he said. "It's not like I close my eyes and picture it first. It's a feeling. I don't know if other painters work that way. I think dancers do. You don't create movement in front of a mirror. You feel something. You try to express it. It's something inside you. C'mere."

He led me into the garage. There were some signs face down against the wall.

"This is what people expect from me."

For your convenience, shopping carts are equipped with electronic alarms that will sound if cart is removed from shopping center.

"Real signs," he said. "I didn't make them up. I stole them. Look. They make no sense."

For your comfort and convenience, bathrooms will be closed to student use during school hours.

I said, "This country went to hell when MAD magazine went under." No kid grew up in those days without knowing advertising is always false. The magazine was subversive enough to spark Congressional hearings.

Bobby said, "People in my community, we always knew

that everything the white establishment said about us and about freedom and justice was a lie. But yeah, MAD proved there were some Anglos who understood it too. Anyway, MAD didn't go under," he said. "It's just like everything else now. Owned by Warner Brothers. They put out parodies of the latest movies...just a way to bring cheap advertising of big budget films to the comic book losers who otherwise wouldn't know what's playing."

"You know what Devon said? TV commercials are a public service. How else would you know about products?"

"And I get a grant to work with those kids," Bobby said.

"I've got an advertisement for you," I said. "Just one more poster, Bobby. Actually, it could be a flyer. We could hand them out." I wrote it out for him:

Lose Weight
the Revolutionary Way!

Our advanced
Fully integrated SYSTEM
allows you to achieve
the weight You desire
PROGRESSIVELY
through a planned and
coordinated program of:

marches
hunger strikes
metabolism-boosting anger

Apathy? or Activism?
The choice is yours!

"OK," he said, "I'll print it. But that's the last one. Why don't they pay an artist to create art? Why don't we pay social workers, therapists and babysitters to do their jobs instead of giving artists grants to do it and not as well as a real therapist or social worker could? I'm not a patient man," said Bobby. "I'm getting old, and I just want to do my work. Cesar, see, was patient."

After he died, I remember the way his son put it: Cesar Chávez was the most impatient patient man.

"That's right," Bobby said. "Impatient because he worked all the time. I mean ALL the time. Patient because he never expected real change to come during his lifetime. But see, these canvases, these are my revolutionary shoes."

He bent over one of his paintings, checking a detail through a magnifying lens. He offered me the glass. I looked, unsure of what I was looking for and handed it back.

"Cesar had nothing when he died, but he had everything," Bobby said. "I'm not asking for much. I want time to paint. Look at these shapes, man. Top heavy, bottom heavy, awkward, overgrown, see, it doesn't matter. They're all buoyant."

I found myself staring at the sweet brown dome of his lowered head. He looked up and our eyes met. A flutter. Foolishness.

"These are my fields," he said. "These are my grapes."

Chapter Twenty-Three

Bernice was pissed at me again. "How could you go and get arrested when I need you?"

She was right. Protest, arrest, it had only served to console me. I felt better about myself but my dissent had changed nothing. It wasn't refusal—like Loy's.

Bernice dabbed at her face. "Devon quits. Jennie doesn't show up. If they'd held you all weekend, we'd've been screwed. You are so irresponsible."

"Yeah, I'm a regular criminal," I said.

Bernice sighed and acknowledged that Augusto Boal said it's more of a crime to found a bank than to rob one.

"That was Brecht," said Amory. He was in an Uncle Sam suit, towering above us on stilts.

Bernice waved her hand at a big long aluminum hose-like thing on the ground. "Jennie was supposed to carry the oil pipeline."

Gorilla Theater had been preparing this action for months. Bernice was dressed as a Colombian peasant. Bobby and I wore camouflage gear, the name Occidental Petroleum painted on our helmets and we carried AK47s made of cardboard. He'd refused to make more puppets, so I bought stuffed animals—cottontop tamarins—from the gift shop at the zoo. Mounted first on shoulder pads and then sewn onto Sara's shirt, they traveled with her—and us, as we marched—while leaving her hands free to roll her chair.

Ruby had stayed home so there was room for our sign—US Out of Colombia—in Sara's lap.

"I need to talk to you," she said.

I didn't answer.

"Where's the sound?" said Bernice. "I want to hear you. What's the matter with you? Afraid to be heard? God forbid you should make a loud ugly noise!"

"Well," I said, "tamarins aren't actually loud. Cottontops chirp, they chatter a bit, they squeak."

Sara squeaked.

"A great big unashamed ugly sound!"

I pointed my AK47 at Bernice. "They're little animals," I said. "About the size of squirrels."

"Didn't you ever hear of the mouse that roared? Roar! All of you! Roar!"

We danced down Wilshire to the offices of Occidental Petroleum, Bernice blowing on a clay whistle except when Bobby and I shot her dead which wasn't personal—it was in the script. Each time she fell to the pavement, Sara roared and sprinkled flour over her body, and then Bobby and I would shoot the tamarins and Sara would tip herself forward and squeak.

You need good visuals if you want to make the TV news, and that's what we had to offer. All morning, the cameras never stopped: television cameras, cameras aimed out of police cars, cameras in the hands of men in suits who we guessed were FBI.

That evening we gathered at Sara's. Ruby took turns with us, wriggling onto one lap and then another as we channel surfed. Nothing. Nothing. Nothing. Till at last, Channel 4. There we were! And there was the news anchor identifying our action as a demonstration against the war in Iraq and using it in a segment about how taxpayers were getting stuck with the bill for the additional police presence at demonstrations.

Amory cursed. Bobby shrugged. Bernice dabbed and surfed channels.

As we were leaving, Sara maneuvered her chair to block me.

"I need to talk to you," she said.

"I've told you. I don't want to talk about him."

"It's not him this time," she said. "I know there's a lot of Jennie Kims, but is our Jennie Kim married to a soldier in the Army Reserve National Guard?"

"Loy," I said. "I'm listening."

We watched Ruby roll on the carpet and wrestle with a stuffed tamarin and its still-attached shoulder pad. Sara rubbed lotion up and down her arms.

"Two agents showed up at the paper today," she said. "They wanted to see me. My editor had turned over a letter. It was delivered a couple of weeks ago but a copy editor never gets news tips. It went straight to my editor even though it was addressed to me."

I held my breath.

"According to the agent, the letter was unsigned. It was from a guy saying he was in the Army Reserve California National

Guard. And he'd gone underground rather than go to Iraq. He was calling on soldiers to refuse to go. Telling people to mobilize for a general strike to stop the war. So, you know, that's mutiny and treason and conspiracy and I don't know what else. The decision was made against publishing it."

"Why?"

"Oh, you know. Ethics."

"Like the media is so ethical."

"Ethically do you publish the Unabomber's manifesto? Do you play Osama bin Laden's tapes? In the letter, the man said he'd sent out ten copies. It sure looks like every other publication made the same decision. You haven't heard about it, have you?"

No. But Loy had said, I shouldn't be hiding. I should be doing something to make it stop.

"They wanted to know why the letter was sent to me. And if I knew who sent it."

I'd told him to contact her, but discreetly. This wasn't what I'd meant.

"In the letter, he accused the government of disappearing his wife. Jennie Kim. They wanted to know if I knew her."

"Yes," I said, "it's our Jennie Kim. What did you tell them?"

She sighed and rubbed her arms. "That half the Korean women in LA are named Jennie Kim."

"This time, I sure wish it were one of the others."

"I couldn't find out anything," Sara said. "After they left, I tried. The government is refusing to release names of people detained. They won't confirm or deny. They can pick people up and hold them indefinitely. You're never told the evidence against you.

You don't have a lawyer. No means of appeal. You're allowed no communication with the outside world."

"I thought that was just foreigners," I said. "Jennie's a citizen."

"I've been learning what I can. There's a US citizen in Indiana, born in Egypt. They picked him up on an anonymous tip from a neighbor. Disappeared him for a while, but he did eventually get released. There's a computer programmer from Oregon, still locked up. They can call you a material witness and then they can do anything to anyone. Anonymous tips," she said. "Someone doesn't like you. You're in a child custody fight. Someone's competing with you for a job or a promotion or a boyfriend. It doesn't have to have anything to do with politics. Your neighbor's pissed because you don't mow your lawn. Jennie have any enemies?"

"Yes," I said. "Well, not really an enemy. I know who reported her."

"Do you know why?"

"Stupidity," I said, and added, "Now he's sorry."

"That may be good news," said Sara. "If he goes back to the FBI and admits it was a spite call. If he just explains..."

David caused it. Now he'd have to fix it.

First I had to make a run over to feed Monk and Chessie and Ninja. An adult day care center had opened up on Temple next to Western Exterminator, freaking me out for a moment as their signs overlapped. More flags had sprouted in the neighborhood. Rumors had spread. Someone had tied yellow ribbons around the cactus in Jennie and Loy's front yard. Someone—presumably someone else—had left a pile of shit on the porch. I cleaned it up, gave the cats food, water, and affection, then hurried home because I owed Molly some quality time.

The agents were waiting. They didn't look much older than Amory and Devon. One was slim and clean cut and white. The other was a small Asian man named Chun and I wondered if he merely represented Bureau diversity or if it was believed his cultural background would give him insight into Jennie.

"You're not in any trouble," he said. "If you cooperate."

I wasn't sure why there were two. They didn't have a good cop/bad cop thing going. Interchangeably unflappable and professional, courteous, is what they were.

"Why do you have his power of attorney?"

"To handle any business his office doesn't, while he's with his unit."

"We're freezing his accounts."

"Then I'll need to come up with the money to pay his mortgage myself."

"He won't be coming back here."

"Jennie?"

"We can't comment on that."

"Look, they're my friends. Am I going to be in any trouble if I pay their bills?"

"You may not have to worry about that. The house may be subject to confiscation."

"Jennie's having a baby," I said. "What will happen to the baby?" I looked at Agent Chun, thinking he would be the more sympathetic.

"We haven't acknowledged holding her."

"But if you are." Maybe Chun was being especially hard on her. I turned to the white guy. "When the baby's born, what happens?"

"We can't comment on that."

"Will it go to her parents? Will you see the baby's taken care of? If her parents can't manage, I will." I'd met her parents twice. I had no idea if they'd be able to take on the responsibility. Perfectly nice people, but not very comfortable with English, which made it easier to smile at them than to talk, and let's not forget that, according to Jennie, her father was a superpatriotic rightwing businessman. "Will you please put that down in your file, that I've volunteered to take care of her baby?"

"We're not at liberty to discuss that."

No, we're not at liberty.

IF IT CAME TO THAT, I hoped her parents would take the baby. I sure didn't want to.

But I would have to. What else could I possibly do? Late though it was, I drove to The Castle.

David was gone.

Where was he? No one was saying. Marcia took me aside. "He went to PVM."

"And where is that?"

"I don't know," she said. "Somewhere in the desert."

"But I need him. Now."

Once I started crying, I couldn't stop. I went home and watched TV in spite of myself. Pictures of mass graves—fault of Saddam (but no weapons of mass destruction, though their discovery was trumpeted every couple of days and then the claim quietly withdrawn) and pictures of armless, legless, burned and mutilated children—our handiwork.

I went to the garage, pretending my car needed an oil change. Actually, it did need an oil change, but I was there looking for Dmitri. I had hoped for—expected—a Nureyev, a Baryshnikov. Dmitri was a dark stocky man in a dark blue jumpsuit. Not what I'd imagined, but still, I could see David trembling before Dmitri's insistence, defenseless at last.

"Do you know where David is?"

He wiped his hand on his dark blue jumpsuit and I stared at his fingers, stained from working on engines, the hairy knuckles, the— oh shit—wedding ring? as his dark eyes shifted away. "You are the wife?" he asked.

"No. And she's an ex-wife."

"I don't know," he said, and I cried.

I cried when a former student was gunned down and killed by the police for being a passenger in a car they thought looked too good to be legitimately in his South-Central neighborhood (though to change its image the neighborhood's now called South LA).

Something had been switched on inside of me, and it didn't switch off. Everything seemed to reach me now. Designated mourner or no, this time I would attend.

Bobby was sitting on his front steps drinking beer.

"Will you come with me?" I said. "Please."

There was no candlelight vigil. No one was gonna stand around in the street in Roland's neighborhood after dark whatever name you gave it. So middle of the day, we were supposed to protest at the police station.

Bobby drove. This looked like the place to be if you wanted a carpet or a new transmission or a motel you wouldn't find in Triple A. Big churches, little churches, churches surrounded by barbed wire, a storefront church with the weekly schedule painted on the flat façade like the menu at a taquería.

"Send a kid from this neighborhood to Iraq, he has a better chance of living out the year," Bobby said.

You couldn't tell just from looking.

A man sat in the open trunk of his car listening to his cell phone and spitting into the street. Around the corner, at the school yard, kids were playing ball while a mother sat outside the fence with a baby in a stroller, keeping one eye on the game.

"This community has a great public housing program," said Bobby. "It's called prison."

The neighborhood stretched low, under big sky, for miles. The police station commanded the heights, a beautiful building as fortresses go, all gray, dusty rose and dusty green stone, with bright sculptures of Aztec dancers over the entryway, too big, too strong to tear down.

Maybe fifty of us standing there. A pretty brown-skinned girl with blonde streaks in her hair gave everyone a sunflower.

Across Broadway in front of the brake repair yard, protesters were chanting No Justice, No Peace!

I started to chant with them. The girl touched my arm. "No," she said. "That's not what we here for."

"That's what I'm here for."

She took a place on the steps and addressed the crowd. "Friends," she said. "Let's start with a moment of silence. It's going to be a moment of prayerful silence for Roland, but also for the police officer. I want you to reach out with your hearts to the police officer who killed him."

Surely they couldn't hear what she'd said, but the protesters across the street got louder.

Someone in our group said, "What kinda shit is this?" and went across the street to join them.

"If that's too hard, at least for now," said the girl, "just try silence. Just try a moment of silence."

As if he knew I was ready to cross the street, Bobby put an arm around me and stilled me.

"We been shouting a long long time," the girl said. "We been shouting no justice, no peace and it ain't brought us neither one. Ain't made no difference. It did for a while. Made the world take note. But not now. Now it's not making the difference we need.

"I know Roland's mother don't see it my way," she said. "I respect her grief. Shit, I'm grieving and I'm angry too. I loved Roland. We was gonna get married. Doesn't matter now one way or the other. But we need to stop the killing and that mean we need for the police to see us, really see us. And for that, we need to see them. That cop, that officer, who killed my Roland? He made a mistake and I know he's suffering with that hurt. Different suffering from mine, and from yours, but he's suffering, too."

There were police on the steps. There were police at the barricades. They wore helmets and riot gear, but they could hear this. You couldn't read their faces, whether she had surprised them, whether any of this got through to them. I almost wished they would charge us. I almost wished for violence. I would welcome a blow to the head to stop the racing of my thoughts and purify my confusion.

"Please," she said. "Nothing else has worked. Please. We gotta try."

You looked at this kid and you wanted to give her the Nobel Peace Prize. Instead I figured she'd end up fucked. Six months from now, she'd forget Roland and be pregnant by someone else.

"Tell that officer your heart feels for him. Struggle with your heart."

The struggle was hard, impulses switching and tearing inside me.

I tried to believe this girl would have a good life. I tried to believe it was possible not to hate. I thought, this is the hardest thing I've ever done and I crumbled again at the very thought, the possibility of such belief.

Chapter Twenty-Four

BOBBY HAD A TATTOO on his back, an armadillo. "Supposed to cure insomnia," he said.

"Does it work?"

He said, "I don't think we're going to sleep tonight."

When he moved inside me I cried so hard he asked if he'd hurt me.

"No. Yes." I couldn't be sure it was pain, maybe just parts of me stinging like a foot waking up, or too much sensation, like a blinding light. I touched his shoulder and the touch reverberated deep inside me. I'd forgotten how feelings could echo.

I tried to loose his ponytail. I was a child of the Sixties but this was the first time I'd been to bed with a man whose hair was longer than mine.

"Leave it alone," he said.

Lips against lips, mouth on neck, thinking how on earth did I ever live without this, but like a gorilla who needs to maintain some modicum of privacy, I will keep to myself most of the details but because I've already condoned drunk driving (though only by Jennie), I don't want to go on record in this day and age blithely endorsing unsafe sex. So safe sex, yes, something people are very aware of even if they don't practice it, and apes and monkeys (as far as I know) never stop to think about. Condoms, yes, and caresses, and the sweat, the endearments, the transit from bed to shower to kitchen to bedroom again. I'll just say Bobby would surely be more difficult to live with than Molly, but she was no comparison to him in bed, that yes, like me, he had a bit of sag and paunch, but the hollow where his thigh and pelvis met had the same smooth beauty you'll find in a leopard.

The body can only do so much. We spent much of the night in talk.

"Viejo," I said. "Any of what she said make sense to you today?"

"Yeah," he said.

"Remember, cops are pigs."

"Some are," he said. "A lot of them, they get caught up in the closed system, Us vs. Them. Gotta be possible to break that down. It's not like they don't have a conscience."

Why does that word make the tears well?

"When you shut down your conscience, do you think other things shut down too?" I asked.

"You have a conscience," Bobby said.

"No," I said. "Yes. Maybe."

"You're right about shutting down," he said. "Without a conscience, I think people stop feeling even pleasure. When I get a job in one of those multi-million dollar McMansions? You walk into a bedroom and there's so many pillows and bolsters on the bed, there's no room to stretch out and sleep. These are houses you can't live in."

"I've been cynical," I said.

"Cynicism trickles down," he said. "Decency is weakness. Win by any means. Crime pays. Violence pays. Lies pay. That's what our kids are learning."

"It didn't used to be about greed," I said.

"I did theater once before," Bobby said. "Back then, you know? Teatro Campesino. You ever see *Las dos caras del patrón?*"

I remembered it. Performed in the fields on the back of a flatbed truck.

"You know how in the end, the farm worker changes place with the grower but says he doesn't want the big house on the hill and the big car."

"Yeah."

"I saw a revival of it this year. And afterwards this woman—Anglo woman—in the audience stands up all upset. Why shouldn't the worker get the big house? Why shouldn't the worker get to drive a fancy car? Back then with Cesar? The idea was fairness and justice. Let people have a decent life. Raise healthy children who could go to school. It was never about greed."

"I'm trying not to hate, but I hate him," I said and Bobby knew I meant Bush.

"Pity him," he said. "He has so much to answer for. If he ever looked at what he's done, the repentance would overwhelm him."

"I'm not holding my breath."

Bobby said, "He's running scared, maybe wondering if he's really predestined by God to be saved. Maybe that's why these bastards feel they have to accumulate more and more and crush everyone else. They're trying to convince themselves they really are the Elect of God, because if they aren't, they're going to hell."

Bobby's religious zeal made me uneasy.

"You're a believer?" I asked.

"In the wonders of creation," he said, "and the oddity of all existing things."

Lying in his arms... how on earth had I ever convinced myself I wanted David?

"I've got to find David," I said.

"You and David. You're, uh, still..."

"No," I said. "It's not like that."

"Hey, tell me if this is true," he said. "I read there's less difference between human chromosomes and chimps—"

"We're 98.74% the same—"

"—than there is between human men and women."

"True, if your DNA changed just a smidgen, you'd be in a cage and I'd be watching you. But the differences between men and women? I'm not jumping into that debate."

I kept my opinion to myself, that men are pack animals, like dogs. They get neurotic if they don't know exactly where they fit in the hierarchy. Women live in herds. If you've ever seen a herd, sometimes one ole gal will try to take the lead. Then the others horn and butt her, not desiring her place, but punishing her presumption.

"You ever been married?" he asked.

"Yes."

"Kids?"

"I couldn't imagine bringing children into an alcoholic home."

"You drank?"

"Yes. Or no. I mean, I drank, but I didn't *drink*. He did. I wondered after. Would having kids have straightened him out? He wouldn't get sober for me. Would he have done it for them? See, I'm still second guessing myself. What could I have done differently? Or better? Could I have stopped what happened? I keep thinking if I'd made the right choice I could have saved him. Which means I'm still caught up in this egomaniacal vision of myself as having the power to influence events. But even when we're not guilty, we're responsible, right?"

I needed to shut up or Bobby would be sick of me even before we rolled out of bed. Sometimes I didn't know how anyone could stand me. Molly put up with me. Jennie used to put up with me and I missed her.

Thank you for living with me is what I said to Molly every morning and every night. I wasn't sure what I could and couldn't say to Bobby.

I pictured Molly baring her throat so I could stroke her there. What would she make of the smell of sex on my genitals, my skin? Why couldn't I go back to the way it was, content to live quietly alongside thirteen pounds of claws and fur?

I said, "The advantage to having a past is you can refer to it instead of moving forward. If you were once a fully realized human being, people may not notice you aren't any longer. You?"

"Me, what?"

"Were you married?"

"Yeah. And I've got some kids I don't see."

I had no idea.

He said, 'I wasn't real good to live with when I got back from 'Nam."

"I didn't know you were there."

"If you recall, people like me didn't have a way to get out of it."

"There was the Chicano Moratorium," I said.

"You don't have to tell me what there was."

My toes had been curled inside his toes. He moved his feet.

"My husband was a conscientious objector," I said. "And the day came when he felt ashamed of it."

"That's bullshit," Bobby said.

"He was ashamed that he knew a way out and most guys didn't."

"We should have all objected." He stretched his arm against mine and clasped my hand.

"He was ashamed and—to make it worse—ashamed of being ashamed. Survivor's guilt. Or something broke in him. But forget I said that. A drunk doesn't need reasons to drink. I wish you spoke Spanish," I said.

"I do," he said.

"I mean only. I mean instead of English. I'm talking too much. The more you listen to me, the less you'll like me." I believed that, but I couldn't stop. "Now he's killed someone," I said. "A conscientious objector, a sincere pacifist, and now he's a killer." Des was big and he carried himself as if he knew his size could intimidate, even the way he moved was gentle, to put people at ease. "He was charming when he drank a little," I said. "Angry when he drank a lot. Like that's the only time he could express it, when he was drunk and could believe it wasn't under his control, and then he never remembered anyway. His anger, it was like it didn't exist, it never happened."

"Did he hit you?"

"Never. I haven't seen him in years. He's in prison."

"Where?" he asked.

"Corcoran."

"Bad," he said.

I read the newspaper. Guards at Corcoran staged gladiatorial contests between inmates, bet on the outcome, and sometimes used the melée as an excuse to shoot prisoners dead. Sara told me all the windows were painted over so the cells got not a glimmer of natural light. "Bad" had to be an understatement.

"Maybe it's what he deserves," I said.

"You could visit," Bobby said. "You could drive it and back in a day."

I said, "I don't want to see him."

"Why not?"

"Sara sees him. I don't have to."

It was the same old story. Women always wanted to help him and understand him, like Sara, starry-eyed, telling me, I can't explain, but there's something...

"You still love him?" Bobby said.

"I'm not sure love plays a part in my life."

Bobby said, "Visiting him would be entirely safe if it didn't."

I loved Molly. At least some of the time I thought I did. I neglected her a lot these days but she still curled her tail around my arm when I brushed her. It thrilled me when she bared her throat in absolute trust. That didn't mean I could do anything with her that I wanted. She didn't like to be held and would wriggle right out of my arms if I tried. A cat trusts without relinquishing self-sovereignty.

If you lived with an animal, human or otherwise, you had to accept getting hurt. The worst time was when I put my hand just behind Molly's hind legs as she prepared to leap. I knew better, but craved contact. I knew she'd take a step back, balance, extend her claws before her spring and sure enough, she dug into the back of my hand, ripping through layers of skin and flesh as she made her move.

In turn, she accepts the pain that I've inflicted. I've stepped on her—more than once—though of course I never meant to. When Molly was a kitten, I'd have nightmares that a dog had attacked her and I used to wake up thrashing and screaming. No wonder she grew up to be a skittish cat. I said I loved her and then let her whimper for attention while I sat zoned out in front of the television night after night. She wrapped herself in my hair at night, purring; I got a haircut. She lies beside me, shifts when I roll over. She retracts and sheathes her claws when we wrestle, but I have to watch my hand when I tease her with a bit of yarn or the strip from a priority mail envelope. Trusting doesn't relieve you of the responsibility of looking out for yourself. This requires vigilance, not paranoia.

Bobby said, "Looks like the only growth areas for employment in California are prisons and war."

"So who do you love?" I said.

"My paintings. No one else cares about them, so I have to."

He made coffee. I showered. At home Molly would have watched me. She'd watch me brush my teeth, intent, alert, as though every move I made was significant.

I picked up our scattered clothes. At my place we'd have to be more careful. She was a good cat but she'd pee on clothing if you left it on the floor and I realized that this thought implied what I was trying to avoid, which was expectation.

If Mirady came back, was I finished? Were there other women? His paintings didn't look like he worked with models.

He said, "I drank when I got home from 'Nam."

"People spat on you."

"That's bullshit," he said. "I don't believe that ever happened."

Like feminists burning bras, I thought. A story.

Bobby said, "You talk to someone who was in WW II. The good war. Let me tell you, it doesn't matter whether you get a parade. It doesn't matter that they treat you like a hero or they don't. It's the things you saw and the things you did, had to do. It doesn't matter whether they call it shellshock or battle fatigue or PTSD. I came home, I was a local hero for a while, till I blew it. The parades, the dancing in the streets, that's to make the people who stayed home feel good. It's the civilians who miss out when there's no celebration. That's the last sacrifice soldiers make for the folks back home: to keep smiling and dancing, to stick your chest out when they pin the medal on. When soldiers get fucked up, put the blame where it belongs, on the experience of war."

"I didn't know," I said.

"There's a lot you don't know about me."

"Do you want to tell me?"

"No," he said. "See, the country should never forget, but I have to."

Chapter Twenty-Five

The statue of Saddam toppled for a photo op. US troops released an Iraqi serial killer from prison by mistake while the US government remained unable to figure out how to release Muslim men judged innocent but still detained at Guantánamo. People who didn't understand that civilization began with the cat reported the plunder of civilization's cradle.

Why were string games called Cat's Cradle? Why did the Cahuilla believe unless you knew cat's cradle figures, your spirit couldn't pass into the afterlife?

President Bush declared victory in Iraq. Gorilla Theater declared victory when Michael got flown to Columbus to be reunited with Melissa.

It was hard to believe in victory when soldiers and civilians in Iraq kept dying, or to feel victorious while witnessing Lyle's distress. He lifted a log and spun around, then smashed it against the wall and I was pleased at first to see him taking out his frustration on something other than himself, but then, he went back to tearing at his arms and biting at his own legs with new sharp grownup canines.

I wasn't supposed to interact, but I presented. I turned my back on him, stuck out my rear, and looked at him coyly over my shoulder. "You used to want me," I said. I tried to distract him from his pain but my power over him was gone. He went on hurting himself in his frenzy.

I tried not to think about Bobby.

I spent a day sweltering in the heat with the Sumatran rhino. Not a primate, but I do what I'm told, in this case trying to monitor that he stayed in the shade because too much exposure to direct sunlight could make him go blind and if you're tempted to say Just like masturbation, save your breath, I've heard it before. He at least got to wallow in the mud while I could only watch.

Six French journalists were detained at LAX, interrogated and subjected to body searches and handcuffing before being sent back to France. They were not allowed to attend the food show they'd been sent to cover, in apparent retaliation for their government's criticism of US foreign policy.

An infamous primate trafficker collaborated with US Fish and Wildlife in a sting operation. He entrapped prospective buyers by offering to sell them an agent dressed up as a gorilla.

A live gorilla is worth close to $100,000—at least that was the asking price, which is much more than a dead one, but they're easier to transport once butchered. All over Africa, gorillas and chimps are protected by law but the law has, you might say, no teeth. People eat them. Bodies are smoked, heads stewed and, given our kinship, this is practically or—some would say actually—cannibalism.

With gorillas just about exterminated in the Congo, of course we launched a protest. People have to know, but our slogan NO MORE BUSHMEAT! was taken as a direct and rather vulgar threat against the president.

The police were not amused. We were arrested and, as I was now a habitual offender, they kept me overnight.

The deputy said, "You're worried about gorillas when there's a war in the Congo basin. More than three million people dead."

Everything in my life had begun to conspire, to make me care about people.

"I hadn't heard about that," I said.

"I'm not making it up."

He didn't let me make my phone call. No way to get anyone to feed Molly, Chessie, Monk, and Ninja. They all survived a couple of missed meals, but when I walked in the door to see Molly pushing her empty food bowl around the kitchen with her nose, the guilt undid me. I could no longer be responsible for them all.

THERE WAS AN OLD MAN sitting on the porch drinking beer at Jennie and Loy's, with two big horrible dogs—pit bulls—at his feet.

He called out to me. "El negro y la chinita, ¿dónde se fueron?"

I hesitated from the walkway, at the bottom of the stairs.

"Come," he said. "Don't be afraid."

He was a neighbor, worried that he hadn't seen Jennie or Loy.

"Reynaldo," he said.

"Rae."

We shook hands.

"*Mi tocaya*," he said. Namesake.

Some of his teeth were missing, others were gold.

"I sit on my daughter's porch all day," he said. "Better here. Keep trouble away." The dogs, he said, had been trained for fighting and his daughter had rescued them. She didn't approve of treating animals that way and she didn't approve very much of his drinking.

"I'll hire you," I said.

"I don't need money."

"As long as you're here guarding the house, will you feed the cats?"

"I don't like cats," he said. The dogs thumped their tails. "Neither do they."

I packed Monk, Chessie, and Ninja in carriers and took them to The Castle.

"Just temporarily," I told Weezie.

Her smile was habitual but I believe she was delighted.

"Any word from David?" I asked.

"The whole point of Neoproctology is to liberate yourself," she said, "but they move in on you like an occupying army." She touched my arm. "I don't like it here."

Marcia told me to take the cats and go. "Weezie's in enough trouble. They already say she has way too many."

If you spend the whole day running around accomplishing nothing, you might as well be a soccer mom. I drove back to Bobby's.

"Would you? Please?"

"I don't like cats," he said.

What was the problem with these men?

I unloaded the litter box anyway. Ninja dashed to it and hid inside. I brought in the cans of food and boxes of frozen French fries. Monk scurried under the chair. Chessie investigated the room, tail held high.

Cats watch you with interest but their bright eyes never turn mild with affection. A cat forms attachments with a willing heart, but doesn't need to. The way Bobby looked at me? He watched me like a cat, but as Chessie regarded him with a bright searching look, then climbed into his lap and purred, I saw Bobby's eyes turn soft with what certainly looked like love.

WITH THE CATS TAKEN CARE OF, it was time to get on the road. I had to find David. Which meant I had to find the detour that Jennie took that day that took us through the town with all the pink colons. I also wanted to find someone to do the driving so, much as I wanted to avoid her, I called Sara.

She picked me up and we headed east. At the rest stop outside Palm Springs, the winds were so high, for all her strength and fabulous biceps she couldn't make any headway in her chair. I had to wheel her to the bathroom, both of us pushing hard against the wind.

Onward. We drove past dairy farms, the cows all squeezed together like cattle in a feed lot and smelling just as bad.

"I guess the vegans are right," Sara said. "Milk's as bad as meat."

I wondered if her captors let Jennie keep a vegetarian diet wherever the hell it was that they were keeping her. I wondered when she was due. It was possible the baby was already born, prematurely, due to stress. I imagined a baby's tiny fingers, a baby at Jennie's breast.

I gave bad directions. I gave good directions. I gave directions I wasn't sure of.

We saw palm trees that actually looked like palms—open hands with fingers spread. We saw sunflowers and willows where there was water, parched grass the color of sand and wheat where there wasn't.

Trapped in the passenger seat, belted in, mile after mile, I had to listen.

"I thought you wanted to know," Sara said. "How to live after enormity. That's what Kenny Desmond can teach you."

Dirt baking in the sun and dust, like the road to Baghdad. And the pink colons, interrupting whatever more about my ex she intended to say. The golf course, all irrigated and green. Low barracks-like wooden buildings with the windows all smashed out and further down the road what looked like a luxury hotel under construction, the windows not yet in.

There were a couple of guys in hard hats. We drove up. "Is this going to be a resort hotel? Condos? Time share?"

Part of the structure was still just the wooden frame, part already stuccoed and painted mustard with terra cotta and brown trim.

"It's church housing."

"Oh," I said. "Is there some kind of hospital or rehab clinic here?"

"I wouldn't know. Wouldn't surprise me. They've got everything else."

We didn't spot a likely looking building, though we did find a stone church, three giant windmills in a row—not the kind that harnesses power in the desert—but decorative and Dutch-style, with tulips painted on each base, a circular building with two signs, one identifying it as an aquarium and one that said CLOSED.

"Let's try the café," Sara said. There was a little storefront, the name PENNY'S inside a yellow diamond. "I almost always get information when I hang around in a café."

I got out. Sara opened her door wide, reached behind the seat for her folded-up chair. I wanted to watch and I wanted to look away as she slowly set the chair up and maneuvered her way from car to seat. At Penny's café, the front entrance had steps but, luckily, the back door had a ramp.

A woman came out from behind the counter to greet us. "Raw or cooked?"

"You mean like Levi-Strauss?" I said.

"The blue jeans?" she said.

"The anthropologist," I said.

"She's talking about the menu," Sara said. "The cuisine. You can get cooked food or raw food."

How did she know? "Can we see both menus?" I asked.

"Raw sits there, cooked sits there," the woman said, "and raw has to be ordered in advance."

"Oh, and you had an advance order..."

"No," she said.

"So you already knew we were cooked," I said.

"That, or in for a disappointment," she said.

We sat on the cooked side.

"Really nice place," Sara said.

"Thanks. This was always my dream. I always wanted to

serve healthy food with the personal touch. Not everything has to be a franchise or a chain. I always wanted to open my own restaurant."

"So you're Penny?"

"There is no Penny. Just that we—my husband and I—modeled the place on Denny's, except for the food, of course, and we offer a complimentary breath mint on your way out the door although with a detoxified diet, you never really need one."

Denny's would have had better air conditioning. We each ordered the cold lentils.

"Why is the cooked food ready but raw food you have to order in advance?" I said to Sara.

"Don't ask me."

"Are we avoiding purines or pyrines?"

When the woman brought our food, I didn't ask but assured her we were really into the low skatole-producing diet. "And purging our bodies of toxins," I said.

She nodded. "Some say the desert sucks the moisture from your skin but I can feel it sucking out the poison." She pursed her lips and made a sucking sound as she walked away.

"He's so spiritual," said Sara, prodding at her lentils rather than eating them.

"David?"

"Kenny!" I could tell she was getting pissed at me but I didn't care. "I was so full of poison for so long," she said. "Knowing him released something inside of me. The rage went away. The rankling sense of unfairness, injustice. I could forgive."

"That's ridiculous," I said. "Kenny isn't the one who hurt

you." If anyone was going to forgive him, it should be me, and I didn't intend to.

"You've never really lost anything," she said.

It didn't seem proportionate to mention a small piece of ear. Or that I missed Jennie so much. "We're here about David," I said, "not about my ex-husband." I motioned for the check. "You're the journalist. Interview her. Get something out of her."

Sara gave the woman who wasn't named Penny a big smile. "I love the desert," she said. "You're lucky to live out here."

"Funny, I was scared when I first moved here."

"How long have you been here?" Sara asked.

"Almost ten years. I'm ashamed to say, but I was scared of the Indians. Now I drive through the reservation, just to look. I like to see how things keep getting better. They were so poor before the casinos. Like nothing you've ever seen. And talk about discrimination? Couldn't get work. People around here took their land, then wouldn't hire them. But now they're doing fine, and giving a lot to the community. School systems probably couldn't run without the money they contribute. Of course now, they're building their own school and I'm not sure what the county's going to do. It won't trouble *us*, of course, we've got our own school."

"That's what I admire about the Church," I said. "Providing everything." Sara's chitchat wasn't getting us what we needed to know. "Like rehab," I said.

"The doctors don't offer me any hope," said Sara.

"My sister," I said. "Completely bamboozled by her psychiatrist. I hear they work miracles at PVM."

The woman who wasn't Penny stared at us.

"You're not hosts," she said.

"We've been to seminars," I said, "and I spend a lot of time at The Castle."

"I see," she said. She slapped down the check. "No need to tip."

I paid at the counter, picked up our mints, and left, and I stared at the sky while Sara got herself into the driver's seat.

"Well, that was a waste of time," she said. "We should have gone to Corcoran."

"Don't start with that," I said.

She pulled over at a barbecue joint.

"We just ate," I said.

"That wasn't a meal," Sara said.

We ate meat.

I WENT HOME and googled "Neoproctology" "PVM". If I hadn't been so emotional, if I hadn't been running from one demonstration to another, if I hadn't been distraught with fear and grief, if I hadn't wasted time in jail over bushmeat, if I'd been thinking clearly and thinking straight, if I hadn't spent the night in Bobby's bed, if I'd had time to stop and think, by all rights I should have put this together a whole lot sooner. The screen showed me the first ten hits and even before I checked out any of the sites, what I was reading was "Neoproctology" "PVM" "Basoba".

Basoba was where Jennie and I gave that woman a ride. The woman who hid her face when we drove past the pink colon mailboxes, who was careful to assure us *I'm not going to say anything bad about the Church.*

I was going to have to go back to the reservation and, culturally insensitive or not, I would have to ask questions.

SARA SAID SHE'D DRIVE ME only if I'd agree to go with her to see my ex. What could I do? I turned down the ride. Bobby had a plastering job. I wasn't going to travel with Bernice, so with Jennie gone, if I was going to go, I would have to drive there myself. I dodged potholes, detoured around the streets closed where a gas line just blew up, and others marked with yellow tape where the police had established a perimeter around a crime scene, tried to take a short cut through hills where there were no sidewalks and where I swerved to avoid the cyclists just the other side of each blind curve and the Hasidic families walking on the Sabbath, back to the flats with gridlock at every intersection where there was no left-turn arrow, gritting my teeth when buses too wide for the narrow lanes threatened to sideswipe me, tried to enjoy all the signs in languages I could not identify, rolled the windows up against the downtown stench of the homeless encampment that made me choke with the question of how we—America—had let this happen, and then steeled myself for driving the freeway.

I've already told you what I think of that. Plus, heading inland meant heading into the smog, windows down, as the temperature was near 90 and my car overheats when you turn on the A/C. I had a six-pack of water and juice boxes of GatorAde.

Smog hid the mountains. It wasn't till maybe ten-twelve years ago, after pollution control had cleaned up the air, that I realized there were mountains to the east. They had suddenly become visible. Now, thanks to SUVs, they were disappearing again. If you can disappear a mountain, I thought, people are easy.

Chapter Twenty-Six

A DESERT PLANT WITH BRANCHES like thin twisted wire gave the house a skeletal kind of fence. That was how I recognized the place. A tiny black puppy ran out in front of the car and I braked in time. A black dog watched from the porch.

I pulled over, parked, took off my sunglasses, put on the regular ones. They'd been heating on the front seat and the metal frames burned against my face.

First impressions matter. I tried to compose myself, then remembered this would not be a first meeting. We'd already met. If I'd done something to offend her, it might already be too late. You don't always know what you've done. At the zoo, I wasn't allowed near the elephant who had taken a passionate dislike to me. An elephant sizes you up, so to speak, immediately, and if the verdict is a bad one, you'll always be in danger if you dare get close. I reminded myself I was here to see a human woman, not an elephant. I just wanted her to like me.

The puppy trotted behind me as I approached the porch. Ruby had made me somewhat less wary of dogs, giving me at least some reason to trust that the bitch lying there might not bite.

She barked, I called Hello, a woman opened the door, fork in hand, and studied me through the screen. I recognized her immediately, even without the red sweatshirt. Short black hair with some white in it, a great manicure, details I'd remembered without remembering I'd noticed.

"You with the EPA?" she asked.

"No," I said. "We met several months ago."

"Oh, yeah. You're a teacher," she said.

"No. Yes," I said. "I mean sometimes."

"We get a lot of teachers about this time of year. Something to do with their certification." She had a soft voice, very soft and precise. "Something about diversity training."

"That wasn't me," I said. "I was here with a friend? You had a white girl who needed a ride?"

From inside the house, I could smell something delicious frying.

"I remember...You were with the Japanese girl."

"Korean, actually."

"In the SUV."

"It was a big car," I said. "Please. I'd appreciate it if I could talk to you."

She opened the door. "Come on in, then."

I hadn't been in a Native home since the last time Des and I vacationed in New Mexico. We used to go for the ceremonies and dances. That had been one of my ploys—take him to the reservations where booze was not allowed. I was no shaman, but I believed this would cure him: the piñon smoke, the golden aspen branches trembling, the women standing on the roofs of Taos Pueblo. We'd watch the dances, we'd vibrate through our whole bodies to the drums, and he'd have a wonderful time, even sober. At the Shalako rites in Zuni, we were invited into a home where the family had dug down their floor, lowering the livingroom several inches so the headdressed dancers could fit beneath the roof. We left the winter air outside, so cold and dry it cut your lungs like knives, and squeezed into a room filled with heat and firelight, the smell of uncured sheepskin, smoke, the drums pounding, hour after hour, as we added our own beating hearts and smell and body heat. My bladder ached and then I forgot it, as I believed Des could forget his need, awed by the experience and the people who had granted us this privilege. On the way home, Des gave me the slip in Gallup, went on a binge and it could have all ended there. But I found him in time, where he lay passed out in the snow. Two Navajo men helped me carry him to our motel. We saved him and he survived to kill.

"Nice and cool in here," I said.

"Casino money paid for the A/C," she said, "and I try to keep the lights off. Sit down and let me finish cooking. You eat meat?" she asked.

"Yes. But you don't have to..."

"Processed meat?"

"Processed?"

"Bologna," she said. "Sit here."

I could hear her moving around in the kitchen. Another dog, an old one, stretched out on the floor. It felt funny to be sitting in her home while she bustled around in there, like this was a restaurant and I was being served. Fried bologna. I never would have thought that it would smell so good. She'd probably serve it on white bread with mayonnaise. Were there other Native American traditions on view in there: oil cloth tablecloth, Jell-O molds? But she'd told me to wait in the living room.

Was it OK to look around? In a white person's house you'd be expected to look around and comment and compliment, but I tended to get things backwards. Why was I nosy as all get out in this home while faced with Bernice I considered personal questions very rude? If I complimented something, like for example the chair I was sitting in because I was making an effort not to really look too closely at anything else, would custom dictate she would have to give it to me as a gift? Stuffed animals on the shelves, a bit of embroidery on top of the TV, framed photos I wanted to go over and look at but didn't, a couple of gourd rattles, a woven basket. *Family Circle* and Oprah's magazine on the table. And—I couldn't believe my prying eyes—a copy of Augusto Boal's *Theater of the Oppressed.*

She brought in a tray, sandwiches (yes, white bread with mayo), Diet Cokes, potato chips.

"I'm Cheryl, by the way," she said.

"Rae."

We held our plates on our laps and I put my glass on the side table, purposely next to Boal.

"Oh! You're reading *Theater of the Oppressed,*" I said.

"My daughter brought it home from college."

"My friend, the one you met, and I, we were in a street theater group, inspired by Boal."

"You've actually done this stuff?" she said.

"Yes, well, a little, not like I'm an expert or anything."

"I was upset Lucinda was taking a theater class. Waste of time, I thought. I wanted her to get a useful education. So she told me to read this, and I have to say, it's made me see possibilities."

"Oh, endless," I said, though I can't say I meant it. "If you can change the script, you can change the world."

"And you've done it? I have questions," she said. "I want to use the techniques here. Theater, seems to me, it's a better way to build a team than sports. It's not competitive. It's like our old games here. Not about who wins and who loses, but about something shared. It's how people learn to work together."

Why dampen her enthusiasm? "In theory," I agreed.

"We can use theater to open up the debate on toxic dumping. You get everyone in the act, they can't shoot all of us."

That belief, I thought, was also open to debate.

"I came to see you," I said, "because this friend of mine has disappeared."

"The Japanese girl?"

"No. Yes."

"You have trouble settling on one or the other, don't you?"

"I mean Jennie Kim isn't Japanese."

"Oh, Korean," Cheryl said.

"And she's disappeared," I said, "but that's another disappearance. I'm here because of someone else. That white girl you had us drive? The Neoproctologists have some kind of facility here, right? She escaped from the rehab center, didn't she? And I think they're holding David there. And right now I think he's the only one who can help Jennie."

"Mind if I smoke?" Cheryl lit up a cigarette. She offered me one.

"No, thanks." It wasn't even American Spirit.

"I had quit," she said. "I started again when we had to bury my nephew."

"Have they arrested anyone yet?"

"No."

"Who decides who gets to use the land here?" I asked. "I don't get it. Neoproctologists. Toxic dumping."

"That's a complicated story," she said.

"I've read they torture people out there."

I'll interject we'd never heard of Abu Ghraib then, or seen the pictures, but how can you not know? When people have power over others in secret, if you just stop to think...

"Look," she said, "from what I understand, what goes on out there isn't much different from basic training."

"My friend Bobby says basic training desensitizes you to degradation, all these rituals to humiliate and dehumanize so you can—"

"Yeah, do all kinds of things to your enemy. Boys get trained up that way," said Cheryl. "Pain makes 'em identify even more with their group, their cause. Call it boot camp, fraternity hazing. Football practice. But here? Thing is, these people—especially the girls—think they're headed to a spa and when they have to do push-ups out in the sun, they start whining. Hello... this isn't Palm Springs."

"I read they kill people. Or make them commit suicide."

"Take the veil," she said. "That's what they call death, or what we call death. They don't see it quite the same way."

Did that mean Dr. Jim was dead? Was that what I'd heard? that he was "in veil"?

"I don't believe they kill anyone," Cheryl said, "and I've talked to the runaways enough that I believe I would know. But the way I see it, whiners or not, if they want to leave, they should be free to go but it's like the Army that way too. Once you volunteer, you're not free to get out. I don't think that's right. They're watched pretty close out there. And it's not my business, but the way I see it, if someone gets away and we cross paths, I try to help them."

"But these reports of torture...?" I said.

"You ever hear of the Sun Dance? Sometimes people in trouble need a bit of pain and blood sacrifice to get their spirits right. You ever hear of S&M? Some people like it."

I said, "But if it's consensual, it's not torture. Like sex is not the same as rape."

"I try to keep an open mind," she said. "Or you might think I just don't care what a bunch of crazy white people do to each other. Long as they leave me and mine alone." She gave me a long look. "You want to see the place, we can drive out there. In your car, of course. I have to carpool to my job in town though I suppose you can't call it a pool when I don't have a car or license either."

"I hear you. Jennie always used to drive," I said.

I wondered what her job was. She didn't do manual labor. Not with that manicure. An anthropologist would have felt free to ask but without a dissertation or a pending grant report as my excuse, I let it go.

Cheryl said, "Guards might stop us at the fence line, but if you want...We'll say you're with the DNA."

"Navajo?" I asked.

"What? Oh, you thinking *Dine*? Navajo? No, I'm saying DNA. Chromosomes, genetic testing." Again she hesitated. Looked at me. "I guess I can tell you."

"I'm not asking to know tribal secrets or anything."

"I don't know any. Folks that know can be close mouthed. I have no cause to censor myself. I'm no repository of anything. My father had secrets, but they could only be passed to a son. My mother was Luiseño from down around Hemet. Where I'm Basoba," she said, and she ran a finger down the inside of her arm. "It's my blood. I'll tell you about the DNA, but first you tell me about that Jennie Kim."

I told.

"See, this is what my people learned a long time ago. You can have every right in the world on paper, but you need to be able to enforce those rights and protect them. Doesn't matter what the paper says. It can all be taken away tomorrow. Come out the back," she said.

The backyard was dirt, beaten down and swept, and shaded with a tarp.

"It's not much," Cheryl said, "but I figure we can rehearse here. I don't want to do it in the cultural center where everyone can watch us prepare."

"You'll perform here?" I asked.

"No. In front of the tribal council. Only they don't know it yet. You'll help?"

"Yes," I said. "I don't know a damn thing. But if you can use me, I'll help."

Even now that I'm living on the reservation, I don't have the whole story straight. Back when Cheryl tried to lay it out, it was hard to follow.

"Don't feel bad," she said. "That's what the judges say. In olden times, we'd get to court and they'd find against us 'cause we didn't have the documents. Now they say we have too many."

The story—history—went something like this:

The Basoba band of Kumeyaay people lived on the fence. That is, in the desert east of San Diego where the border now divides the tribe between Mexico and the US.

"The government separated us from our families in Mexico, but then the Bureau goofed and mixed us up with some Luiseño to the north. We're Kumeyaay but don't confuse us with Pauma or Pala. When we finally got a reservation, they put it down not as Basoba, but Luiseño. Then when the Cahuilla were driven off their lands, some of them came to us. Folks from Santa Something and San Something Else and Diegueño intermarried with Cupeño and then Soboba, which made them not that far removed. When the Bureau made lists of tribal enrollment, they put down anyone who claimed it. People who'd married in. People who'd leased land. People who trespassed. We'd say, Hey, those people aren't Basoba, but the Bureau marked them down anyway, and soon there were more of them than there were of us, and they were dominating the votes in council."

"What about sovereignty?"

"What about it?" she said. "I'll allow the Bureau does draw

the line somewhere. A lot of hippies came around in the Sixties and they didn't make the enrollment. About ten years back, some white woman shows up. A voice told her she's Basoba, and we're supposed to believe that, and she's a shaman."

"Marcia!"

"She called herself Orange Blossom. Some of the fellows took to calling her Smudge Pot. Yeah, some of us used to work the orange groves, when there still were any. Some of us had orchards. But they diverted the river water, took our springs. The water rights were reserved to us in 1890. We've been in court just about as long. Each time we win, but the decision is never what they call implemented.

"Well, we're not allowed to marry cousins, so most of us ended up marrying Luiseño anyway. And speaking English, Spanish, and Cahuilla. I know I'm Basoba. Half the people here, I don't know what they are."

She told me this in the car. Windows down, slow on the dirt roads, dust coming up filling my nostrils and throat, dusting me red-brown.

"I talk a lot," she said. "Just like to run my mouth. I get lonely sometimes, my husband being on the Powwow Trail."

I didn't know if this meant he was actually attending powwows or if it was a euphemism for infidelity, abandonment, or death.

"Some of us, especially me, want to see some genetic analysis. Prove for once and for all who's Basoba and who's not. It matters to us, because we've got individual allotments plus tribal trust land. It matters to you 'cause we'll tell them at PVM you're checking whether any of them want to be part of the DNA test. On the chance one of them's got Basoba genes. Long shot of course, but I've never yet seen a white man wouldn't take a long shot if it meant getting his hands on Indian land. Can I have some of this?" She popped the straw into a box of GatorAde. "The Bureau has to approve all outside contracts, and they wouldn't sign with the forensic scientist I found. I came up with a college professor who'd do it with a grant, so we didn't need a contract, but you can't get a grant without a timetable, and you can't get a timetable from an Indian. So. The whole damn thing's on hold. And most likely, it won't prove a thing but that we're all related to the chimpanzee."

"We are, of course," I said. "I work with primates at the LA Zoo."

"That pay well?"

"It doesn't pay at all. You know how it is in LA. The more money you have, the more likely it is that you don't work, or that you do something unproductive and utterly useless."

"Me, I'm versatile," she said. "Basically a bookkeeper. Billing, accounts receivable, they have me doing inventory work too. They keep me busy and I swear, if you don't stand up to them now and then, they'll ride you like a horse. With spurs. Of course, not so much anymore. Since the casino, they all think we're just rolling in money. He's afraid if he oversteps the line with me, I'll walk and stay home doing my nails."

"Your nails look great," I said.

"It's the undercoat," she said. "The primer. That makes the difference."

"Even when the bottle says One Coat?"

"You've gotta think of it as part of the product name," she said. "Not instructions for use."

I think this is more or less what she said, along with lots of specific dates and she cited lots of rulings. I understand these days you're allowed to reconstruct dialogue, tell events according to your own selective often self-serving or self-flagellating memory, change them as necessary to suit narrative considerations, go for metaphoric rather than factual truth, and still call it nonfiction. So take all of this as you find it and keep in mind that at the time I was stupefied with the heat.

"You'll find most people here are remarkably law abiding, remarkable when you realize we have no rule of law. Enforcement in the hands of the state. The state delegates it to the county. The county don't bother. See, I don't even know who you are, but I'll tell anyone. Nothing spreads more than complaint. Complaints and rumor, does a much better job than the daily news."

She didn't sound angry, but she didn't let go.

The windshield was covered with dust. I tried the wipers and soon ran out of wiper fluid which in any case just smeared. We couldn't waste our water, but I stopped and wiped the glass clean with tissues, then with my hand. It dusted over soon again.

"We could use the water rights," she said, "though I've pretty much given up on that account. Mostly doing it to get to the bottom of things, find out who's really in charge here and where the dumping's coming from."

The first settlement we came to, I didn't know any better then, and thought this was it. But the Neoproctologists with all their money? I couldn't believe David would live in a shantytown like this. And it wasn't fenced or guarded, though if you didn't have your own transportation, it would be a long hot walk through the desert. No wonder that girl had looked exhausted and sick, if she ran from here. Slapdash pieces of trailer leaning one panel up against another, extension cords running everywhere. No flowers. Nothing but dust. The makeshift home in Tijuana was luxury compared to this.

I slowed down and the dust cleared enough so I could see some faces.

Not Neoproctologists. “Basoba people?” I said.

“No. Migrants,” Cheryl said. “Though who knows? We should test them too. A lot are from across the border and for all I know we’re cousins.”

The families in Tijuana were migrants, too, come to the border looking for work. They came from villages where people shared strong cultures and looked out for one another. In Tijuana, people show up from all over, all strangers to each other. Everyone’s been ripped off. No one trusts anyone. People don’t speak to their neighbors. Building houses together was not just for habitation, we were told. It was a way to reweave community.

Cheryl said, “Jerome Muñoz let a few families move onto his land a couple years ago. See, they come to pick dates, work for the growers, but the growers don’t provide housing and won’t pay enough to cover rent. The towns don’t want these folks anyway. So more of them came. Nowhere else to go. The Bureau and the feds trying to get them evicted, health hazard, code violations, illegal leases, whatever, but the state and county are fighting the feds in court because they sure don’t want to end up providing.”

I reached for a water bottle and took a swig. The water was hot enough to brew coffee.

Some months later I would ask, "Any restrictions on how many cats you can have?"

"As many as you want, till the coyotes get them."

Not an answer I liked, but still. What looked to me like squalor might look like home to Weezie. I would ask Muñoz if he had room for one more—an elder.

Children waved as my wheels spun dust up into their faces.

"Where do they go to school?" I asked.

"I think they mostly don't," she said.

I was scratching at my arms and legs, almost as bad as Lyle, sand fleas or distress or something.

"Even the other Mexicans don't like those people," she said. "They're Indians."

We drove through the encampment and reached a gate. It wasn't padlocked, just held closed with a loop of wire. Cheryl got out of the car to open the way.

"They'll stop us further along," she said.

We raised such a cloud and made so much noise, I knew we were giving them plenty of notice.

The Neoproctologists didn't just have a fence topped with razor wire, the fence was electrified, too. Two uniformed men came out of the guard shack, weapons drawn. One of them holstered his gun and spoke via walkie-talkie to someone somewhere.

Our ploy didn't get us past the gate. "They'll ask the hosts." The guard stroked the holster with his trigger finger. "Come back in a week. We'll let you know."

When we returned, he shook his head—"No participation is desired"—and left us standing with our fake genetic sampling kits, baggies and cotton swabs.

Another wasted trip: to Bobby's.

The whole point of leaving the cats with him was so I wouldn't have to go back and forth all the time, but I drove down to his place with shopping bags full of cat food. I didn't phone ahead because I was afraid he might tell me not to come.

He wasn't home. I waited on the porch and Chessie—the indoors/outdoors cat—purred in my lap until he got bored. Chessie got up and walked away and so did I—just a little too soon because by the time I got home, Bobby's message was already on my machine.

Thanks for the cat food. I played it back. *Thanks for the cat food.* Nothing about sorry I missed you. Maybe he was just skittish like Molly. I listened for subtext, for affect. For affection. *Thanks for the cat food.*

I hit the remote control to turn on the TV. All sides in the conflict in Liberia asked desperately for peacekeeping troops. I stared at pictures of mutilated civilians, piles of bodies, the slaughtered and dead, footage of armed Marines with orders not to intervene as they guarded the delivery of beer to the US Embassy.

I played Bobby's message once more, then hit the number 3 key to delete his voice.

"You're here again!" said Cheryl. "You must be in love with this David guy."

"No," I said.

"Then why are you so anxious to find him?"

"I don't know." It had started out for Jennie's sake, but it was more complicated than that. I was supposed to think like a mountain and think like an ape. Loy complained I couldn't think like a black man, but the truth of it was I didn't even know how to think like myself. "I don't know."

"You know what I don't know," Cheryl said. "Why's everyone making such a fuss now about Bush telling lies? The claims about uranium and aluminum rods, and Tony Blair's fake dossier—they were all exposed as lies before we went to war. Before the killing and the dying started. It didn't seem to matter when it still mattered."

I said, "We're not very good at stopping people when they want to save the world."

Cheryl narrowed her eyes at me. "You told me once you're a teacher."

"I was. Certified for high school."

"If you really want to hang around here, we're finally opening up an Indian school. I understand they're still short some teachers for September."

"Here on the reservation?"

"No. There's a piece of land about twenty miles from here. Basobas, Sobobas, Luiseños, Cahuillas, we've all been disputing whose piece of land it is. So we decided to put up an Indian school for all of us. The kids will take a bus over there instead of into town. You'll teach there, live here, and we'll do some Theater of the Oppressed in the yard."

"Why me?" I said. "Why on earth would you trust me?"

"You say *I don't know* a lot. It's a good place to start."

"So now I let you run my life."

"You came knocking on my door. You want to walk your own path, you don't go around asking for help," she said.

We have forged an alliance but not—at least not yet—a friendship. Sometimes Cheryl speaks to me from the heart but she's always quick to add "and I don't care who hears me say so."

Chapter Twenty-Seven

THE UN HEADQUARTERS IN BAGHDAD was bombed, the special envoy killed. You remember all this, don't you? The terror continued in Afghanistan. The killing continued in Israel and Palestine. A leader of Hamas was assassinated by Israel and 100,000 Palestinians poured out into the streets. The dying continued in Africa. A California woman in a wet suit was killed by a shark that mistook her for a seal.

I did what I'd promised myself I wouldn't do. I wrote to Des.

He wrote back. The envelope was stamped MAILED FROM STATE PRISON. I didn't know if this was to warn my letter carrier about me, or me about the sender.

Rae, he wrote,

Until I heard from you, I didn't realize how much it would mean.

It was a long letter, mostly printed, sometimes sliding into his instantly recognizable sloppy script. He still didn't know when to use apostrophes. After a couple of paragraphs I had to put the letter down and curl up a few moments with Molly till I was calm enough to read on.

Sara said he could answer questions: How to go on living

after enormity. How to stop good people before they go too far.

My own enormity, how I could have countenanced Jennie's drunk driving. I don't know how to explain. I could only speculate: I'd been good for too long. I wanted to see it all as innocuous fun. I wanted to do it over with no one getting hurt. I wanted to live as though the past had never happened.

I lay with my head against Molly, the letter on the bed beside us. And because I had to read the letter but couldn't bear to be alone with my ex-husband's words, I read it aloud to my cat.

Kill and forget it, he wrote. *Kill and forget it. That's how they perverted the Buddhist message. It became the way of Zen.*

What I've learned, he wrote, *its not the innocent Zen we imagined we understood when we were young. The Way was born of atrocity. It matured in repentance.*

I have plenty of time in here to read. Would you believe they don't allow the Sports Illustrated swimsuit issue, but you can get your hands on Hitler who wrote, by the way, that a philosophical system stays pure, that's why its better than a political party. A party must compromise it's stand. A philosophy never does, and in this as in everything else, you see how wrong he was. Any message can be perverted. Islam, Christianity, Judaism, even gentle Buddhism.

He wrote how medieval warlords took simple peasants who lived by the Buddhist message of peace and taught them to kill.

All is ephemeral. Everything is death. The gong that sounds and then fades. The flower that opens then droops, withers and falls. You can kill and forget it. Everything passes. Amnesia is a lovely drug. Kill and forget.

Zen enabled the action, Des wrote, but the warlords lied. The experience could never be forgotten. Zen had to provide an answer in the aftermath. Lock yourself away and fix your concentration on the tiniest, slowest motion. Collect pebbles and sit still for ten years just to watch them change. Wash a single paving stone on hands and knees, keep your bloody hands so busy you can never again unleash the monster.

Instead of the silence of a monastery, instead of camellia blossoms drooping, falling, Des lives with the noise and danger, the stench of angry men, light from a single window, barred, I imagined, up high. The way of Zen: a century is a moment, and each moment can expand to last a century.

Prison is not a place conducive to meditation but it's a place where one must find meaning in meaninglessness.

That's where I am, fallen out of time as we know it. There is nothing productive or worthy about this, but its a way a person can do no further harm. Its' a way to survive year after year of brutal living and remorse. Sara interrupted this. Not a welcome distraction, this breaking my detachment, and hearing from you now gives me hurt and shame. I'm glad for it, not because it feels right for you to punish me, but it feels right to once again feel something.

All those years you wanted me to say "My name is Des, and I'm an alcoholic."

Now theres no question of forgiveness or making amends, only of getting through the nights and days.

My number is D01745 and I'm a killer.

Chapter Twenty-Eight

THERE USED TO BE A TUNNEL at the Museum of Tolerance. As you passed through, recorded voices shouted every ugly bigoted epithet at you, voices filled with hate. And you came to understand on a most visceral level the hate in hate speech, how it wounds both body and mind.

The last time I went there, I was with Jennie and the tunnel was gone. Instead there was a wall on which words lit up and you had so many seconds to eliminate all the bad words. Some of the bad words were perfectly good English words with no pejorative connotations, depending on context. Slope, slant, queen, chief.

"There's nothing wrong with these words!" Jennie said. She didn't erase them and a message soon lit up scolding her insensitivity.

"You don't get it!" she shouted at the wall until a guard came over. "You just don't get it!"

Jennie wasn't always so clear about language. I remember her laughing. "Do you know that song? When my English wasn't so good, I thought it said, Two sun to two come caring, the hatchet peter toner paw." One day a friend spread out the map and showed her: Tucson, Tucumcari, Tehachapi, Tonopah. Not one English word to be found there. How can you disappear a person so innocent she's capable of getting lyrics as screwed up as that?

Life abounds with unanswered questions. How can a person stay sane or even partially intact in prison? How dare Sara imagine she can "forgive" him? What gives her the right? What does Molly think without words? What goes on in PVM Rehab?

Loy said I couldn't think like a person of color. You can't get any whiter than David. Could I think like David?

I tried to imagine the hold Neoproctology had on him. I imagined the hold it could have had on me though I of course would never have fallen for anything as absurd as Neoproctology in the first place.

According to Neoproctology, PVM Rehab is psychoanalysis speeded up. No drugs, and no blaming the mother, since Dr. Jim very much loved his own. Breakthrough, breakdown, and life-transformation guaranteed within six months.

They say people go for three reasons. Some because it's a prerequisite for moving up in the hierarchy. Some because it offers knowledge. Some because it offers cure.

So: How is this achieved? According to the UN, torture is inflicted by or at the instigation of a public official. What happens in the desert is voluntary and private and so what happened to me at PVM cannot be classified as torture.

Up till now, everything not only happened just as I've told you but almost all of it can be documented, too. It doesn't work that way when it comes to Dr. Jim's Rehabilitation Center.

What actually happened to me was —or so I believe—a heat and dehydration-induced hallucination. But what happened in my mind was clearly based on the rumors, affidavits, reports, court testimony of people who've been (or claimed to have been) there. From Mirady, I knew about the School of the Americas in Ft. Benning, Georgia, where the US Army trains Latin Americans in the techniques of interrogation and torture, and Mirady told me the kinds of things they do. Besides which, as I've already mentioned, through re-earthing I've expanded my consciousness. Most people re-earth themselves in order to think like a mountain and think like a wolf while I am trying to relearn how to think like people. You must bear in mind, however, that there are people in this world very hostile to the Church, willing to say anything. The Church says criticism comes from toxic minds. The Church insists none of the rumors, accounts, or affidavits is true.

According to reports, the average stay at PVM is six months, but like any hospital stay or nightmare or prison term or shamanic trance, time as we know or knew it shatters. Six months may be an estimate, an average, a metaphor, a lie. It doesn't matter. Once you're Here, there is nothing but a long relentless Here.

You might put the whole thing down to my driving home from Basoba, temperatures in the triple digits all through the Inland Empire and I was out of water and GatorAde. The hot wind through the windows and the seat belt alarm beeping incessantly on the passenger side even though no one was there. Skin gone clammy. Body wracked with stomach spasms and chills. Getting off the freeway, pulling over somewhere, looking for a

7-11, but I could go no further, parked on a side street somewhere, anywhere, doors flung open to let in air, engine off but I could still hear the alarm, beeping, beeping, everything spinning around me. Helpless.

Then you hear voices, memories.

Bernice said we needed a mission statement: "Every organization today has to have one."

Jennie wasn't interested in joining an organization.

Amory said *mission* turned him off. It sounded religious.

For Bobby, it was too military.

Devon wanted to know what a mission statement was.

I could feel my autonomous nervous system shut down at the very words.

Molly's mission is to live. To find a balance of autonomy, security, and relatedness, i.e., to be fully human.

To be fully human and allow the same to others. Isn't that enough?

It has to occur to any thinking person who's lived through the 20th-century and the opening years of the 21st, that any mission larger than that can become an enabler, a justifier, an engine of atrocity.

So: the highway patrol found me and gave me water. But before that, before that....A Church van picked me up. The van was white with dark tinted windows and a discreet little pink colon painted on the driver's side door. A man dropped a black hood over my head, guided me to the seat and strapped me in. The door slid closed with a bang.

I wasn't alone. I could tell there were other people, I couldn't say how many, but there was their breathing, the smell of their sweat. I could tell that much, and the anxiety of our beating hearts, and when the paving ended and when the dirt road began.

I could tell they all wanted something more.

When the door swung back, we stumbled out into desert light.

Hoods off. Clothing off. Strip!

Most people will hesitate.

There are things you think about, later, though while these things shock through your system, during the during, there are intimations only, no words.

Did you know the immigrants to Ellis Island had to strip and step naked into disinfectant showers? Authority tells you to do it and you do. When doomed Jews stepped into the gas they surely thought Business as usual. Same old shit.

Sometimes shit is what it all comes down to.

Look at yourself before you look at others and say Why did they allow it? How? Why?

Ten of us or maybe eleven maybe twelve under the desert sun, racing naked and barefoot. There were cattle prods. The prick of cactus on legs and feet. People cheering us, jeering us on. I fell, skin clammy, shivering in the heat, cold sweat, breathless, my insides clutching. Zap. Zap. And the tables where they probed us. The harsh insertions. And shit is what it came down to.

Down in a ditch. The pit had already been used. We stood ankle deep in human feces, and as the enemas took effect, we didn't need to squat, we released, we spilled, we spewed, splashing one another with filth, gagging, choking.

Is that the healthy rounded odorless shit of a practising Neoproctologist?

No! It stinks!

The cattle prods and prodding voices, the sudden shove of hands.

Smell it! Get down in it!

Crawl in it! Roll in it like dogs! Lick it up!

We're not talking about the slight fecal aroma that is added to artificialized food—this is true—to enhance flavor. We're not talking about the erotic predilection, vice of the powerful, reputedly shared by historical personages as diverse as Queen Victoria and Hitler. We're not talking about the infant's pleasure of fingerpainting in shit.

You can say I'm making this up, but it's happened so many places so many times, in the humiliation of prisoners, in the training of paramilitary squads and secret police, spurt after spurt of shit and the gagging and the vomit and the observers taunting.

Not the aberration. Not the fringe. There is nothing here we have not been prepared for.

You're full of shit, so wallow in it.

Caesar, the gorilla, had no compunctions about scooping up a fresh mound in his human-like hand but he knew it was offensive or he wouldn't have thrown it at people who bugged him. The gibbons turn their backs and moon people they don't like and if they really don't like you, they both moon and fart. Leona ate her own shit and it didn't bother her at all. I always wondered what Molly thought, every day burying her feces in the litter box and then watching me just as diligently dig it up. I imagined Jennie changing the baby's diaper. There was nothing disgusting in this. It was nothing more nor less than a sign of life. Good for David, I thought. Teach him to accept the things of the body, but he was here because the Church condemned his body's needs.

What is to be done with a love that won't perpetuate a species? Who are we, who will not, do not, or cannot breed? Who are these people who think they can save us?

I was broken sick but at moments still more curious than afraid, and time would pass and one day I would be one of them, clothed, taunting the new arrivals. Having transcended humiliation, I would feel no pity for someone else's.

I learned: You can endure anything, even what you inflict.

This happens all over the world. Techniques are shared. A global culture of force.

The sensory deprivation of the black hood. The electrodes, yes, the rods hitting the feet, the hanging positions, the swollen hands.

Goddamn you, David. How perfect: the body known as a thing that cannot know pleasure.

The pain blows you out of your head. You dissolve. You are nothing. You endure if you believe in something, belong to something, and as Bernice had made clear, I did not.

People have stayed sane reciting poetry. Me, an English teacher, and not a word came to mind. Instead I pictured Molly, stretched out on the windowsill, watching; happily licking a piece of white paper; clawing away at an Express Mail envelope which is just about her favorite thing.

You can go into dark places when you feel safe. You feel safe when there's a little cat playing at your feet.

A cat can cooperate but she won't obey. In PVM I could no longer name the difference.

There is a world of atrocity and pain, and there is also a world where cats stretch their bodies and lie in the sun and in fact I was in that safe world, that quiet world, staring into space and imagination. I was in the normal ordinary world, home again, Molly at my feet, but my fevered mind kept carrying me back, to there, where a partner inflicted pain.

They never said *victim*. They always said *partner*. You must be exquisitely attuned. You must be able to gauge each physical and emotional response, so that you push the experience to the outer limits without ever crossing the line to lethal harm.

I understood I would never again in my life know anyone as well. I would never feel myself so known. I would never again experience such intimacy.

GatorAde, electrolytes, water. I came back to myself but even then some certainty of self was broken.

Months later, I would see David for real in the PVM clinic and he would tell me I very nearly got it right.

Chapter Twenty-Nine

In the meantime, I missed my husband. With all my heart, I missed Des. I'd tried to write him out of my history, but he kept coming back as though denying him was denying part of myself.

Don't think for a moment I ever forgot. It was Des who each morning pressed the reset button as though the night before had never happened. It was different for me. I remembered everything, though it became like something in a history book—a bomb that dropped, a coup d'état, a war, where the dead are already dead. You can know the fact and avoid the meaning.

His little niece stayed with us once. She was nine years old. "Is it true?" she asked one day. "Is it true the United States dropped atomic bombs on Japan?" I answered and she started to cry. "The United States is evil. My country's evil. I hate this country!"

I told her it was OK to love her country. I told her she should.

"I'm evil," she said. "We're all evil."

I held her and told her none of it was her fault. I told her she wasn't evil and that I loved her. Part of me was proud of her, but I told her that people thought they were doing the right thing, saving lives by ending the war. I told her no one knew how terrible the bomb would be. I made excuses.

Des was not willing to be responsible for what he had done himself the night before. This child considered herself accountable for things that had been done by others long before she was born. That was the moment I decided Des and I would not have children.

I fought him for the car keys. I begged. "If you ever hurt someone, how will you forgive yourself?" And then he ran her over. I still can't say her name aloud. Hearing it brings back her face, brings back what it was like sitting in the courtroom, looking at her and at my husband.

How do you incorporate what you've done and are capable of doing? How do you go on?

We went on. I didn't leave him. I visited him in prison each week. I thought about the luck of the draw and my good DNA. Not an alcoholic tendency to be found in my lucky genes. Legal fees and the civil suit took all our savings, and the house Des—we both—had worked so hard to restore. I found us an apartment, telling myself I could have been in his place. I could have been every bit as destructive. I could have let everyone down, just as he did.

He got sober in prison. He started drinking as soon as he got home.

"You ran someone over. You left her crippled under your car."

"You think I don't know that?"

"You'll kill someone before you're through." I felt bad as soon as I said it; I knew I'd hurt him. Back then I said, "I wouldn't blame you if you had diabetes. I don't blame you for alcoholism. We just have to learn to manage your disease."

I wanted the car keys.

"I'm not a child," he said.

"Let me handle our money."

"You don't trust me," he said.

"Not if it means trusting the way you drink."

"I like to drink," he said.

When he drank the bitterness came out: resentment, disappointment.

I said, "I'm not going to pretend anymore that it's OK."

But I did. We went on and the end only came the morning when he didn't want me to have Molly.

I took out the recyclables and came back with a calico kitten purring in the pocket of my shirt. I could hear him in the kitchen, the crush of the beer can in his hand, then the pop as he opened another. That's how he drank in those days. Pop the top off the can, drain it in a single gulp, crush it, pop open another.

"I found her on the deck," I said.

"Put her back there. Cats regard me with contempt."

As they should, I thought. Crush. Pop. I maybe hated him by then. "A cat regards you as an equal and you can't take it. She's not impressed just because you're a white male."

"That's not fair," he said.

"No, life's not fair. What's gotten into you, Des?" I didn't know Bobby then, but I wanted someone Bobby-like, who could go into multimillion dollar mansions and see only if they were comfortable to live in. Des used to be that way. When, how, had he changed?

Pop. Swallow. Crush.

I didn't realize I was shouting till the kitten began to whimper and squirm. I lowered my voice but didn't quit. "You think the world owes you? Can't get what you want, so you trash it? You'd trash the whole world if you could. You just trash it all, don't you?"

"I'm not a white male," he said. "I'm not a hero. I'm not the American Empire. I'm just me."

"You're just a drunk." I walked around him for my pocketbook and keys. The hell with him. The hell with politics. The hell with whatever used to matter. "I'm going to the pet store. Molly needs things."

He said, "I know a cocktail waitress name of Molly."

After the pet store, I got on the freeway and drove 45 minutes to the center of LA. I spoke to Molly as I cruised around scanning the For Rent signs. No one's gonna put you back. No one can take you away. Mollycuddle, Mollycule, no one can separate us now. When I finally stopped and filled out an application, I assumed the landlord would reject me. My credit was ruined, I was crying, and the kitten in my pocket was covered with fleas.

Chapter Thirty

When you visit someone in prison in California, you can't chew gum or wear an underwire bra. You are not allowed to carry writing materials or books. You can't bring gifts or carry your own Tampax and I knew from sad experience that the vending machines on the inside were often out. What you can bring is $30 in singles or change in a clear unlined plastic purse. I owned such a purse in the days when I drove to Lancaster every weekend to see him. When he came home, I threw it out, never expecting to need such a thing again, so now I headed up to Corcoran with money and ID in a Ziploc bag.

Was I out of my mind? It used to take an hour to Lancaster, up through the Antelope Valley and the high desert. I'd wait for the first sight of Joshua trees, the sign I was getting close. Corcoran? Three hours up and three back for a one-hour visit with someone I'd insisted I didn't want to see.

Up over the Grapevine and through Bakersfield, where he was born, a place with problems of its own, but when he took his stand, it was in Mississippi. The night we first met, we talked for hours, comparing the situation of sharecroppers and migrant workers. How American we were, each of us keen to fight injustice as long as it was far from home.

Now the landscape was dry and flat, the horizon marked by things storing other things: fuel depots, silos, water towers, cylinders and structures for which I had no name. Past acres of oil pumping units dipping their beaks and on through the Central Valley, the California I'd first known when I left Ohio 35 years ago, drawn west by Cesar Chavez. I'd come for La Causa, not for glamour, and yet none of it was the California I'd expected. California was San Francisco hippies and Hollywood stars. California was redwood trees and surf. I'd never pictured this: dry flat land where tumbleweeds the size of trees blew—still blow—across the road, where the sight of green broke your heart instead of lifting it: the vineyards where scab labor harvested the grapes, the lettuce fields where the men worked with the brutal short hoe. (Who was the politician who said Mexicans were meant to be stoop labor? That's why God built them low to the ground?)

Today's politics: a red, white, and blue billboard: STOP TERRORISM! GET US OUT OF UNITED NATIONS NOW!

There were vineyards everywhere along the road, on any random patch of ground, vines trained over stakes and wires. There were shakers in the almond orchards bringing down the nuts and a big white plastic bag blown and twisted against barbed wire like a broken-necked swan. There were memories.

THE HEARTBEAT OF AGRICULTURE—a faded sign at McFarland where I'd once interviewed families whose children were dying from carcinogenic pesticides. I wrote up their stories for *El*

Malcriado, back when I still imagined I might become a journalist. These were the places where I'd marched and the dust kept blowing and I leafletted and picketed and organized.

There were popcorn clouds and thunderheads and wind. There were what looked to be a thousand head of Holstein crammed into a small lot and reeking. There was a prison in Delano and a prison in Wasco and a prison in Avenal. I traveled through the California gulag to where Des was waiting.

I hoped he'd found peace, but I didn't want to hear about it.

Don't talk to me about Zen. Don't tell me how spiritual you've become. At the end of this road, I don't want a revelation. I don't want to hear how that child's death led to knowledge or growth. I don't want you to make me hate you.

Did I color my hair for the visit? Yes. Did I wear lipstick? No.

Did I go because I thought it would make Bobby like me?

I'm not trying to tell you it was the right thing or wrong thing. Going to see him is simply what I did.

I got off the highway and went in the direction of the guard towers and lights. At the State Prison, they told me I was in the wrong place. He was in the Substance Abuse Treatment Facility. That made sense, till I found out the place was built for treatment but never used as such. Before it opened, the State transformed it to a maximum security lockup but never bothered to change the name. Maybe taxpayers imagine someone's being treated?

Parking near the handicapped space, I felt strange, like a voyeur or a spy, thinking I knew exactly where Sara had parked when she came to see him.

I waited in one line and then another.

There were people of all races. Ordinary people. Many of us dressed in black, not in mourning, but because so many other colors were forbidden. The people didn't look hard bitten or downtrodden. The guards pleasant enough and polite, but gave no quarter.

The ordinary girl ahead of me bit her nails while her ordinary mother listened to the guard who said, "She's been coming in under your authorization, but now she's eighteen and she has to be processed on her own."

The girl said nothing.

"It's her eighteenth birthday," said her mother. "She wants to spend it with her father."

"Not without authorization. And she doesn't have it."

"We applied for her weeks ago."

"She wasn't eighteen then so her request was denied."

"But it takes a month to process. You know her," said the mother. "You've seen us every weekend for the last two years. It's her birthday."

"It's her eighteenth birthday, which means she can't come in."

When the guard called my name, I turned over my Ziploc bag and glasses and wristwatch and shoes.

She examined them and said my pants were too baggy.

"It's just I've lost a lot of weight," I said. "Kind of stressed out over the Bush Administration and the war."

"Baggy attire is prohibited."

I pulled out my copy of the Visiting Rules and Regulations. "Look. It doesn't say baggy. It says sagging."

"Your clothing sags on you," said the guard. "And you're not allowed to carry paper. Or those tissues."

"Can't you just strip search me?"

"We may do that anyway," she said, "but not until you throw those pages away and return in non-prohibited attire."

The birthday girl said, "My pants might fit you."

You never know who will be kind.

We exchanged clothes in the bathroom and then they let me through the metal detector and gave me back my shoes. A door opened and I entered a cage. Another door opened and I was in the yard, alone in the wind and a space that felt more exposed and empty than you can imagine in spite of the towers and razor wire and electrified fence to hem you in.

Before, Des and I used to have contact visits and I could stay all day. A child-killer, he's in protective custody now, so it's different. You only get an hour.

We sat separated by glass, and said nothing. It was not that we had nothing to say, but all we did was look. I used my shirt sleeve to wipe my eyes.

I'd thought there were feelings I could shut off, a past I could move past, block off in order to go on. Is the core what persists or what we throw away?

We looked at each other and looked and looked and it doesn't matter to me whether you can love him or not, whether my words have or have not convinced you he's worthy of it. For better or worse, I was overwhelmed to see him. The speechless surprise: that the sight of him made me happy.

The realization that I still love him shook me to the core, making me see that I still have one.

After the visit, he wrote me again:

Why did you love me? I'm asking you because you're probably the person who knows me best. Ana won't see me and I can't really ask her to. So tell me, if you can, why did you love me? Tell me something I did—anything—that was worthwhile and good. Remind me, if you can, that I'm more than this. Let me believe I can still be useful.

I wanted to say I haven't given up on you, but I held back. I wasn't sure that I meant it.

Chapter Thirty-One

GIVE NOTICE TO THE LANDLORD or not? I was moving to Basoba, but I didn't want to give up the place. This was the only real home Molly had known. It was here we'd got rid of her fleas. The vet gave me drops but as soon as I applied them to her fur, she screamed and threw herself around in what looked like a fit. I took her in my arms and saw fleas by the dozen as they scurried out of her fur to the safe naked corners of her eyes. Then she lay still and trusting on my lap as I plucked the bugs out one by one with tweezers. I didn't trust the steadiness of my hands, but she did.

She'd sat in every window, she'd raced around, cornering hard on the hardwood floors.

Hold onto the apartment or let it go?—it was the only place where Jennie would know to find me.

I opened up packing boxes and Molly jumped into them. If she understood what I had in mind, would she dissent? When I do anything she objects to, Molly takes my ankle in her mouth but she registers her protest without breaking the skin. Molly never bites. Now when I lifted things down from shelves, she panicked at shadows. She chased dust.

Books, papers, photograph albums were easiest to pack, but most distracting.

Des with his hair full of plaster, working on our bungalow. A man strong enough to refuse to kill, too weak to escape the fate of killing.

Sunflowers and a ladder against an adobe wall in Taos.

I'm wearing a cowboy hat and Des has an arm around me and we're both smiling, happy, raising shot glasses toward the camera.

A glass of wine is no more harmful than a word like *slant*. It all depends on who uses it and how it's used.

Glassware had to be wrapped in newsprint or bubblewrap.

Clothing in two piles (never on the floor, of course): Goodwill and Keep.

A little at a time. A little more packed each day. Delaying.

Then the phone rang. Of course it had been ringing all along. Telemarketers. But this time:

She said, "We're home."

Of course "we" wasn't Jennie and Loy. It was Jennie and the baby, and Jennie could hardly be the person I remembered.

She used to phone and say Guess what time it is? Cocktail hour.

Name that sound. The ice clinking in her glass.

I drove over.

"I'm sorry I didn't call you right away," she said. "I was with my parents, and then I—we—needed time alone." She nursed Loy, Jr. and rarely raised her eyes, but she wasn't looking at him with maternal adoration, she was staring at the floor, or at nothing. "The FBI's been asking me about Loy for months," she said. "I couldn't tell them what I don't know. Do you?"

"No," I said.

"I suppose they've released me to lure him out of hiding, or to follow me to him."

I wanted to tell her as much as I did know, but it was hard to believe the house wasn't bugged.

"My parents," she said. "They were always OK about Loy, but they're not OK about his deserting."

"Do they know President Bush was a deserter, too?" I said.

"They keep telling themselves his disloyalty is why I got arrested. It's easier for them than understanding it was the other way around. Where are the cats?" she said.

"With Bobby."

"I want them," she said.

I wasn't sure I wanted to see him.

"Phone him. Make sure he's home," I said, and rattled off his number.

She looked at me, surprised that I knew it by heart.

Loy had taken the big car. Jennie was driving her mother's, already equipped with an infant car seat. I held him while she unlocked the door and his skin was every bit as soft as people say a baby's skin will be.

"They wanted to take him from me," Jennie said, "put him in foster care but it was all delayed. Official disagreement about appropriate racial placement."

Sometimes racist stupidity works in your favor. Our eyes met and we started to laugh and I could believe the Jennie I'd known had not been crushed, that she was still herself somewhere inside.

Then it was as if laughter gave her confidence. "This Administration is going to be so discredited, they'll have to grant amnesty. Loy will be welcomed back," she said.

We didn't know it then, but what would happen was we'd hear from Loy after the Mexican government assured him it would refuse to extradite. Then Jennie and the baby would cross the border with two cats to join him.

"We didn't forgive the Germans who went on with daily life under Hitler," she said. "When your government does wrong, you're supposed to leave."

"Not when it's America," I said, surprising myself. "We'll get our country back."

"You think so?" she said.

In the meantime, we could get the cats.

Jennie panicked, caught in Dodgers game traffic. Too many people, too much of a crowd for someone who had spent months in solitary.

I couldn't imagine what she'd been through. It made me shy.

"How will you live?" I asked, meaning what will you live on?

"I don't know," she said.

NINJA HID FROM US but Monk came running at the sound of Jennie's voice. Then he froze a few feet away, fluffed up his coat and studied her.

"Yes, it's me, sweetheart."

She handed me the baby. I looked into his dark eyes which seemed so calm in spite of what they must have seen. I thought, If you tickle him, he'll laugh. That can't be taken away. But I was still awkward with him then and only held him.

Jennie held out her hand and Monk took the last few steps toward her. He sniffed at her fingers. He meowed insistent as a car alarm, then rolled over and over in ecstasy.

"Chessie hasn't been doing well," Bobby said. "He hasn't been eating."

"Have you been giving him French fries?" I asked.

"Yeah, yeah," he said. "When he wouldn't eat the frozen kind, I tried making them fresh."

"And you said you didn't like cats!"

Bobby said, "He was falling over when he walked and now he hardly moves at all."

"Have you taken him to a vet?"

"Of course. What do you think I am? And you! You just drop the cats off with me and disappear," he said.

"Don't say disappear in front of Jennie," I said.

"So where have you been?"

"Busy," I said. "I'm moving to Basoba, to the reservation, and I could ask you the same."

Chessie lay on a towel in the bathroom. He was listless till we came in, then he opened his eyes and began to purr before he half-shut them again.

"The vet thought he'd had a series of small strokes, and I guess he's had another. He gets worse." The vet had suggested putting Chessie to sleep. "He doesn't seem to be in pain. I just couldn't do it," Bobby said. "For a while he'd eat a little bit or drink a sip if I put it right in front of him. So, are you going to take him, too?"

"Of course," Jennie said.

Bobby scratched Chessie's head lightly. "I mean, I don't think he has much longer." Chessie let his head flop down against Bobby's arm. Bobby said, "I think you should leave him here. He's kind of used to me."

THE MAN WITH A VAN came to move my stuff. I drove out to Basoba and Jennie followed with the baby to see where I was going to live. These days she packs a diaper bag instead of margaritas.

"Can we stop for lunch on the way?" she said. "I remember there was a place I could see from the freeway."

"Steak house?"

"No. Breakfast 24 hours a day."

"That's just nauseating," I said. "Omelets, pancakes, waffles." It amazes me that people eat that stuff, let alone enjoy it. "I could understand if eggs benedict grew on trees. A fast lazy way to fill up. But to think that people actually go to the trouble to prepare that crap!"

"You can have bacon," she said. "Sausage. Something evil."

It was beginning to sound like we were back to normal except that in the restaurant, which had a full bar, she stuck to iced tea.

"I would never risk his safety," she said, with a kiss to the top of the baby's head.

IN SOME WAYS, Jennie never quits.

As soon as we arrived at Basoba she started bugging Cheryl.

"Does the school have elementary grades? Can the bus pick up the migrant children too?"

"I don't know," Cheryl said. "We'd have to take it up with the Tribal Council. Intertribal actually. Some folks might not want them in the school."

"Those children really need that education," Jennie said.

Cheryl said, "I suppose you're right."

CHERYL ALSO SAYS it's not a good idea to go out alone after dark, but that night she walked with us out into the desert's empty spaces.

"You're not afraid of anything," Jennie said. Cheryl didn't answer. "You're fighting powerful people. You know what they did to your nephew. They could kill you."

"You have to die sooner or later."

"Ah, the warrior mentality," I said.

"Don't start with that shit!" Cheryl said. "We were never warriors. The Basoba were farmers. We had settled towns and we cultivated the land and when the white people took our land they took our nice little houses and orchards and our fields ready for harvest."

"I'm sorry," I said.

"We can be warriers," she said. "Just not the way you mean it."

Jennie rocked the baby. There were stars above, but no moon.

"I'm not looking for a windfall now from all the suffering that went before."

I looked in the direction I thought was north, toward PVM Rehab, and wondered what was happening to David. If he tried to escape, we would be here to help him. I knew who Jennie was thinking about.

Cheryl said, "Plenty of folks here are as materialistic as any white man and they'll take whatever they can get. Me, I'd be satisfied just to hear the Old Ones honored. I'd be satisfied with an apology and the truth. Oh," she said, "wait. Listen. Here they come." She beamed her flashlight slowly over the desert floor, through the chaparral. "See, they're not afraid of the flashlight."

A solitary creature came into the light.

"Stephens Kangaroo Rat?" I asked.

"I don't know whose," she said. "I suspect he's free. Go ahead," she said.

I reached into the bag of corn chips and the kangaroo rat came right over.

"Do they bite?" asked Jennie.

I almost flinched but made myself hold still and the wild creature ate from my hand.

Chapter Thirty-Two

At the end of September, at the demonstration against the occupation of Iraq, I got the first intimation I was going to lose Jennie. We were marching side by side, till she broke away to approach the contingent of military wives.

"My husband's a deserter in hiding," she said.

I expected them to turn against her, but they embraced her and she marched with them, leaving me to join the Aztlán folks asking for the return of California to Mexico.

By the end of October, Jennie had joined Loy in Tijuana, and California caught fire.

The brush burned, the trees burned, then the houses burned. The San Manuel Band of Indians took in refugees from around San Bernardino and the mountain communities. At Basoba, the reservation was too barren to feed the fires, though smoke stung our eyes and enveloped the world as far as we could see with haze. Ash flaked down and covered every surface. Some people wore particulate masks to filter out the crap and some took breaks inside the air conditioned casino, though I doubted the thick secondhand smoke was any better than the toxic ash.

The tribal council called for volunteers to head to northern San Diego County to rescue the horses left behind by rich people running from the flames.

Cheryl enlisted my help at the rodeo grounds. I wasn't used to horses or any animals that size, but these were remarkably calm for what they'd been through. No one even thought they might need blinders and they weren't freaked in the least by our masks.

I pitched hay into stalls and carried in buckets of water. Cheryl checked which horses had hind shoes. She came back with a chestnut mare.

"This girl can take company," she said. "Bring over that flea bitten mare." None of the horses looked that bad to me. "That's the color, Rae. The gray one with the clusters of red and brown."

I stroked the mare's face and head. "My kitten used to be flea bitten," I told her. I looked into her eyes. "It's not your fault you live in a Republican county. You're not the one who voted down the bond measure every year to pay for a fire department." She wouldn't budge.

"Yank the stud chain," said Cheryl.

"I can't do that," I hollered back. Then to the mare, "You didn't tell those creeps not to pay taxes."

"It won't hurt her," Cheryl said. "It's just to get her attention."

"What a nice star you've got on your forehead," I said. "Your coat will look so nice once we brush out the ash. Come on, girl. Come into the nice stall."

"Give her a tug," said Cheryl.

"She's awful big," I said. "Come on, sweetheart. There's food and water and Cheryl made sure that other horse doesn't have hind shoes." I patted her sleek ashy neck. "Those people who owned you got what they deserved."

Cheryl said, "Take it easy. You're talking about people who just lost everything."

"Some decent people may have got screwed, outvoted by the greedy scum."

Cheryl said, "Enough propaganda. Just lead her in."

"I'm trying." The mare's nostrils quivered and I watched the busy movements of her mouth, like the orangutans who can use their dexterous lips for jobs that chimps and humans would do with hands. "You're a good horse. You didn't tell them to ignore brush clearance. You didn't ask to be owned by selfish Republicans who need to be bailed out when they won't pay their fair share."

Cheryl took the halter from me and yanked the stud chain and the mare followed her into the stall.

"You know a lot about horses," I said.

"No," she said. "It's cars I know. Auto mechanics."

"I thought you didn't drive."

"If you knew everything that can go wrong, you wouldn't either," she said.

"Yeah, like your brake cylinder going without warning."

"Never walk behind a horse," she said.

I knew that much. "Do they bite?"

I asked Jennie's question because I missed her. I didn't expect an answer.

"You come across a mean cuss now and then," Cheryl said, "one that will nip you, but most of the time, if they do, it's an accident. They don't see good close up, and they're liable to mistake a finger for a carrot."

She gestured with her index figure. The chestnut mare took it. The mare chomped down and ground her teeth side to side and Cheryl shrieked with pain. The flea bitten horse shied. I grabbed for the halter, missed it, got a hold of the lead rope, but she reared and it tore from my hand and whipped my face and next thing I knew I was kicked and in so much pain, it makes me all but pass out just to remember.

There were a lot of voices and a lot of hands. Someone said the road out to the hospital in town was closed by fire. Someone said something about good neighbors. Then a needle jabbed me with something that made me float, and there was an ambulance and a man repeating it again, "We're good neighbors. People need to know that we're good neighbors." He was leaning over me. His breath smelled of onions and when he moved back I could see the pink colon on his shirt and that's how Cheryl with a fucked up finger and I with a shattered knee got past the barriers all the way to PVM.

I remember the clinic and me asking, "Is Cheryl going to lose her finger? It's all my fault," and someone telling me, "She'll keep the finger but you're going to need some hardware in that knee."

"Can't you just give me a new one?"

"All we can do now is stabilize you. No surgery for you till the gash heals. Too great a chance of infection."

I thought I heard Cheryl's voice, asking something about leases.

Then things happened, then some more things. On Percoset you know what going's on or think you do but it's more like reading about it than feeling it.

"Do you want a flu shot?"

The voice was familiar but I didn't recognize him at first. The beard made David positively simian.

"There's an epidemic coming. They trained me," he said. "I'm just here doing my job. Otherwise, I don't think they'd let me talk to you."

"I've been looking for you," I said. "There's people ready to get you out of here."

"What for?" he said.

I told him every awful thing I had imagined.

"Quite accurate," he said. "You got it very nearly right."

"You've got to get out of here," I said or think I said.

"Why? It's been the most meaningful experience of my life."

"You've been tortured," I said. "Brainwashed."

"Like most people, you display a certain bias against torture. While I was being tortured, a Level IV host asked my partner and I—"

"My partner and me," I corrected him.

"He asked if we wanted to change places. My partner said yes and I said no. It was only the third or maybe fourth time that they asked that I was unselfish enough to agree. I wanted to give him what he'd given me. What I found out."

"Which is what? That Dr. Jim's a closet case?"

"You still don't understand about torture. What I did to the baboons was wrong. Not because I caused them pain and suffering. But we used them to learn for our own purposes not for theirs. They gained nothing. There was no mutuality of response."

"You were responsive with Dmitri," I said.

"They made me confess."

"Confess! What for? So you're gay! You can have a real life, a full life—"

"My God, Rae, that's the least of it. Just listen. These people are brilliant. They gave me a drug to paralyze my vocal cords. They tied my hands so I couldn't gesture or write. Think what it's like! You're being tortured to confess, pushed to the limit, all your defenses down, and the only confession you can make is a silent one, in your own mind. You'll lie to a torturer. Isn't that what people do? They always lie. You might lie to a partner, but the only thing you can do with yourself is tell the truth."

"Then be true to yourself."

"I used to think if I could see inside me, there'd be nothing there. Instead, Rae, there's all these dark places. Once you see that, the only thing to do is turn yourself over for cure."

The conversation is vivid in my memory, though I can't say for sure whether it was David or the Percoset talking.

"Forget everything I told you before," he said. "All you need to know is that I'm happy."

Someone who'd never been happy in his life, I thought, might easily confuse another state with happiness.

"Do you want that flu shot?" he said.

"Sure. Stick me."

As YOU GET OLDER, time moves faster, yet so much can happen in just one year.

Another year from now? The presidential election was coming—and I foolishly believed that was all we needed. We'd have liberty, justice, a government with a conscience. Jennie and her family would be able to come home.

Instead, Loy's working in a Mexican clinic. Jennie's got a gig indexing depositions and doing abstracts for a law firm—long-distance, electronically. A big boring corporate case that will likely provide an income as long as needed.

In a year, Loy, Jr. will be walking. Maybe I'll be walking again without crutches and with less pain once the hardware—two pins and a figure 8 wire—get removed from the bone.

Will I see Des again? "Thank you for going to see him," said Sara, but I didn't want to talk about it. Something dark had lifted off my heart, but that didn't mean I had to see him again. It didn't mean I wouldn't.

For this year at least I'm settled in at Basoba.

I have a nice little house though the ants keep getting in—a hassle for me, unending entertainment for Molly.

The new school is air conditioned as comfortably as the casino, and without the cigarette smoke. The grounds and bulletin boards are still bare, but that will change. The migrant children aren't enrolled this term, but it looks like that will change too.

"There are two kinds of songs and stories, two kinds of legacies," I tell the kids. "The private and the public. I know there are songs that belong to just one person in the tribe, and those songs are secret and go silent unless that person chooses someone to pass it on. And then there's culture that's shared. There's a legacy that belongs to everyone, and that means it belongs to you as much as to anyone else in the world."

I want to tell them the story from Chaucer. I want to tell them there's two kinds of sovereignty. The sovereignty of a nation, but just as important is self-sovereignty. But I don't.

Instead we've been doing theater games in Cheryl's yard and we're trying to follow Boal and do it in a grassroots and democratic way. The kids themselves name the issues that concern them. So far, we can't get anyone interested in toxic dumping. The kids are survivors of centuries of violence, but the boys have problems with their parents, and the girls have problems with boys.

I'm frustrated as all hell, but Cheryl says we have to give them time.

She says we're getting them ready to be a generation that will question, that will speak up.

She's given up on the DNA. "No, I have not given up," she insists. "It's that I see it different." She says a label doesn't make someone Basoba; it's how someone lives. And these kids, she says, will live Basoba lives: "They are not gonna roll over."

I keep thinking about Chaucer's story. The knight is punished and sees the error of his ways. The old hag has her youth and beauty restored and the two of them live happily ever after. But the story begins with a young girl's rape. What becomes of her? How does she go on?

I don't want to tell that story till I can say she's all right. Till I know what the violated girl needs.

Lately I've wondered if the old crone is what the young girl became. If trauma—the violence and bitterness, the shame and rage—cast the evil spell. To break it, the knight had to be sentenced. He had to know he was guilty and he had to change. Then, to be herself, the woman needed to forgive.

Chapter Thirty-Three

LET ME BACKTRACK HERE to a day before the fires. Yom Kippur, the Day of Atonement. I first laid eyes on Bernice, Yom Kippur 2002. One year later, Gorilla Theater met for the last time and Jennie said goodbye. She stuck around just long enough to mark our troupe's demise.

It was Jennie who insisted I stop at The Castle to pick up Marcia and Weezie. If they had to be included—and I couldn't refuse Jennie—I figured I could at least return the briefcase.

Cheryl rode in from the reservation with me. I wanted her there to see if Marcia and Orange Blossom were one and the same, but a host with a twitch in her left eye told us Marcia had run off.

With a guy, I assumed.

"With our antique candle snuffer."

We found Weezie in a private room, moaning in bed with her eyes closed. A nurse with the colon logo on her uniform sat on a chair beside her, crocheting. Half a dozen cats lay across Weezie on the bed.

"Weezie?"

Her eyelids flickered but didn't open. The awful sounds

seemed to come from her whole body, not just her sunken mouth, and it looked way too late to think of moving her to the Muñoz encampment.

The nurse smiled at us and said, "The veil will lower soon."

Weezie's smell was no worse than usual.

"She'll outlive us all," I said.

"There's nothing to fear about the veil," said the nurse. "See, she's smiling."

"She always smiles," I said.

When I lowered myself onto the bed, one cat looked up, yawned, then licked her paw. The others didn't budge.

"Look, but don't touch," said the nurse. "Her skin tears."

"Weezie," I said, "I brought your briefcase back. How long has she been like this?"

"The light coma? About a week."

"A lot's happened, Weezie," I said. "The White House leaked the identity of a covert CIA operative to punish her husband for criticizing Bush policy. I thought it would outrage everyone, but they weren't even afraid of getting caught. Like gangsters everywhere, they want you to know that if you cross them, you have good reason to be afraid."

"Why are you bothering her with this?" said Cheryl.

"She used to care," I said, "and she, at least, isn't telling me to shut up. Weezie," I said, "you know what else he's done? Violated the Geneva Convention, not just about the prisoners, but privatizing whole Iraqi industries and turning them over to American firms for profit. He's gutting the Clean Air Act and allowing mercury in our drinking water."

"Really?" asked the nurse.

Of course there was more—much more—that hadn't yet come to light. And there would be more after he was gone.

"Protecting us from terror? He blocked the security screening of cargo planes—save the industry some money."

"Stop it," said Cheryl. "It's the end. Let her have some peace."

"She's had peace for fifty years," I said, "ever since they cut up her brain."

"She can't hear you," said the nurse.

"At least she has an excuse." I stroked her cool spotted hand before the nurse could stop me and I placed the briefcase beside her. One cat panicked and scrambled off the bed. A gray tortoiseshell sniffed at the leather, touched the handle with a paw and licked it. "I appreciated reading the files, but I want you to know, it's still all out in the open. Nothing is secret. Everyone knows."

We waited by the bedside a minute, and a minute more. Weezie kept smiling.

CHERYL AND I had the longest distance to travel so of course we were first to arrive at the zoo. We followed the curving path past the gerunuks and the lions, up to where the snack bar looks out over the giraffes. Sara wheeled her way up next, followed by Jennie and the baby.

In recent years, I haven't observed the Yom Kippur fast, but the day felt solemn. I resisted the hamburgers in spite of the aroma from the grill and Cheryl's plate. Sara licked at an ice cream cone. Jennie ate French fries, in memory of Chessie, I thought, while Loy, Jr., in the sling against her body, didn't fuss or cry. From what I'd seen, he spent most of his time either nursing or sleeping which made him, so far, less demanding than a kitten.

A school group passed, the children shouting "A squirrel! Look! A squirrel!"

Cheryl said, "Bobby's been visiting Rae every weekend."

"Every weekend?" I said. "Three."

"Well, you've only just moved out," said Cheryl.

"He finds inspiration in the desert," I said. "He loves the light."

Sara, of course, wanted to hear about Des.

"He's got me asking the same question," I said. "How to live with what you've done. If you can't face it, you keep doing it. And maybe we can't face our own guilt unless we have a way of living with it."

Bernice arrived, eyes streaming. Bobby followed and kissed me in front of everyone. Amory and Devon showed up together.

"Has anyone heard from my father?" she asked.

This was a few weeks before I got kneecapped and saw him, so I, like everyone else, said no.

"Is it true that Neoproctologists torture people?" she asked.

"Probably," I said. "Anyone can become a torturer." I told her about the famous Milgram experiment—famous to everyone but her generation, I supposed. "Obedience to authority. Ordinary people were perfectly willing to administer painful shocks to others when told to do so."

"That's just the sound bite version," said Amory. "The part no one ever talks about? Milgrim's followup experiments. Nine out of ten subjects resisted authority and refused to administer the shocks as soon as there was someone else in the room objecting. Torture stopped in the presence of dissent."

"Wow!" said Jennie.

"Amory!" I said, "I'm so glad I know you!"

"Thank you," said Bernice.

Jennie said, "Please repeat that. Please just say it again!"

Amory shrugged and went back to biting his cuticles.

Then it was time for Gorilla Theater's last curtain.

We walked the last steps past the colobus monkeys and the blue-eyed lemurs, up to the green gate and the empty enclosure, the former home of the drills.

They're all gone now—Leona and Becky to Columbus, Lyle to Atlanta where the Species Survival people have introduced him to the Scarlett O'Hara of baboons.

We stuck flowers in the fence and we lit candles.

"We failed you," said Bernice, "but we won't stop. We will dissent."

We'd received some sad news, and we grieved.

Michael had been sent to Columbus to be reunited at last, we thought, with Melissa. The zoo housed him instead with the fertile baboons he was expected to impregnate.

Michael and Melissa could hear one another, smell one another, but were not allowed to be together, or to touch. They couldn't kiss or groom each other. They couldn't sleep wrapped in each other's arms.

Michael paced in circles. He got as close to her enclosure as he could. She vocalized with little cries, with chicken-like clucks, a voice he would have recognized anywhere. His tension mounted and his grief. They found him one morning stiff on the ground, shunned in death by the nubile females he had scorned.

So broke that noble heart. Melissa didn't long survive him. She sat in a corner, refused to eat, and followed him soon to the grave.

"I'm sorry, Melissa," said Bernice. "I'm sorry, Michael. I'm sorry, Becky. I'm sorry, Leona. I'm sorry, Lyle. Let this be a lesson," she said.

If there's anything I hate about being human, it's this desire to learn lessons from the deaths of others, to impose meaning on the destruction we wreak. But this time, I believe Bernice was right.

"I'm sorry," said Cheryl.

"Forgive us," said Bernice, "for what we've done."

We held hands before the enclosure. The drills were gone and this was our last time together, too.

The year ends, but not the story. The crimes go on and the greed and cruelty while this record stands, partisan and partial, a small challenge to amnesia.

"Yo, pecador," said Bobby.

"I'm sorry," I said.

"I'm sorry," said Sara.

Amory mumbled his apology and then Devon, "I'm sorry."

How could we blame the zookeepers with their good intentions, baffled as they were by the loving heart?

Jennie said, "I'm sorry."

We left our candles and flowers at the gate and headed together to the chimpanzees so Loy, Jr. could begin to know them and we could ask them, humbly, to forgive us.

Acknowledgements

Deep gratitude to

- Marc Estrin and Donna Bister who bring art and activism together in Fomite Press and in their own creative work.
- Dr. Cathleen Cox for creating and directing the research department at the Los Angeles Zoo and for (I hope) forgiving my trespasses as I make imaginative use of what I learned there.
- My fellow animal behavior observers and all the extraordinary other-than-human animals for allowing me into their lives.
- Theater artists Hector Aristizábal, Alexandra Chun, Jennie Webb, and L. Trey Wilson for years of friendship, inspiration, exploration, and shared struggles.
- Rosalind Bloom for "Circus Fellini," the oil collage that hangs on my wall and inspired the description of Bobby's painting.
- Carl Anthony for his exchange with Theodore Roszak in "Ecopsychology and the Deconstruction of Whiteness" which informed Loy's response to *Think like a mountain*, and Michelle Cacho-Negrete for sending the interview my way.
- Judy Witters for her storytelling.
- Susan Martin, la malcriada—¡viva! la huelga—for her friendship and her labors for labor.
- Desi for loving, purring, taking my breath away, teaching me, and making me laugh.
- Suzee Carnel, for the horses.

- Hirokazu Kosaka for his artistry and thoughts on Zen.
- *Santa Monica Review* and the Rainstorm Press anthology, *Through the Eyes of a Storm*, where portions of this novel in somewhat different form first appeared.
- I also want to acknowledge the liberatory thought and work of Paulo Freire (1921-97) for *Pedagogy of the Oppressed* and Augusto Boal (1931-2009) for *Theater of the Oppressed*.

About the Author

Diane Lefer is an award-winning fiction author, playwright, and occasional rabble-rouser. She has studied primate behavior for the Research Department of the Los Angeles Zoo for almost twenty years and brings attention and affection to the rescue cats at the Amanda Foundation. Her ongoing collaboration with Colombian exile Hector Aristizábal includes Theater of the Oppressed workshops in the US and abroad, their nonfiction book, *The Blessing Next to the Wound: A story of art, activism, and transformation*, and their play *Nightwind* which has toured the US and more than 30 other countries as part of the worldwide movement to end the practice of torture.

Fomite

A fomite is a medium capable of transmitting infectious organisms from one individual to another.

"The activity of art is based on the capacity of people to be infected by the feelings of others." Tolstoy, *What Is Art?*

Writing a review on Amazon, Good Reads, Shelfari, Library Thing or other social media sites for readers will help the progress of independent publishing. To submit a review, go to the book page on any of the sites and follow the links for reviews. Books from independent presses rely on reader to reader communications.

Visit http://www.fomitepress.com/FOMITE/Our_Books.html for more information or to order any of our books.

As It Is On Earth
Peter M Wheelwright

Dons of Time
Greg Guma

Loisaida
Dan Chodorkoff

My Father's Keeper
Andrew Potok

My God, What Have We Done
Susan V Weiss

Rafi's World
Fred Russell

Fomite

The Co-Conspirator's Tale
Ron Jacobs

Short Order Frame Up
Ron Jacobs

All the Sinners Saints
Ron Jacobs

Travers' Inferno
L. E. Smith

The Consequence of Gesture
L. E. Smith

Raven or Crow
Joshua Amses

Sinfonia Bulgarica
Zdravka Evtimova

The Good Muslim
of Jackson Heights
Jaysinh Birjépatil

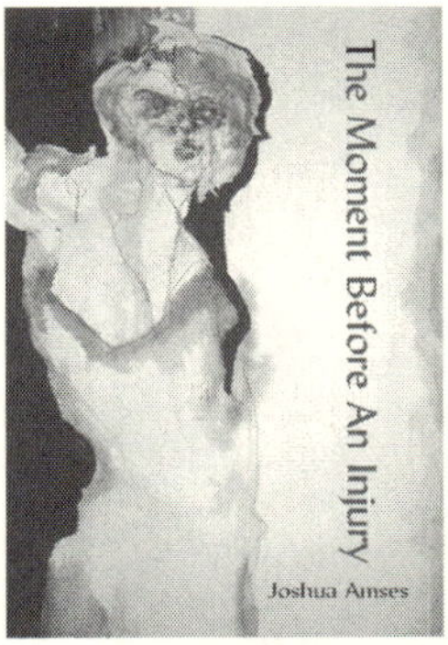

The Moment Before an Injury
Joshua Amses

Fomite

The Return of
Jason Green
Suzi Wizowaty

Victor Rand
David Brizeri

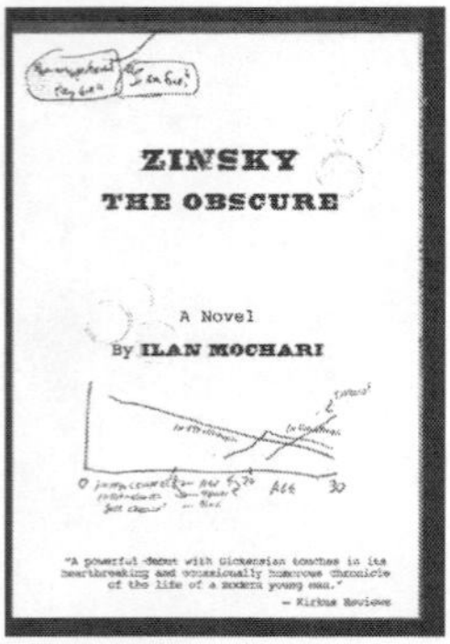

Zinsky the Obscure
Ilan Mochari

Body of Work
Andrei Guruianu

Carts and Other Stories
Zdravka Evtimova

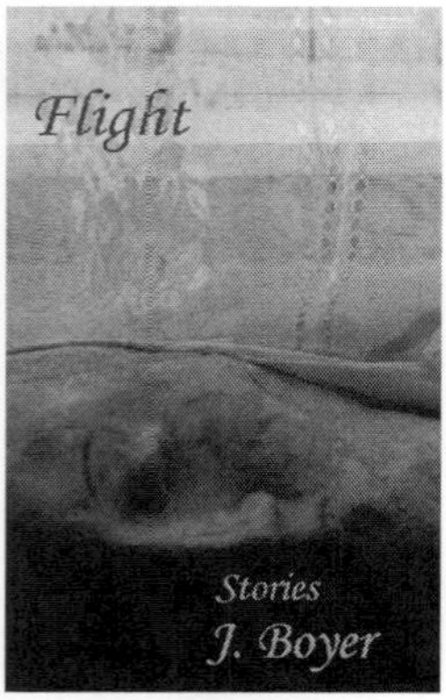

Flight
Jay Boyer

Love's Labours
Jack Pulaski

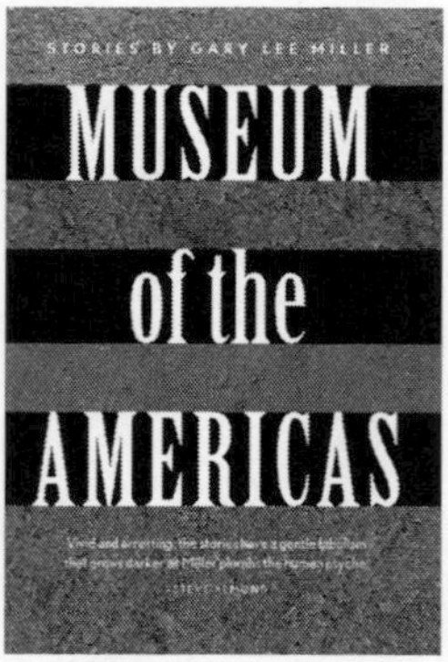

Museum of the Americas
Gary Lee Miller

Saturday Night at Magellan's
Charles Rafferty

Fomite

Signed Confessions
Tom Walker

Still Time
Michael Cocchiarale

Suite for Three Voices
Derek Furr

Unfinished Stories of Girls
Catherine Zobal Dent

Views Cost Extra
L. E. Smith

Visiting Hours
Jennifer Anne Moses

When You Remeber
Deir Yassin
R. L. Green

Alfabestiaro
Antonello Borra

Cycling in Plato's Cave
David Cavanagh

Fomite

AlphaBetaBestiario
Antonello Borra

Entanglements
Tony Magistrale

Everyone Lives Here
Sharon Webster

Four-Way Stop
Sherry Olson

Improvisational
Arguments
Anna Faktorovitch

Loosestrife
Greg Delanty

Meanwell
Janice Miller Potter

Roadworthy Creature
Roadworth Craft
Kate Magill

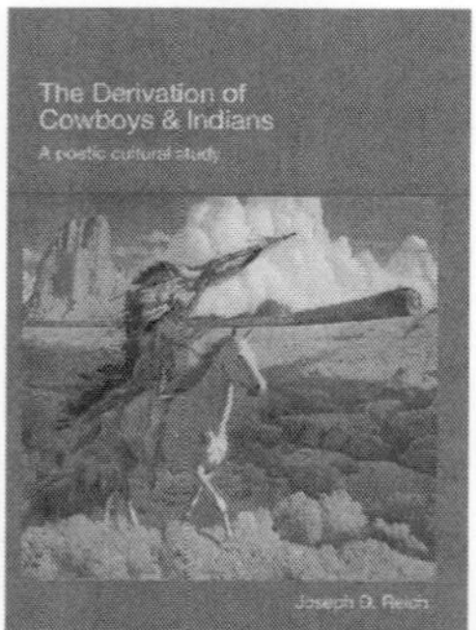

The Derivation of
Cowboys & Indians
Joseph D. Reich

Fomite

The Housing Market
Joseph D. Reich

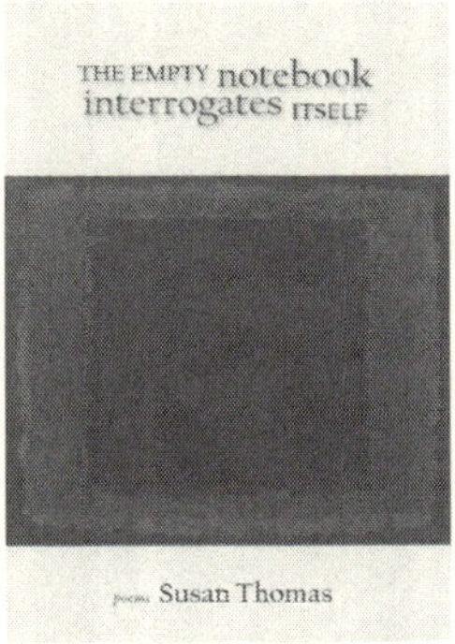

The Empty □otebook
Interrogates Itself
Susan Thomas

The Hundred □ard
Dash Man
Barry Goldensohn

The Listener Aspires
to the Condition of Music
Barry Goldensohn

The Way □ one
of This Happened
Mike Breiner

Screwed
Stephen Goldberg

Planet Kasper
Peter Schumann

My Murder
and Other Local □ ews
David Schein

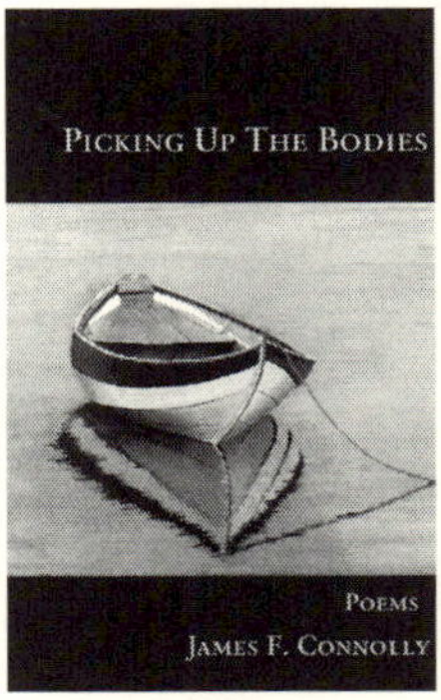

Picking □ p the Bodies
James F. Connolly

Fomite

The Falkland □ uartet
Tony Whedon

Companion Plants
Kathryn Roberts